Translated from
by Christine

Enigma

Rezvani

Dedalus

Dedalus would like to thank the French Ministry of Foreign Affairs in Paris and The Arts Council of England in London for their assistance in producing this translation.

Published in the UK by Dedalus Ltd, Langford Lodge, St Judith's Lane, Sawtry, Cambs, PE17 5XE

ISBN 1 873982 28 3

Distributed in the United States by Subterranean Company, P.O. Box 160, 265 South Fifth Street, Monroe, Oregon 97456

Distributed in Australia & New Zealand by Peribo Pty Ltd, 58 Beaumont Road, Mount Kuring-gai, N.S.W. 2080

Distributed in Canada by Marginal Distribution, Unit 102, 277 George Street North, Peterborough, Ontario, KJ9 3G9

First published by Dedalus in 1998
First published in France in 1995

L'Enigme copyright © Actus Sud, 1995
Translation of Enigma copyright © Christine Donougher 1998

The right of Rezvani to be identified as the author and Christine Donougher to be identified as the translator of this work have been asserted by them in accordance with the Copyright, Design and Patents Act, 1988

Typeset by RefineCatch Ltd, Bungay, Suffolk
Printed in Finland by Wsoy

This book is sold subject to the condition that it shall not, by way of trade or otherwise, be lent, resold, hired out, or otherwise circulated without the publisher's prior consent in any form of binding or cover other than that in which it is published and without a similar condition including this condition being imposed on the subsequent purchaser.

A C.I.P. listing for this book is available on request.

Dedalus Europe 1998
General Editor: Mike Mitchell

Enigma

THE AUTHOR

Born in 1928 of Persian and Russian parents, Rezvani divides his time between his homes in Provence and Venice.

A man of many talents he first came to prominence as a painter, before establishing himself as a major novelist, dramatist and poet.

THE TRANSLATOR

Christine Donougher was born in England in 1954. She read English and French at Cambridge and after a career in publishing is now a freelance translator and editor.

Her many translations from French and Italian include Jan Potocki's *Tales from the Saragossa Manuscript*, Octave Mirbeau's *Le Calvaire*, Sylvie Germain's *Days of Anger* and *Night of Amber*, Marcel Béalu's *The Experience of the Night* and Giovanni Verga's *Sparrow*.

Her translation of Sylvie Germain's *The Book of Nights* won the T. L. S. Scott Moncrieff Prize for the best translation of a Twentieth Century French Novel during 1992.

institut français

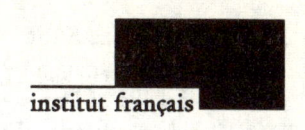

French Literature from Dedalus

French Language Literature in translation is an important part of Dedalus's list, with French being the language *par excellence* of literary fantasy.

Séraphita – Balzac £6.99
The Quest of the Absolute – Balzac £6.99
The Experience of the Night – Marcel Béalu £8.99
Episodes of Vathek – Beckford £6.99
The Devil in Love – Jacques Cazotte £5.99
Les Diaboliques – Barbey D'Aurevilly £7.99
Spirite (and Coffee Pot) – Théophile Gautier £6.99
Angels of Perversity – Remy de Gourmont £6.99
The Book of Nights – Sylvie Germain £8.99
Night of Amber – Sylvie Germain £8.99
Days of Anger – Sylvie Germain £8.99
The Medusa Child – Sylvie Germain £8.99
The Weeping Woman – Sylvie Germain £6.99
Infinite Possibilities – Sylvie Germain £8.99
Là-Bas – J. K. Huysmans £7.99
En Route – J. K. Huysmans £7.99
The Cathedral – J. K. Huysmans £7.99
The Oblate of St Benedict – J. K. Huysmans £7.99
Monsieur de Phocas – Jean Lorrain £8.99
Abbé Jules – Octave Mirbeau £8.99
Le Calvaire – Octave Mirbeau £7.99
The Diary of a Chambermaid – Octave Mirbeau £7.99
Torture Garden – Octave Mirbeau £7.99
Smarra & Trilby – Charles Nodier £6.99
Tales from the Saragossa Manuscript – Jan Potocki £5.99
Monsieur Venus – Rachilde £6.99

The Marquise de Sade – Rachilde £8.99
Enigma – Rezvani £8.99
The Mysteries of Paris – Eugene Sue £6.99
The Wandering Jew – Eugene Sue £9.99
Micromegas – Voltaire £4.95

Forthcoming titles include:

The Dedalus Book of French Horror – edited by Terry Hale £9.99
L'Eclat du Sel – Sylvie Germain £8.99
L'Anglais décrit dans le château fermé – Pieyre de Mandiargues £7.99

Anthologies featuring French Literature in translation:

The Dedalus Book of Decadence – ed Brian Stableford £7.99
The Second Dedalus Book of Decadence – ed Brian Stableford £8.99
The Dedalus Book of Surrealism – ed Michael Richardson £8.99
Myth of the World: Surrealism 2 – ed Michael Richardson £8.99
The Dedalus Book of Medieval Literature – ed Brian Murdoch £8.99
The Dedalus Book of Femmes Fatales – ed Brian Stableford £8.99
The Dedalus Book of Sexual Ambiguity – ed Emma Wilson £8.99
The Decadent Cookbook – Medlar Lucan & Durian Gray £8.99
The Decadent Gardener – Medlar Lucan & Durian Gray £8.99

Alban Berg

My propositions serve as elucidations in the following way: anyone who understands me eventually recognizes them as nonsensical, when he has used them – as steps – to climb up beyond them. (He must, so to speak, throw away the ladder after he has climbed up it.)

Ludwig Wittgenstein

I

The Maritime Affairs Investigator and the Literary Expert head down towards the port. Cutting through the warehouses, they come to the dry dock where the *Uranus* lies, steeped in blue by the dusk that is gradually obscuring it.

'There's nothing more surprising than coming upon a yacht, like the *Uranus*, in dry dock,' says the Maritime Affairs Investigator, as they both climb the iron ladder drawn up by a tow tractor and left resting against the smooth hull. 'See how the water-line is marked with lots of blood-stained scratches,' says the Investigator when they are halfway up. 'They all tried desperately to climb back aboard but couldn't find the slightest grip. But we'll examine those marks more closely in daylight, since we've made a strange and very surprising discovery. If you come across the deck with me, we can go down and take a look at the cabins. Everything's been left the way it was. Apart from the manuscripts, which my friend the Criminologist and I had removed from the various cabins, nothing's been touched, either at the controls or on deck. The library's just as we found it, and so is the kitchen, but for the perishable goods that were thrown out after being itemized.

'Let's go down this corridor,' says the Investigator, showing the Literary Expert the way. 'Here you have Karl Knigh's cabin, the most spacious of all, with his teak-wood desk, and the two beds over there, his own and his young wife Lotte Knigh's. We found Karl Knigh's manuscripts in impeccable order on the desk, and also in the drawers. Lotte Knigh's, or rather her notebooks – you can examine them later – were found in the wardrobe, behind her dresses. As for the rest, the untidiness has been scrupulously respected; everything's been photographed, identified and registered so that the file on the mystery of the *Uranus* should be quite clear and comprehensive. Now, let's go through this door, if you would?' continues the Investigator. 'Then you can take a quick look at the cabin that was occupied by Rosa Zhorn-Knigh, Kurt Knigh, and

Gustav Zhorn. Apart from the same untidiness as in old Knigh and his young wife's cabin, nothing unusual, except for this sheet of paper pinned to the wall, with these lines of verse on it. We assume they're by Kurt Knigh.'

> Cain, indeed! see in that fell moment how the blade rises
> comes down on the greenish tomb
> The bronze glistening before it pierces the earth
> rising again a dull sticky black
> First human blood to darken the world –
> son of Cain our father!

'And there are more lines on the back, in the same handwriting.'

> The triple goddess rules the world when out of chaos
> springs the dark god Uranus
> On the secret clefts of Mother-Earth he showers rain
> in clear streams
> Grass flowers trees birds originate in the hollow places
> as well as the first creatures
> Half-flesh half-soul in being – ourselves cast into the
>   abyss by Arno!

'Uranus? Do you think that by pinning up these verses containing the name of his father's boat, Kurt Knigh intended to give us a posthumous clue to interpreting this mystery?'

'If I'd come across these verses before my thesis on the Knigh family was published, I'd have been happy to be able to include them,' says the Literary Expert. 'May I keep this sheet of paper?'

'Of course. You'll be able to add it to the various manuscripts we've had delivered to your room at the hotel. Would you follow me this way? Now, let's go through this bulkhead. That brings us into the forward part of the yacht. This is Franz Knigh's cubby-hole, which is so cramped that you wonder how he could have worked in it. A pile of handwritten pages was found on this shelf by the porthole. The cubicle next door is where Julius slept. His manuscripts filled three old suitcases lying open on the floor. And that's it!' said the Investigator. 'Did you note carefully how the writings of the various members of the Knigh family were distributed, as the Criminologist and myself found them on boarding, when the coast-guard patrol-boat brought us out to meet the deserted *Uranus*, being towed in by the trawler that came alongside it, adrift at sea?'

'But . . .'

'I know what surprises you. No servants aboard? Isn't that the question you were about to ask? Well, believe it or not, there were no sailors or maids or cook on board. Ordinarily speaking, there should have been some Thai or Pakistani, or at least one of those standard Greek waiters that you get on yachts. But this wasn't your standard yacht. Karl Knigh liked to sail alone with his family, his "literary family", as the title of your thesis puts it. Accept this, if you will, as a writer's whim, the eccentricity of a famous and overbearing man. We may as well admit it: if there'd been any servants on board, this tragedy wouldn't have occurred and we wouldn't be here now. Inevitably the ladder would have been let down, and the whole Knigh family would have easily climbed back on deck. But there are absurdities like that, which you have to accept or reject. At sea, all terrestrial logic disappears. The sea is a vast living body of illogicality, where everything that happens is illogical. The province of Maritime Affairs, in which I specialize as a professional investigator, is above all else the province of the illogical. I am the most dedicated, most dogged investigator precisely because every maritime investigation explores the irrational, most of the time. And that's what I like about this very special kind of work, and why my friend the Criminologist — who's a poet as well — also enjoys maritime investigations. People who take to sea are very different from other people. Nothing is ordinary at sea. A crime that occurs at sea is no ordinary crime. An accident at sea, on the other hand, is something ordinary. Even the most unordinary accidents are ordinary at sea. Numerous inexplicable incidents occur every day on the world's oceans. The movement of these huge volumes of water not only distorts perspectives but, by causing the eye's unsteadiness, inevitably destabilizes the mind as well. "Many poets describe the sea as *playful*," my friend and collaborator the Criminologist keeps telling me. He's been writing for years, but no one's ever managed to see, let alone read, his poems, which he only talks about to those he trusts. Yet everyone knows, from hearsay, that he's written masses of them. What he does like talking about are themes. "It's themes," he says, "not the subject, that guide the creative mind. There's nothing worse than a subject, an idea," he always says. "What's important for a creator is the irresistible excitement that derives not just from one theme but various themes presenting themselves simultaneously, to the point of furiously jostling with each other. The mind then gets worked up into a frenzy, and plunges with delight into this sort of chaos of divergent ideas." That's what my friend the Poet Criminologist says. You'll meet him shortly. He's to join us at the Yacht Club, as soon as he frees himself from certain obligations that his life is tragically burdened with. We recently investigated a shipwreck in which more than eight hundred people perished after the bow hatch of a ferry opened . . . But if you come this way, we'll return through the control room, which also functions as a library-saloon. You see how the helmsman, while at the wheel of the *Uranus*, could carry on talking to his guests settled comfortably under the book shelves lining the walls of the spacious common-room cabin.'

'I notice,' says the Literary Expert, studying the titles of the works in rows up to the ceiling, 'that gathered here are all the great classics representing the finest, most innovative, and most unexpected of what the human mind has produced in every age. The *Uranus* was a wonderful floating library . . .'

'That, from one minute to the next, lost not only its readers but its living authors.'

'Therein lies the enigma! That a yacht should sink with its occupants, its library, even the manuscripts it was carrying – nothing could be more unexceptional. The ocean floors are, as they say, paved with these treasure-houses containing, within a limited space, a symbolic cargo representing humanity. We accept extinction, we accept the image of it, the idea, the sorrow and secretly, perhaps, the comfort of being relieved of that certainty of knowing there is nothing to know. But what's upsetting and causes despair is being confronted with an everlastingly lost world.'

'You mean: books without readers?'

'Exactly! Speaking of which, that puts me in mind of a very strange story published by Franz Knigh, in which he describes a world so automated that when human beings suddenly disappear — due to a fatal epidemic, or something of the sort — *everything* continues to function with no remaining trace of human existence. Oil is self-extracting. Nuclear power stations operate for nothing and for no one. Energy distributes itself, powering factories that produce machines that were already self-generating, so would go on self-generating, self-renewing and self-issuing for ever after mankind had been wiped from the face of the earth. And, of course, there's the amazement of travellers from somewhere or other in space who come upon this dead world, inhabited solely by self-activated and apparently self-motivated machines, pointlessly reproducing, without the slightest hint of any *knowledge*, the phantom gestures of a humanity long since extinct.'

'In a way,' says the Maritime Affairs Investigator, 'the same amazement we feel at the magnificence of a shell vacated thousands of years ago by the mysterious creature that mysteriously created it.'

'Yes,' says the Literary Expert, 'except that a fossil shell is an object, a petrified remain. What's terrifying about Franz Knigh's idea — and you can't help mentally pursuing it — is that some lifeless activity should go on and on for ever, in our image, as it were. "Without art," said Franz Knigh, "is that not all we would be: activity for activity's sake."'

'Did you meet him many times?'

'Yes, quite a few. He lived in Hamburg, where he was conducting some interesting experiments on the senses. As a matter of fact, he'd invented the most astounding machine — I'll explain to you how it worked.'

'Be careful,' says the Investigator, 'and come down the

ladder backwards. Now, it's time we went over to the Yacht Club. My friend the Poet Criminologist is sure to be there already, waiting for us.'

II

They are now at the Yacht Club where the Poet Criminologist has just joined them.

'This is the French Literary Expert!' says the Maritime Affairs Investigator. 'He's here at last!'

'We've certainly been looking forward to your arrival,' says the Criminologist. 'I read your thesis on "The Knigh Literary Family", and we thought you were just the right person to help us decipher the Knigh family's manuscripts found aboard the *Uranus*.'

'We've just come from the dry dock,' says the Investigator. And turning to the literary scholar who is an expert on the Knigh family: 'It was my friend here, the Criminologist, who had the idea of calling on you. "I think his presence here with us is absolutely essential," he told me. "This scholar is thoroughly acquainted with all the writings of Karl Knigh, as well those of his brother Julius, his sons Kurt and Franz, and also those of Rosa Zhorn-Knigh. For many years now he's taken an interest in the Knigh family, the clashes that have constantly set the family members against each other, their loves, jealousies, hatreds and conceits, everything! Without him," he said to me, "we'll never solve the mystery of the *Uranus*. Because it was no accident that took place: the ladder was deliberately pulled up." Isn't that what you said?'

'Absolutely! It emerged from your thesis on the Knigh family – and I was particularly struck by it, so much so that I persuaded my friend the Investigator to invite you to work with us – that the metaphorical ladder had long since been pulled up, among them, and the conflicts that divided and at the same time united the members of this strange family were bound to end in tragedy. But not to such a puzzling disappearance!'

'Since the three of us are destined to be working together,' the Maritime Affairs Investigator cuts in, 'I took the liberty of telling him what an excellent criminologist you are ... and secret poet, too ...'

'Now, let's not talk about poetry! It's only the criminologist who's taking part in this investigation. The poet always stays in the background, watching in silence. There's a young poet I admire – one who naively claimed to be a count – was it not he that said: "Must I write in verse to set myself apart from other men?" I'll not add anything to that. It's true, I write some verse but rarely do I allow anyone to read it. My verse tells of my confused desire to express in poetry what I could not otherwise express. I write at night, and during the day I collaborate with my friend the Maritime Affairs Investigator in his inquiries. On the one hand I'm someone who writes, and on the other someone who investigates loss of life. I'm fascinated by what's called *loss of life*. I like diverse ideas brought together. At first sight poet and criminologist seem incompatible, and although these two terms are diverse, yet I see the delightful convergence between them. I'm fascinated by derangement. Why should an apparently normal person become deranged for no comprehensible reason? Do you know that there's an institute in Berlin, the Kaiser Wilhelm Institute, where they cut up the brains either of famous men or of particularly inventive killers into something like twenty thousand slices twenty-billionths of a meter thin? There, Lenin's brain was cut into thin strips, so too was Maxim Gorky's brain, and Stalin's, just as the brains of most twentieth-century politicians and scientists have been cut up, and the slices preserved between two glass slides, so that they can be studied in centuries to come and whatever compelling conclusions be drawn. Einstein's brain has also been cut up and preserved for future researchers. You can't imagine what a terrible state Vladimir Ilitch Lenin's brain is in. That's a notorious case of derangement. Of course, every human brain is inevitably deranged. Most of the time this derangement makes no difference. It doesn't lead to any visible derangement in what's called the real world. It's quite possible for a normal man – so described by his neighbours – to murder his wife and children, for the gentlest person suddenly to turn into a wild beast, as they say. But most of the time derangement remains hidden and disappears with anonymous extinction. And yet, what surprises we'd have if an in-depth study were to be made of the brain lobes of the first person picked at random from the crowd!'

'You think that a deranged member of the Knigh family might have pulled up the ladder while the others were swimming round the boat?' says the Literary Expert sceptically.

'We've examined every possible explanation,' says the Investigator.

'And what about the person who remained on board, assuming that person wanted to watch the whole family perish?'

'That's the real puzzle,' says the Poet Criminologist. 'You knew them – do you think that one of them could have been sufficiently deranged to want such a death for themselves after that of every member of their family?'

'In my view,' says the Literary Expert, having pondered for a moment, 'they *all* had that desire in them. Yes, they *all* toyed with that terrible desire. Except that none of them, in my view, would have actually been capable of it.'

'On land, I've no doubt, but at sea very often the impossible becomes possible,' says the Investigator. 'It so happens that my friend the Criminologist and I had to investigate a terrible shipwreck, a huge catastrophe in which more than eight hundred people drowned. And, believe it or not, with one surprise leading to another in the course of our investigation, we got so much caught up in the game, as they say, we forgot the large number of deaths caused by that shipwreck. It was only the game that concerned us, the game that every investigation represents.'

'Did not a French poet say: "The fly does not reason well at present. A man is buzzing in its ears." Are we flies? It's surely because we're not flies that we *play*, so as not to reason too well. What would the brain of a deranged fly look like? For there are such things as deranged flies, since there are so many men who think of themselves as *normal* flies.'

'Your eternal paradoxes!' exclaims the Maritime Affairs

Investigator. And declaring before the Literary Expert as his witness, he says, 'You couldn't find anywhere a more pleasing wit than that of my friend the Poet Criminologist, a wit more classical, more eighteenth-century in the way that it plays with profound ideas, while giving the impression that these ideas merely skim the surface of a supposed reality. Every investigation, as a matter of fact, demands a great propensity for play. Can you imagine, on that ferry that sank to a depth of ninety metres a kind miracle of elementary physics occurred: two men survived in one of the usual pockets of air that generally form in the metal-plated cabins to which the crew are confined. By chance, the ferry had not settled on its side; it was standing on the seabed upright, with its big bow hatch gaping open like the dislocated jaws of some enormous whale. It was through there that our divers managed to get into the wreck. Imagine their surprise when they drew level with the crew's quarters and thought they heard tapping, a regular, even rhythmic, tapping, they later recounted. No doubt about it, someone was rhythmically tapping on the ferry's metal-plating, at ninety metres' depth. One of our divers immediately swam into the crew's quarters. Sure enough, it was true! A large air-pocket had formed in one of the cabins. There, huddled on an upper berth were two black guys who'd joined ship heaven knows where. They were clinging to each other, with their teeth chattering. They didn't understand how they'd come to be in the dark for so many hours with water up to their waists. After much to-ing and fro-ing, our divers managed to get the necessary equipment down into the wreck and to convince the two black guys that they were imprisoned in the sunken ferry, and that they had to proceed with the utmost caution. You remember those two poor guys, half dead with cold and fright?' the Maritime Affairs Investigator says to the Poet Criminologist.

'Of course, we were there together, on the deck of a boat put at our disposal by one of our big oil companies, when the two survivors were brought out of the decompression chamber. Apart from their extraordinary fright – retrospective fright, to tell the truth, that made them tremble even more, said the divers, than when they were underwater – they seemed in good shape. Only a few hours after their rescue, they were cheerfully tucking in to a hearty meal, and they suffered no after-effects from such a terrible experience.'

'And do you know what saved them? The irresistible need, and such a humanly desperate need, to play.'

'What do you mean?' says the Literary Expert. 'I don't understand.'

'Yet it's marvellously simple. Trapped in total darkness, in the wreck lying on the bottom of the sea, they began tapping regularly on the metal-plate wall in the crew's quarters. And gradually their purposeful tapping turned into an almost musical rhythm. It was these syncopated rhythms, terribly muffled though they were by the depth and density of the water, that our divers were amazed to detect. So, already half drowned, and almost certain of a horrible death, those two black guys couldn't help transforming into a *game* what were supposed to be cries for help,' continues the Maritime Affairs Investigator. 'And, you see, what tremendously surprised us when we examined closely the hull of the *Uranus*, scratched all around, was to find strange symbols engraved on it, with a ring-stone, we think, by one of those desperate individuals, just before drowning. So, besides blood-stained scratches, the proudly enamelled cliff-face of the *Uranus* conceals a bizarre message, as you'll see as soon as the photographs of these symbols have been enlarged.'

'That reminds me,' says the Poet Criminologist, 'of prisons where those condemned to death, who have nothing left to hope for, can't resist leaving some written trace of themselves. In the face of that kind of death, we know, it's impossible that there won't be some trace telling us that, when about to be "humanely" put to sleep by injection or electrocution, Mankind, in these doomed individuals, has felt the disturbing need to *play* with symbols, offering to their future decipherers the enigma which is what the last sign from someone who is going to be put to death represents.'

'To *play*? Do you really think so?' says the Literary Expert.

'Yes, I do. To *play* at challenging this world that will go on without you, that will still exist without you. It's almost the opposite of the game children play of frightening themselves. How else are we to explain the truly weird symbols engraved on the hull of the yacht, which quite closely resemble those I happen to have seen on the walls of cells where prisoners condemned to death lived their last moments?'

'But in the case of the *Uranus* . . . The symbols are bound to say something, expose the culprit, or at least give some clue to those who would try to understand the reason for such terrible desertedness,' says the Literary Expert.

'We thought so at first. But as you'll see, the symbols aren't rational, I assure you,' says the Investigator.

'Unless, on the point of drowning, one of the members of the Knigh family tried to write down a name, or even just someone's initials, but feeling such intense panic at drowning, couldn't write anything coherent. So many criminals have been exposed by having their names written by their victim's bloodied finger,' says the Criminologist. 'For instance, there was that famous case you had in France, of that elderly millionairess, a well-read woman, apparently, who, although inflicted with an incredible number of stab wounds, managed to drag herself to a wall and, using her hand that was wet with her own blood, to write the name of her assassin as well as a few other words, in which, puzzlingly, there glared the most inconceivable spelling mistake. That spelling mistake appalled France infinitely more than the murder itself. The crime, the truly unforgivable crime, was there, on that wall. It had the effect of an electric shock rousing France from its literary and grammatical torpor. It wasn't a crime of bloodshed but a crime of misspelling.'

'I'm very curious to see the blown-up photos of those markings found on the *Uranus*'s hull,' says the Literary Expert rather thoughtfully. 'I may have an idea of what they might signify. A strange intuition. But let's wait until we've seen the photos you mentioned. I think I know which of the Knighs would have made this inscription. If it is the person I'm thinking of, we've yet more surprises in store.'

'Go on, tell us,' says the Poet Criminologist with forced jocularity.

'It would be premature, I assure you.'

'It's getting late,' says the Investigator. 'Let's accompany our literary friend to his hotel. I suggest that tomorrow the three of us meet at my office at the Maritime Affairs headquarters. I think we'll have the photographic enlargements by then. I'll be waiting for you with great impatience,' he says to the Literary Expert. 'In your room you'll find several parcels tied up with string. They're the manuscripts that were discovered in the various cabins of the *Uranus*. I hope you'll forgo a little sleep if not to study them at least to do an initial sorting. As you'll see, there's a considerable pile.'

III

'I was just now with the Literary Expert,' says the Poet Criminologist the following morning, as he enters the Maritime Affairs Investigator's office. 'He won't move from his room. I found him on his bed, among the Knigh family's various manuscripts. There he lay, fully dressed, reading in the smoke-filled room. The chairs and armchairs, the table, the floor and his bed were buried under bundles of paper that he had apparently sorted into unequal piles, according to their different authors.

'"I haven't slept a wink," he told me, "and I'm afraid that my discoveries will keep me from sleeping for a long while yet. I'm thunderstruck!"'

'He actually said that?' the Maritime Investigator cuts in impatiently.

'He expressed himself in those obviously exaggerated terms, but the Knigh family's papers must surely contain revelations that have seriously shaken him.

'"As an expert, I'm devastated," he said to me. "I'm very much afraid that several years' work and literary study devoted to the Knigh family are in danger of being cancelled out at one fell swoop. If my thesis weren't already published and in wide circulation, I'd have destroyed it immediately. You can't imagine my devastation and at the same time my extraordinary excitement."

'When I asked him to explain himself in more detail, he showed me several thick notebooks that he had placed at the head of his bed.

'"These manuscripts that you see here are particularly eloquent. I set them aside because they already throw a little light on the tragedy, and simultaneously darken its areas of shadow. As an expert, I'm in the most awkward predicament."

'Taking a notebook from the top of a pile, he held it out to me. "Do you see this almost indecipherable writing. What do you think of it?"

' "It looks like a woman's handwriting," I said.

' "You're right. It's that of old Karl Knigh's young wife, Lotte Knigh. It turns out that she was keeping a secret diary. But not the kind of diary one might expect of a young wife more interested in herself than in the literary output of this astonishing Knigh family, whose collated writings constitute a body of work truly unique in the history of not only European literature but world literature," the Literary Expert told me with a morbid excitement that I find rather worrying.'

'Worrying?' says the Investigator in surprise.

'Although he's extremely likeable, this literary expert doesn't seem to me as sound as a genuine expert ought to be. The way he identifies with the Knigh family – and has done for so many years! – makes me anxious for the future of our investigation into the *Uranus* tragedy. How are we to keep on top of all the elements of this puzzle without being overwhelmed by the Literary Expert's inordinate excitement? These literary types are often over-excitable. In this particular case it's understandable. I too feel drawn this way and that. The poet in me is excited. The criminologist wants to keep his level-headedness.

' "Doubtless something unique has happened," I said to the Literary Expert, "but we must keep our cool. Phantom ships abound in maritime chronicles. Remember that big derelict sailing-ship, adrift at sea, with a human figure on deck that seemed to be laughing and waving?"

' "And it was just a corpse," the Literary Expert immediately replied, "quite simply a dead sailor, torn to pieces by a sea bird, whose devoured face left his teeth exposed." And he added, "Is that actually from Edgar Allan Poe or Baudelaire? Of course, the image is Poe's, but here the description so readily replaces the image that one wonders . . ."'

'Let's get back to the manuscripts,' says the Investigator. 'What was it, more precisely, that he read in them?'

'That's just what I asked him. "Without wishing to detract from the literary side of our investigation," I said to him, " – and never forget, in this family tragedy the criminal aspect alone should be our primary concern – what did you read last night, then, that was so extraordinary? We're relying on you to enlighten us about these posthumous writings of the Knigh family."

'"Have no fear," replied the Literary Expert, "you'll be kept informed of my discoveries. But do realize, and tell your friend the Maritime Affairs Investigator, that I need some time. Have a little patience."'

'But how long is he intending to keep us waiting before giving us even a superficial report?'

'That's exactly the question I put to him. He showed me the manuscripts and said, "I can assure you that the answer is to be found in this mass of writings. I'm not saying they're the key to the puzzle but, as it were, the casket in which the key lies, very carefully laid on a little cushion of crimson velvet." That's what the Literary Expert said to me this morning in his hotel bedroom littered with the manuscripts we retrieved.

'"You can't imagine what a poisoned chalice all this represents to me, with my thesis on the authors of these pages already written! Here, we have the unfinished writings of Julius Knigh, in which his inspired *incapabilities*, to use that painful word so frequent in Kafka's *Journal*, emerge more than ever, and in which his profound differences with his superstar brother Karl Knigh are laid bare; here are Rosa Knigh's writings, by certain pages of which, hastily read, I was astounded; here, in an almost indecipherable hand, those of Karl Knigh, mostly free verse, similar to that found pinned to the wall of his cabin; and here I've made a pile of Franz Knigh's manuscripts, the most lucid, most intelligent of all. But it's in Julius Knigh's writings," said the Literary Expert, "that I'm impatient to immerse myself. Julius's inverted thinking is surely the most peculiar, the most out of the ordinary. When I was gathering material for the thesis I intended to write on the Knigh family I went to Spain, to the province of Gerona, where Karl Knigh owned a large house in the port of Pals. From there, Karl accompanied me to Granada, where Julius was renting a room above a *cantina*. The two brothers had more or less not spoken to each other for years. It wasn't that they hated each other. A presence had come between them, a ghost, an absence that oppressed them all their lives, the nature of which I learned of little by little. This absent presence bound the two brothers together indissolubly. Shackled them to the most unbearable remorse."'

'Did he disclose to you the nature of this remorse?' says the Investigator.

'Not explicitly. But I was given to understand that some terrible incident had occurred between the two brothers. And this incident, instead of dividing them, as they inevitably would have been divided by their very different temperaments, on the contrary kept them inseparably yoked.

' "Please ask your friend the Maritime Affairs Investigator to excuse me for not coming this morning," the Literary Expert said to me, "but I'm immersed for the time being in some strangely inverted writings of Julius Knigh. When I met him in Granada, I was filled even then with admiration for the originality of what he wrote, an originality intensified by the different stages of his perpetual drunkenness. But my feeling today is one of dismay when I set Julius's writings beside those of his brother Karl. Do you see that pile on the floor, between the bed and the bathroom? Those are the last writings of the 'great author' Karl Knigh. I've read a few dozen pages that are terribly revealing."

'When I asked the Literary Expert to be more explicit,' says the Criminologist, 'he replied that for the moment it was impossible for him to speak any more plainly, and that he himself felt almost drunk after reading the two manuscripts side by side.

' "These are apparently the first drafts of two huge and ambitious books which, unbeknown to their authors, seem as if they were meant to complement each other. They're two testamentary books, as they're called when the author's still alive, and which often fall into oblivion after his death. Even though it's Karl who's supposed to be 'the great writer', the one by Karl Knigh seemed to me weaker and above all more conventional than that of his brother Julius. Turns of phrase of a kind that suggest to the reader that their author is a man of sobriety and integrity keep cropping up throughout Karl

Knigh's manuscript. And on the basis of this sobriety and integrity, the author enjoins his readers to remain within the sphere of benign moderation and zeal where they have been placed by this writing. His readers must above all admire this sobriety and this integrity. By total contrast, Julius's writings, which so shook me up last night, are amazingly volatile. Both brothers are obsessed by the same idea, the same issue. But one of them acts like a literary beta-blocker, while the other plunges you into uncharted abysses," the Literary Expert told me, visibly affected by the pile of manuscripts we've saddled him with.'

'You worry me,' the Investigator says to the Poet Criminologist, 'from what you tell me, our Literary Expert seems an extremely impressionable expert, and almost painfully sensitive to anything of a literary nature. Moreover, his position with regard to the Knigh family strikes me as too partisan. He champions Julian Knigh, as though, as a "failure", the writer who remained in his brother's shadow reassured him as a scholar. It's well known that scholars tend to hate those whom they select as the object of their studies. And since Karl Knigh was the sun round which the other members of the Knigh constellation gravitated, it stands to reason that our poor Literary Expert should try by every means to do down Karl to the advantage of his brother Julius.'

'I don't think so,' says the Poet Criminologist. 'And I'll tell you why. As you can imagine, the same thought naturally occurred to me when I was with the Literary Expert just now, in his room littered with that heap of manuscripts representing all of the Knighs. But being a little perverse, I twisted that gloriously bitter phrase of Robert Musil about Thomas Mann: "Karl Knigh," I said, "*he's something! But definitely not someone.* Isn't that what you think, and isn't that what Julius Knigh must have thought of his brother?"'

' "Absolutely not," replied the Literary Expert, "that kind of dismissive judgement should remain in Switzerland, clinging for ever, as it were, to the embittered writer who voiced it. Nothing's more dangerous than quotations taken out of context. Those words relate only to the person who uttered them:

the writer Robert Musil relegated to Switzerland by his fellow writers, the 'clever race-horses', the front-runners in the publishing stakes. Karl Knigh was not the type to 'hatch plots', as they say; he may have been calculating, but he always behaved with the utmost integrity. In this he somewhat resembled Thomas Mann," said the Literary Expert. "Just as Thomas Mann was a great bourgeois without rebellion or bitterness, so too was Karl Knigh, even before he was awarded the 'Dynamite' Prize, as Kurt and Rosa called this supreme distinction their father had just recently won. Thomas Mann, with whom Knigh surely had a tendency to identify himself, was a man in a state of mortification. Mann's entire oeuvre was a painful mortification through sickness. It was sickness that spoke, slept, ate, bred and perhaps loved a little. Both his major novels and his lesser works were nothing but hypochondria and morbidity, novels of suffering and shameful pleasures. This is where any possible resemblance between Karl Knigh and Thomas Mann ends," the Literary Expert went on to say, "for unlike Thomas Mann, Karl Knigh was hiding a secret, a terrible secret of which I was not quite certain at the time I was writing my thesis, and which I believe I penetrated last night, in deciphering the papers found aboard the *Uranus*."

'That's what the Literary Expert told me before I left him to come and tell you that he wouldn't be leaving his room today.'

'Well, let's go over there then!' says the Investigator. 'We can use as an excuse the photographs we spoke to him about yesterday.'

'Absolutely not!' cries the Poet Criminologist. 'Not now. We don't want to annoy him. Let's wait until lunchtime. Hunger will inevitably drive him out and nothing will be easier than to carry him off to the Yacht Club where we can grill him,' he adds with a laugh.

'It's imperative that we keep him under control, strictly limit him to the subject of the investigation. We didn't entrust him with those precious documents so that he could reply to his thesis with a counter-thesis that would include not only his literary discoveries but also our conclusions regarding the mystery of the *Uranus*. That material belongs to us. We brought in this Literary Expert to collaborate with us, and not the other way round. What happened? That's what we want to know.'

IV

'Yes, we absolutely must handle this literary expert with care,' resumes the Poet Criminologist in the Maritime Affairs Investigator's office. 'At the point we've reached in our investigation it looks as if he's the only person, with his detailed knowledge of the Knigh family, who might be able to reveal to us by what aberration all the passengers of the *Uranus* ended up in the sea with no one left aboard to let down the ladder.'

'Or, to frame the question better,' says the Investigator, 'who stayed aboard and why would that person have pulled up the ladder? And then how come that person ended up in the water as well, along with the other members of the family? Let's just imagine the unmanned yacht and its passengers swimming round for a day, two days . . .'

'Two days? That's a long time.'

'Don't you believe it! Victims of shipwreck have been known to survive for more than four days, as long as the water isn't too cold. In any case they all kept swimming round the deserted luxury yacht, without finding the slightest unevenness of surface to offer them any grip. The bloody scratches on the enamelled hull attest to the panic and rage that must have seized this bamboozled family cast into that absurd sea by an incomprehensible fate.'

'Indeed,' says the Criminologist. 'I'd like to know what they might have said to each other during those hours, those days of swimming. What a pity that their words didn't freeze in the air, and later unfreeze, as happened literarily, after a memorable sea-battle. "Since there's no one left to tell us what happened," I said to the Literary Expert, "let's hope that with your insight you may at least detect some clue, some premonition, some written evidence of premeditation, of a desire for annihilation! Thanks to modern methods of reading texts, and particularly what are called 'pre-texts', it should be possible to discern the *intention*, where the author was unaware of having made it apparent. This sudden disappearance of the *Uranus*'s passengers opens up a void within us that we absolutely must fill," I also said to the Literary Expert, "since it seems that an accident is to be ruled out."'

'Unless the whole family were partying,' the Investigator breaks in, 'and they all spontaneously jumped into the water, having got tipsy, for fun, as they say, without remembering that the ladder hadn't been let down.'

'Or else, they all jumped into the water – *but one*. And it was only then that that person had a kind of inspiration. The fact of seeing his whole family in the water, in an ocean of emptiness as far as the eye could see, giving him the idea of carrying out a deed he was perhaps planning solely for himself and which this inspiration presented to him as a splendid way of getting rid of all his family in one fell swoop . . . himself included!'

'And not only his detested family,' says the Investigator, playing along with the Poet Criminologist, 'but above all *the Knigh literary family*, with no violence committed other than drawing up the ladder and jumping in after them.'

'Why do you say "detested"?' says the Criminologist. 'Apparently, some of the "great" family crimes are the result, on the contrary, of excessive love. Some of the surviving family killers I've had occasion to question have confessed to me they couldn't bear for their loved ones to outlive them in grief and despair over *their* death.'

'Let's amuse ourselves,' says the Investigator. 'Let's suppose this mass drowning came about as a result of excessive "love". Which of them do you think would have felt this excessive "family love" . . . or this despair? That's the question we must put without delay to our peculiar Literary Expert. Let's go and find him right now. In any case, it's nearly lunchtime.'

Having got to the hotel, they are now on their way up to the Literary Expert's room. They knock. He does not stir. They knock again. The Literary Expert answers, through the closed door, that what he is reading is fascinating and he is not to be disturbed. They persist. Finally the door opens and the

Literary Expert appears, holding a bundle of manuscript pages.

'What do you want me for?'

'You knew them all well? You even managed to win their trust? Then tell us whether you think that any one of them could have murdered the others out of excessive love turned into psychoneurosis? My friend the Criminologist and I were talking about murders within apparently exemplary and trouble-free families,' says the Investigator.

'As a poet and also as a criminologist, I was wondering whether we weren't in fact faced with a typical case of specious logic such as only an Edgar Allan Poe could have invented. Yes, are we not confronted with one of those fallacious arguments in which various information from the most diverse sources converges to form a kind of knot that you wish were even more illogical the more you desperately try to untangle it.'

'If I understand you correctly,' says the Literary Expert, 'rather than find the solution to this puzzle, you'd like us to invent one?'

'Almost,' says the Poet Criminologist, laughing. 'It would indeed be very satisfying for the criminologist that I am to preserve the "artistic" angle. Investigation artists! That's what above all we must strive to remain! Let's not forget for one moment the famous purloined letter left in public view. Its visibility – and therefore invisibility – is only a literary conceit. It's precisely its very obvious visibility that gives us that delicious shiver of literary pleasure and sophistical delight. Poe's poetic crimes don't hold water, as they say; if they did, they'd have no place in books. Actually, there exists an as yet unnamed sickness of the age that the Investigator and I have just referred to: the multiplication of family murders committed by fathers suddenly unable to cope with what's called "life". Family man indeed! A laughably hackneyed association of words! Give us back the sacred, give us back the sacred murder and you won't have any more of this kind of gratuitous crime, these urban crimes dictated by a here-and-now grown incomprehensible. Let's call it two-dimensional crime.'

'As far as the mystery of the *Uranus* is concerned, we don't seem to be dealing with that kind of two-dimensional crime. I wouldn't be surprised if some element of the sacred didn't enter into it. Believe it or not, I was just reading a very peculiar text by Kurt Knigh. Come in and sit down on the corner of the bed,' says the Literary Expert, moving aside a few piles of manuscripts. 'Listen to this. Kurt is with his father at the Yacht Club for the launching of the last *Uranus*.'

'I very well remember the launching of the last *Uranus*,' the Investigator breaks in. 'Karl Knigh was the centre of attention, as usual. His sons and daughter and Zhorn the actor were there, as well as the club regulars.'

'This is what Kurt writes,' the Literary Expert goes on without paying the Investigator any attention.

'*Father took me by the shoulders and, hugging me almost too tightly, said these terrible words to me: "Do you know why I've named all my yachts Uranus? In memory of Charon's boat. Uranus is a god who's long been forgotten. He's the wretched father of all the gods. In the beginning there was Darkness," Father said to me, "and contrary to what one might think, Chaos was born of Darkness. From the coupling of Darkness and Chaos were born Night, Day, Erebus and Air. From the coupling of Night and Erebus were born Destiny, Old Age, Death, Murder, Continence, Sleep, Dream, Discord, Suffering, Tyranny, Nemesis, Joy, Friendship, Compassion, the Fates and the three Hesperides." Rosa, Franz and Gustav were present, and they listened in astonishment to Father's strange words. Julius was also there, in the background, among the other guests. He was smiling oddly.*

'And a little further on, Kurt talks of his hatred of this boat, on which, however, he writes, *we could not refuse to accompany Father. Not one of us has yet found the courage to avoid this absurd family ritual. Not even Julius. Father had still not let go of me, holding on to my shoulders with apparent affection. In a joking tone of voice he finally added these unbearable words: "The god Uranus was castrated by his favourite son, Cronos." What he said took everyone by surprise and he went on in the ensuing silence, even raising his voice a little: "Uranus was asleep and Mother Earth had armed their son Cronos with a scythe and told him what he must do.*

With his left hand, the cursed hand of ill omen, Cronos then seized his father's genitals," Father went on to say, *"and cut them off. He threw the scythe and his father's genitals into the sea but a few drops of blood fell, which gave birth to the Three Eumenides, those Furies who avenge parricide and perjury."'*

'I perfectly recall that strange speech,' says the Maritime Affairs Investigator. 'I'm not surprised that Kurt Knigh felt the need to make a note of it. But, you know, that kind of outburst was nothing exceptional. Karl Knigh was a very courteous, very affable man . . . but he could also say some terrible things. He would in a way shelter behind the myths that he was fond of quoting, and of which he seemed to have a very extensive knowledge, in order to do so.'

'I've another page here where Kurt tries to capture his father's peculiar personality,' continues the Literary Expert. 'Commenting on the *dead weight*, as he puts it, of books by "the great author", "the author of international and even world-wide renown", who is led by vanity, what with all the adulation, more and more to produce the kind of book expected of him, instead of taking the risk of being, as Freud writes somewhere, *the first to*, Kurt has fun playing with the word *novels*. You see, every time he refers to those of his father, what does he do? Instead of *novels*, he writes *grovels* .'

'Let's see,' says the Poet Criminologist impatiently. 'Well, in any event this is telling evidence, if I may say so. We know all too well what this sort of word game signifies. When a person begins to substitute a rhyming word for another word, madness of a specifically literary nature is not far off. Especially, as is the case with Kurt Knigh, if the substituted word has what we might call a criminalizing connotation. That the great Karl Knigh's books should be *grovels,* as I see vituperatively written more or less all over this page, is extremely illuminating in terms of the state of mind of this son who also wrote novels.'

'But not *grovels,*' says the Literary Expert, laughing. 'Kurt, Rosa and Franz all felt a strange sense of superiority towards their father – this wasn't at first detectable but became increasingly obvious the more you got to know them. What they joked about a great deal was that Karl should have accepted, and what's more been proud of winning, what they all three laughingly called *the Dynamite Prize*. "What's so brilliant about dynamite?" Kurt Knigh said to me one day. I was with him, his sister Rosa, and Gustav Zhorn, in Austria. At the time I was researching my thesis on "The Knigh Literary Family", and they very kindly received me at the house on the outskirts of Vienna that had been placed at their disposal by the producers of a film based on Rosa Zhorn-Knigh's first novel.'

'What's so brilliant about dynamite!' echoed the Poet Criminologist. 'Actually, it must be admitted, dynamite hasn't, criminologically speaking, the fascinating possibilities of other means of spilling blood. Imagine Cain blowing up Abel with a stick of dynamite! No more Sacrifice! No more Expiation! And Abraham preparing a bed of dynamite for his son? No knife! No more playing games with God! Anonymous dynamite! And remember that this "Dynamite" Prize, as you say the Knigh children called it, is also supposed to reward those who work for "peace" or, better still, certain scientists who, having taken what else but dynamite as the measure of destruction, seek to multiply the violence of an Apocalypse promised by the *dynamite of all dynamites*!'

'You're thinking of Rosa Knigh's writings,' says the Literary Expert with amusement.

'Precisely! It takes a neurotic young woman like Rosa Knigh to dare to broach certain literary themes that only a few nineteenth-century female writers had ventured to deal with. Remember those Englishwomen oppressed by Anglican puritanism, and those smooth-skinned vicars with dry hands who served as their fathers, uncles, cousins or husbands. All of them fathers, to tell the truth, as dessicated as mummies escaped from their sarcophagi. It's no surprise that these books, full of gusting winds and lowering clouds over the heath, talk of nothing but coffins, white-eyed corpses, and incestuous love affairs recounted from a neurotic female point of view of unparalleled morbidity. It's true, Rosa Knigh managed to create a modern style of baneful prose in which the scarcely concealed, great terror of the father appears in all its horror. The omnipresent father, in possession of the magic ring whose burning ray strips the children of their skin . . . Do you remember that famous photograph of a screaming child, yes! stripped of her skin, with the death's-head mushroom of nuclear catastrophe rising up behind.'

'Rosa Knigh,' says the Literary Expert, 'was a young woman with a totally original mind. I'm extremely impatient to bury myself in her manuscripts, which I've put aside on that chair, there. What I read of them last night leads me to expect some very great surprises. There are pages about her brother Kurt that are quite shattering, and other pages about Zhorn, and especially about her marriage to this unhinged actor whose name she was prepared to take, even signing her most recent books Rosa Zhorn-Knigh. All these revelations are so disturbing! Only the silence of the night can help me penetrate and unravel such writings. In any case Rosa Zhorn-Knigh's books are far from being *grovels*!

V

'When I was researching my thesis on the Knigh literary family, and in particular the Rosa-Kurt-Gustav Zhorn triangle,' the Literary Expert continues, 'I often thought of the Bronte family – those sisters and their drug-addict brother who also wrote poems, unreadable for their arrogance and lunacy, which he would slip between the pages of his sisters' compilation of writings.'

'In the Knigh case, though, it was the brother and sister who introduced a foreign body between them,' says the Poet Criminologist, 'and, if I understand correctly, it was that hurt that fed Rosa and Kurt's writings. And those writings created a kind of indestructible net, as it were, around the young trio.'

'You're right, except that this net didn't ensnare just the three of them, but was part of a much vaster net, and one so much tighter, in which the whole Knigh family was embroiled. Skimming through the manuscripts made available to me, and as yet grasping only an infinitesimal part of them, it appears that, rather than each representing a distinct type of writing, all these manuscripts converge. They seem to me to constitute a whole, as if what we had to deal with here was *a Knigh culture*, with its contradictions, alliances, betrayals, hatreds and loves, its incests supposedly too shameful to admit, which the Knigh children not only admitted but vaunted, like some weapon wrested from the myths that they use now, in the present day, against their father Karl Knigh, he so comfortably ensconced in a bookish and how etiolated a memory of those self-same myths! You can't imagine what a terrible reappraisal of the contents of my thesis I'm struggling with, and to what extent the little that I've already gleaned from these manuscripts calls into question the very image I developed of this family of writers. At the time, I saw in the Rosa-Kurt-Gustav trio not a trio but a loving and, given current mores, almost normal twinship; that's to say, *two-in-one* that had drawn into the orbit of this twinship a third body passing within range . . .'

'Do you know, the same's true of certain rare stars?' says the Poet Criminologist. 'Those famous double stars whose rotation sucks in wandering bodies and absorbs them.'

'That's right, but in the Rosa-Kurt-Gustav case, the force of attraction at first functioned on the principle of *two-absorb-one*, then it shifted, with the result that *one* ended up by absorbing *two*, do you follow? It's reminiscent of the sublime and diabolical Heathcliffe, created by Emily Bronte! "That's him," I said to myself on seeing Gustav Zhorn for the first time, in Vienna. And at the same time, thinking of Kurt before he met Zhorn, I said to myself, "That's him as well, Heathcliffe as he might have been, and as the Brontes' brother was before being, as it were, remodelled by Emily's morbid prose . . . and Charlotte's too." It's not at all surprising that, in that century when women were the living-dead, the two sisters should have written parallel novels, in which the adored brother of the two young girls whose hearts had been poisoned by the venom of Anglican puritanism becomes the incarnation of the Devil. Today, of course it's not incest or perversions that have the capacity to shock, but the violence of a truly insane love, yes, literally insane! It was only too obvious that there was something very violent going on between Rosa Knigh and her brother Kurt Knigh, a kind of amorous electric charge, both despairing and triumphant. The term "amorous electric charge" is one taken from this manuscript here, by Rosa, Zhorn-Knigh as she became. I also came across the same term in that manuscript over there on the table. Which is by Kurt Knigh, whom I should call Kurt Knigh-Zhorn, so admirably did Zhorn succeed in parasitically exploiting that love and uniting himself with that twinship.'

'Yes, indeed,' says the Maritime Affairs Investigator, 'I remember Zhorn from the Yacht Club. Wherever he appeared, the attention of everyone there would excessively focus on him. It might be said that the man had a disagreeable charm. There was lots of gossip about him. One thing was clear: Kurt Knigh couldn't stand his presence . . . and for his part, Gustav Zhorn never missed a single one of those family cruises. He relished Karl Knigh's coolness towards him, and at the Yacht Club I often saw old Knigh visibly stiffen and turn away at Zhorn's approach.'

'Nevertheless,' says the Literary Expert, 'he never refused to have him aboard. While at the same time hating Zhorn, he couldn't do without him. That I know!'

'Yes, it raised quite a few smiles, that evident fascination.'

'Ah, that Zhorn! What a good culprit!' says the Poet Criminologist, laughing.

'Absolutely,' says the Investigator. 'If our instincts were to be trusted, we'd all point the finger at him. And yet we know from experience that when it's said of someone, "we'd all point the finger at him..."'

'That's virtual proof that it wasn't him.'

'Well, believe you me,' says the Literary Expert, 'having known him quite well and listened to him a great deal, of all the guests on the yacht he's the only one I can imagine doing the deed out of sheer perversity.'

'Perversity can't possibly be the motive. To drown so many people and drown yourself along with them out of sheer perversity? No!' cries the Investigator.

'But just so,' says the Poet Criminologist, 'no motive! I've scientifically studied numerous crimes, and my career as a criminologist is strewn, as they say, with hundreds of cases that prove to us that a great many crimes are without motive. To tell the truth, all crimes are without motive. Crime is in itself a motive. Crime uplifts the mind. I don't know how many criminals whom I regard as artists have confessed to me that they couldn't resist the invitation of chance. The inspiration, if you prefer. The crime volunteered itself. The near-possible suggests itself ... or the near-impossible. This deed is not possible; I'm doing it! We ought to know that murder is one of the most natural expressions of the living. One who's alive doesn't realize he's killing; he lives and survives. Death is prior to the crime. But where the "beauty" of it is lies in knowledge of the crime. Before the crime there was murder. But murder doesn't interest us. Death was never denominated by life: that thing's moving – now it's not! There were two of them – now there's only one. That perhaps was the first astonished realization of one who, having stood up on his hind limbs, tried to formulate an explanation for why that thing's moving and why now it's not. Is that not compelling: this thing's moving and now it's not? Something to be cancelled out upon realization that all life's a mirror. By shattering the mirror, as it were. That in my view is a sufficiently strong motive for this mass drowning: a philosophical murder.'

'So that means we now have to find out which of all the *Uranus*'s passengers was the philosopher?' says the Investigator sarcastically.

'Precisely!'

'In short, someone who couldn't resist the philosophical temptation?'

'Precisely! The temptation of "beauty". It was just too beautiful, you understand? There he is, alone on board the *Uranus*, empty sea all around, ringed by an empty horizon; the *Uranus*, motionless, a floating splendour, as bright as a dazzling iceberg; otherwise, blue water and blue skies everywhere! There are six of them swimming around the boat, laughing and calling to each other . . .'

'You say six; there were seven of them.'

'Exactly, which of them got out first? Which of them, looking down over the side at the others from high, high above, on the yacht, was unable to resist? Pulling up the ladder and jumping in as well, because never before, perhaps, had such an opportunity presented itself to an intelligent man who was enough of an artist to be incapable of denying himself such a crystal gem of criminal beauty.'

'You speak as a criminologist aesthete,' says the Investigator. 'That you, a criminologist aware of the possible "beauty" of a crime, might not resist, I could just about accept, but that there should happen to have been one among them – brother, father, sister, daughter, sons, uncle or husband – unable to resist this temptation which you regard as almost natural, I cannot believe!'

'Not at all! You misunderstand me: one that goes against nature, and for that very reason artistically irresistible.'

'But you seem to be forgetting someone,' the Literary Expert intervened. 'What about Lotte Knigh?'

'What do you mean? Old Knigh's young wife?'

'And why not? I've glanced at her diary. It's so weird and complicated, not only in the way it's written, but also because of certain additions and drawings made in Karl Knigh's hand. But more about that later, if you don't mind, when I've had a chance to examine the photographic enlargements of those markings found on the hull of the *Uranus*.'

'But come along with us, we're on our way to my office! The photographs are there waiting for you.'

'No, I can't take everything in at once. I mean, I've had too much new information sprung on me for one night. I'm going to be inundated with just as much, and even more, as soon as I get back to my reading.'

'Lotte Knigh,' says the Criminologist, 'young Lotte Knigh. Now, isn't that a fascinating idea? They all get in the water. She doesn't. She feels sad. She feels herself to be an outsider in this family. She watches them from above, swimming round the *Uranus*, and suddenly *that feeling* comes over her, it's irresistible: the abyss, the irresistible gesture that requires no effort other than unhooking the ladder, yes, letting it drop among the swimmers. At first everyone laughs, then they begin to get panicky, calling for her to throw down a line, a rope, so that she can hoist up that ladder and secure it again. And what does Lotte Knigh do?'

'She goes running off in search of a rope,' says the Investigator.

'Not at all! Excited by the general panic, the shouting, the instructions that maybe even Karl Knigh himself is yelling at her, taken with a sudden fit, she jumps in among the swimmers. Yes! Just like that. On an impulse . . . or in desperation . . . although she's no sooner in the water than she realizes! On contact with the water, she *wakes up*.'

'Are all criminologists so fiendish?' says the Literary Expert, laughing.

'Criminology is indeed a fiendish science. Criminology

teaches you that crime has a power of fascination over men. As I said before, not murder – crime. Cain was a murderer, but the criminals were those of his descent: the ones who knew. Cain was innocent, but not those of his descent. Murder was called crime over the innocent body of Abel. I like the great criminals; the criminologist in me likes the great criminals. Who would ever think of studying the innocent? Who would ever think of studying the social slave? The social slave is a clone, a biological replica who has the Law "Thou shalt not kill" somehow instilled in his genes. The social slave eats, drinks, sleeps, and breeds offspring identical to himself. For millennia now, he's not been *a player in the game*, and for this he's rewarded with a daily handful of corn. And then one day, who knows why, the monstrous angel's roused. And *he* acts differently. Does he think differently? Who knows, but whatever he does, he acts differently. Crime is there, settled inside him, waiting its chance. Before even having killed, the monstrous angel is a criminal. He cuts his way through the anonymous crowd and no one notices that crime is inside him, that he's bearing a crime just as an artist bears inside him the *crime* of a masterpiece.'

'Have you read Julius Knigh's books?' says the Literary Expert.

'No.'

'I'm struck by how close your paradoxes are to his. See these manuscripts that I've stacked up on the table? They filled the three old suitcases that Julius dragged along with him even on the *Uranus*. I picked out these lines of Nietzsche, which appear as an introductory quotation to one of these writings. They suddenly illuminated for me the hidden personality of this man Julius, who's so reserved and so apparently detached from everything.

> *'I must climb more than a hundred steps,*
> *I must climb, I hear you cry:*
> *"You're callous! Are we then stones?"*
> *I must climb more than a hundred steps,*
> *And no one wants to be a step.'*

'Those lines are unworthy of a humanist,' says the Investigator. 'Those lines are unworthy of a *true* poet!'

'And yet,' says the Poet Criminologist, picking up the page that the Literary Expert has just put down, 'and yet those lines get as close as can be to the quiet secret rage that as much oppresses the soul of a criminal in search of his *great* crime as that of the artist in search of the impossible masterpiece. Every poet is a criminal, by default a killer of words instead of human beings. Poet and humanist? Sorry, but the two are mutually exclusive! There are masses of versifiers, masses of humanist versifiers. But call that a poet? Surely not. Did not Nietzsche himself say, "*This isn't a book: what do books matter! Those coffins, those shrouds! Books plunder the past. But here the Eternal Present reigns.*" There's the criminal poet for you, the non-humanist poet, as all the fierce great poets, filled with a love-hate for humanity, have been.'

'I admire your insight,' says the Literary Expert, waving between them a bundle of pages covered with extraordinarily close handwriting. 'Julius achieved the feat of unsettling words. In these manuscripts here are fragments of a beauty, a splendour, that's almost inhuman. Last night, going from one manuscript to another, I couldn't help comparing them and was able to judge to what extent Julius Knigh's writings, like those of Lotte Zhorn-Knigh's in fact, are on a par with that other line of Nietzsche: *The sea laughs, the freakish sea*! And that's only a first impression. Give me a few more days and I think I can promise you a great many surprises . . . And for future generations, too.'

'Enough poetry!' exclaims the Investigator. 'And never mind about future generations! What I ask of you are some clues, or premonitory remarks at least, hinting at the tragedy we're investigating, and for which we've turned to you as an expert on the Knigh literary family. It's of no interest to us whether Julius Knigh's manuscripts are destined to revolutionize the behaviour of future generations. As Maritime Affairs Investigator, I'm impatient not for the editorial but the investigative result of your reading. Your reading of the manuscripts found aboard the *Uranus* should be as unliterary a reading as possible. What does literary quality matter to us right now? It's the shock answer we're waiting for! Who was the killer? How did the killer do it? Why did the killer do it? We have to satisfy curiosity. Not just our own curiosity, but curiosity in general. We'll be writing a report on the *Uranus* mystery, dedicated to the god Curiosity. And not to the pleasure of how the *Uranus* mystery might be expressed. How the answer's conveyed is of little concern to us. It's the satisfaction of curiosity that we want.'

'As a secret poet, I think you're wrong,' says the Poet Criminologist, 'but as a criminologist I'd almost agree. The poet in me detests curiosity, that poisoned sword with which the writer impales the reader. Curiosity requires a final word. And the secret poet, ever alert within me, is against any final word. A mystery should remain a mystery. Now, what about going over to the Yacht Club for lunch?'

VI

'To return to the Knigh family, if you don't mind,' says the Maritime Affairs Investigator when they were seated at a table in the Yacht Club, 'how could old Knigh have possibly agreed to your idea of a literary thesis on the Knigh family? Knowing what he was like, I'm amazed that he went along with it.'

'Oh, he didn't go along with it, as you put it. He agreed to see me, thinking, I imagine, that he would dissuade me from undertaking research of a kind that would involve studying not only his works but also those of his brother, daughter and two sons. I made the trip to Spain where he "consented" to see me, he said, on condition that our interview should take no longer than an hour or two . . . and I stayed a week.'

'So he did agree to it?'

'No, not at all. He didn't agree to anything. But not being able to prevent me, he tried, not only at Pals but later in Granada and again in New York and finally in Berlin, to make me "drop it". Those were his words. "You'll never write this thesis," he told me, while at the same time agreeing to answer my questions. As soon as he saw me, he realized that I'd go through with it. He knew that I was to meet Rosa, Kurt and Franz. Furthermore, he knew that I knew where Julius was. Julius hadn't refused to meet me; he knew that too. How was he going to gain the upper hand and try to steer my thesis firmly in the right direction? So he received me in a little Moorish garden where his work table had been set up. When I mentioned the "Knigh literary family", the old man immediately tensed and Lotte Knigh grew agitated.

'"You mean, you're not planning an academic thesis on my work but a kind of extra-literary investigation?"

'"Not at all," I replied. "With your help, and that of your brother Julius, and your children Kurt, Rosa and Franz, who've also agreed to see me and answer my questions, I'd hope to construct a literary criticism model based not on research into the significance of your extraordinary family's writings but on a semantic approach to this quite exceptional phenomenon. Never has a whole family exclusively dedicated itself to literature, to the extent of producing such a quantity of texts written in parallel. It's this, what I'd call, almost genetic aspect that fascinates me."

'As you can imagine,' the Literary Expert goes on, 'I disguised my real purpose as a scientific study of the written material, when it was *how it affected their lives* that intrigued me. But what most upset the old man was that I put his brother's writings and those of his children on a par with his.'

'Even those of his son Franz?'

'Even those of Franz.'

'Yet Franz is more of a philosopher. I've read his work on the senses. I don't see how it could detract from the novels of the "great" Karl Knigh.'

'Of his three children, Franz was certainly the one he loved least. I later realized why. Franz was the third child – the last – whose birth cost the life of his first wife. For which he never forgave Franz. That he should be here, alive! Through Franz, it was his first wife that he blamed for an untimely departure, as it were. She had gone and died on him, leaving him alone with three children to look after. But at the time he carefully avoided talking about his children and he barely allowed me to mention his brother Julius. He even avoided talking about his own books. He began by holding forth in wide-ranging terms about literature, touching on Browning's *The Ring and the Book* . . .'

'One of the strangest books, and read by very few people!' says the Poet Criminologist. 'You know, in London, a kind of secret society has grown up around that book?'

'That's what Karl Knigh told me, suggesting that a small circle of "anonymous readers" had also "crystallized" – those are the words he used – around his own writings. "Conversely," he went on to say, "everyone claims to have read Joyce's *Ulysses*, a book that no one's ever actually read through to the end . . . or rather, of which everyone's read only the ending. Ah, that Molly!" He fell silent for a moment, with a set jaw and a frown on his face. At that point Lotte Knigh came up to him and rather condescendingly, almost indulgently, laid her hands on his white hair, treating him like an elderly child.'

'Do you know,' says the Poet Criminologist gaily, 'that Isidore Ducasse found a wonderful way to describe novelists belonging to literary high society? "The court-in-sitting clan of novelists".'

'So, you were with Karl Knigh at Pals,' the Maritime Affairs Investigator cuts in a little irritatedly. 'Did he tell you anything from which it might have been possible to predict the tragedy that overtook him and his whole family.'

'How interesting that you should mention Isidore Ducasse,' says the Literary Expert, addressing the Poet Criminologist. 'Do you recall the second song?'

'You're thinking of the famous shipwreck?'

'Exactly! The poet talks of "the soon-to-drown" being happy to prolong their lives if only for a few seconds, "in the swirling vortex of the abyss".'

'I know every word of it by heart.'

'Well, on the second day of our interview at Pals, Karl Knigh, without identifying it, referred to the passage in which the narrator takes his double-barrelled shotgun and fires at the swimmer whose "handsome and resolute head" appears and disappears among the waves. Do you recall that passage, which has a very engaging looseness of style?'

'*At the height of the storm, I saw a strong head with shaggy hair, desperately striving to keep above the waves. He swallowed litres of water, and sank into the abyss* . . . And further on, he adds, *He couldn't have been more than sixteen; for in the flashes of lightning that illuminated the darkness the peach-fluff on his upper lip was just visible* . . ." I could continue to the end, from memory.'

'Even though he didn't identify it, Karl Knigh referred to that passage, you say?' the Investigator says insistently.

'"Tragic *Uranus*!" Karl Knigh exclaimed as we were walking along the beach at Pals. He shook his walking stick at the sea and the sky, brandishing it at the yacht anchored not far off. "Do you want to know what my secret desire is?" he went on with disagreeable sarcasm, so that at the time I thought he was making fun of me, "my secret desire is to see it go down with every member of my family."'

'His secret desire, you say?' the Maritime Investigator cuts in.

'Yes, and still in that enigmatic tone of voice he added, "May not one of us survive! At the same time I'd like to lie in ambush on a rock along the coast and shoot at them with my double-barrelled shotgun as they jumped into the water." He laughed and suddenly changing expression – as he often did, you remember? – he told me this was the subject he had in mind for his next book ... or last book ... I'm not sure exactly which.'

'But you can't hedge between *next* and *last*,' says the Investigator. 'The second word not only puts everything in an entirely different perspective but substantially influences our suspicions. Do you really believe that old Knigh was capable ...?'

'I don't think so. He may have imagined it in literary terms ... But to go from that to killing all his close relatives and himself as well ... to pass from the written word to the deed ...'

'Don't you believe it,' the Poet Criminologist cuts in. 'I've followed at close hand a quite extraordinary case of passing from the written word to the deed, as you put it. It involves a young working-class woman who out of boredom, perhaps hatred of her family, began writing anonymous letters to herself. A need for distraction? Fed up with being just "a housewife and mother"? Who knows? What threat to her did *her* letters make? To destroy her *happiness* as a wife and mother, of course. The kind of *happiness* that this young woman secretly hated. And then, since no one took seriously these letters of hers that made her interesting, she keeps increasing the dose, as it were, with every succeeding anonymous letter. The threats become more specific. In her disguised handwriting, does she not even go so far as to threaten the life of her own child? There's no outrage among those around her. They laugh at this preposterous blackmail. Isn't it natural then, that the young woman should honour the literary contract she's made with herself? She kills her child, which just goes to show them! The written word's fulfilled by the deed.'

'I don't think that Karl Knigh had that kind of "simplicity" in him. Remember, he had a great knowledge of myths,' the Literary Expert goes on. '"I don't want to be a *modern* author," he used to say, "on the contrary, I want to establish myself as a classical author. As much as possible, I keep very close to myths. I want to be as near as I can to them. I'm at home with myths. I love everything about them: the blood, cannibalism, incest, the multitude of gods who *play* a mirror-image of a mankind. All my books," he told me, "are intended to make the ancient myths modern. I want to give them a beauty, an appeal that transcends them and makes them acceptable to us today. Take an everyday news story: for example, the decent family man, as they say, who for obscure reasons, and indeed often for no reason at all – which makes the whole thing even more obscure – kills his children, and his wife, as well as the greatest possible number of relatives . . . and turning his weapon against himself, takes the law into his own hands. Takes the law into his own hands! A family man! The law! Family man," he said, "now there's an expression too recent to give full scope to man's heart of darkness."

'We were walking along the beach at Pals again; we did nothing else for the whole week I spent with him in Spain. He stopped and in the sand, still wet from the last wave, he traced a series of weird signs. By the way, I suspect that the marks on the *Uranus*'s hull . . . but we'll talk about that later! Karl Knigh went on to say: "Although the patriarchal society dates back hundreds of years, deep down we regret the matriarchy. I became aware of this the day that my first wife, Belle, died. Yes, on that day I regretted those distant ages when the Mother-Queen held sway, the Great Goddess, the Queen from Mesopotamia, forebear of Aphrodite Urania, queen of the sacred mountain where Erycina, goddess of midsummer, lived. She killed the sacred King who coupled with her on the mountain-peak. Imitating the queen bee that kills the male by tearing out his sexual organs, Erycina Aphrodite Urania, like the heather bee – *erycina* means heather, don't forget to put that in your thesis, my dear young scholar – make sure you stress the red-heather colour of the immolator bee-Queen, likewise dressed in red, you know, at the time of her amorous relations with Anchises on the summit of the sacred Mountain, as well as that of the unfortunate sacred King's immolation.'

'Wait a moment, now, wait a moment,' the Maritime Affairs Investigator cuts in. 'Wasn't Karl Knigh pulling your leg? I remember that at the Yacht Club if he wanted to put down either one of his children or one of his guests, it was in myths, so he claimed, that he found the examples he needed. To tell the truth, I've always suspected him of having more imagination than memory.'

'Yet what he said about the sacred King being sacrificed on the summit of the sacred Mountain is quite correct,' the Literary Expert continues. 'Karl Knigh was speaking of himself when he referred to the dethroned sacred King. He lived his life in all sincerity as an overthrown king or god. Every line written by his brother or sons or daughter he perceived as an attack on his sovereignty.'

'Don't you think,' the Poet Criminologist insists, 'as our friend the Investigator so subtly remarked just now, that Karl Knigh was pulling your leg? It's well known that when an author comes across a literary expert sufficiently naive to drink in his every word, he can't help pushing his head in the barrel and keeping it there for as long as possible. Do you really think that in cloaking himself with myths he wasn't enjoying himself, drowning you in a kind of storm while at the same time shooting at you, the shipwrecked literary expert, with an automatic rifle?'

'In any event,' says the Investigator, 'having often attended either the launchings of his successive *Uranus*es or the parties he sometimes held here in the Yacht Club to mark his safe return from his cruises, all of us have always thought that Knigh used his genuine – or false – knowledge of myths to sever all communication with normal people like us by means of his erudite talk. It was his personal way of treating us with affable scorn. You had to drink with him and listen to what he said.'

'That's right,' says the Literary Expert, 'Karl Knigh always slightly despised anyone he spoke to. I believe that secretly it was himself he was afraid of despising, or at least that he was so unsure of himself he had to belittle in his mind anyone who came near him. I realized where this arrogant insecurity originated. Gradually, as he talked, I saw the reason for his insecurity and the reason for his arrogance become clear. All his life he'd run up against a wall.'

The Literary Expert stops for a moment to light a cigarette.

'That wall was Julius. The fact is that despite his fame, despite his books and the commentaries, studies and analyses in every language, yes, the "great" Karl Knigh remained all his life head-on up against a wall named Julius. Between the two brothers there was not only a terrible secret that, since last night, I think I *almost* know – I say *almost* because the secret is to be found in their writings – rather like that bank note which is torn in half to serve as a means of recognition between two strangers who've been given the two halves in secrecy – but most important of all, Karl Knigh had become aware of Julius's true literary stature and this was unbearably painful to him.

'Once, when we were on the beach at Pals, he stopped and this time with his walking stick wrote Julius's name in the wet sand left gleaming by the retreating wave. He squeezed my arm as his brother's name slowly disappeared, the next wave little by little rendering the sand smooth and bare, the way it was before. Wait, that's not all! He then traced the names of Kurt, Rosa, Franz, Gustav Zhorn and finally that of Lotte, then his own. And once more he held my arm in a tight grip, the entire time it took the sea to make the wet sand smooth again.

'"Did you see that?" he said. "They are, all of them, to be treated as the subjects of your thesis?"

'"Yes," I replied.

'"You're really determined on it?"

'"Insofar as my thesis will remain purely literary."

'He laughed. "Purely? You know very well that there's no such thing as a thesis that's purely anything whatsoever. Every thesis is purely impure," he said, still tracing those strange signs of his in the sand, "every thesis is constructed on written remains. Just as you somehow have to get your hands on a corpse to dissect, or buy a cat from some grubby street urchin if you want to do a vivisection, your thesis cannot but be literary butchery, because, whatever you say, your thesis, it seems to me, must be closer to vivisection than dissection. Why don't you wait till I'm dead before beginning your literary investigation. I'm an old man. My wife's much younger than me. Can you really not wait until the day after my burial? There's no better distraction for a writer's widow than to speak of the departed! Absence fills itself with words. What could be more natural? And the words of widows are always attended to with perhaps more attention than those of creative writers in their lifetime."

'We walked for a while in silence along the beach at Pals,' the Literary Expert continues, 'and suddenly Knigh said to me, "I don't like your thesis. Already I don't like it!" And still holding me by the arm, in the way that elderly Italian men affectionately stroll along together, he dragged me off to a little *cantina* in the modern port. "Let's sit here," he said, "and drink. I've a most bizarre appointment, in this very place, and I'd like you to be present. Watch, but above all don't say anything. I've a rendezvous here with the future . . . and, as you'll realize, with the past as well, the terrible and insurmountable past. Let's drink!

'"Listen," he said to me a little later, after a second bottle had replaced the first, "you don't seem too bad for a literary expert. You're young, you seem almost too intelligent to be making a career out of me and my family. My children and my brother are all fiercely committed to writing and, I confess, nothing irritates me more. Even Lotte secretly keeps a diary. They all write diaries, poems, stories, and novels too! Have you read Julius's latest book?"

'I hesitated,' the Literary Expert goes on, 'to tell him how much I admired *all* Julius Knigh's writings. That in fact it was through my admiration for Julius Knigh that I came to read the books which he, Karl Knigh, had written, as well as those of Kurt and Rosa, and later those quite exceptional philosophical essays of Franz.'

'And so what did you say to him?' asks the Poet Criminologist.

'Now, really,' exclaims the Investigator, 'he shouldn't have said anything – like any good investigator, to my mind, be he literary detective or criminal investigator.'

'Well, not a bit of it!' says the Literary Expert. 'On the contrary, I was eager to strike the first blow.

'"I infinitely admire what your brother Julius has written," I said, pouring myself another drink.

'After a while he said in a rather subdued voice, "Infinitely, you say?"

'"Yes, I assure you . . ."

'"Right . . ." We continued to drink in silence. "And what about my son Kurt? You're not going to have me believe that you have an infinitely high opinion of his writing?"

'"Let's say, I've a high opinion of them."

'"Really?"

'"Yes, a very high opinion."

'After he'd ordered another bottle, he added in a voice barely audible this time: "And my daughter Rosa's writing?"

'I looked him straight in the eye and then fired my third arrow, surely the most terrible, striking him where it hurt most. "Along with Carson McCullers, Rosa Zhorn-Knigh is without any doubt the greatest . . ."

'"Come, come," he immediately interrupted me, "you know very well there are no women writers . . . Women's writing is worthless writing."

'"I don't agree," I said, pressing my case, "as a writer, your daughter Rosa Zhorn-Knigh outclasses most of her literary contemporaries."'

'Do you really think so, or were you just saying that to see his reaction?'

'It was a goad, a red rag. But I nonetheless consider Rosa Zhorn-Knigh to be a very great writer, although no one can define what constitutes "great" literature.'

'Indeed,' says the Poet Criminologist, 'no one can make

that assertion. It's like what I was saying to you a little while ago about crime. Yes, there's always a little "crime" in all innovative writing.'

'Now, suppose we get back to that *cantina* where you were drinking with old Knigh,' says the Investigator impatiently.

'Isidore Ducasse,' the Poet Criminologist continues, 'the most amoral individual in his writings, suddenly becomes almost mawkish when he declares in his *Poems*: *Good is victory over Evil, the negation of Evil. If Good is celebrated, Evil is eliminated by this congruous act*. He even goes on to say this completely incongruous thing: *Words that express Evil are destined to take on a useful significance. Ideas improve.* I can't believe that the poet who drowns a shipwrecked youth with *the peach-fluff on his upper lip just visible*, by shooting at him with a rifle, could possibly believe in the usefulness of poetry, or more broadly speaking of art. Usefulness!'

'Not now! Now not!' says the Maritime Affairs Investigator, losing his temper. 'It's getting late. It's going to be time for us to go our separate ways. Continue with your reading of the manuscripts! For myself, I have to leave you for an urgent meeting. Can we please get to the end of this *cantina* story? So, this appointment that old Knigh had? Who was it that he had come to wait for, with you, in this *cantina* in Pals?'

'A strange appointment, as you'll see. At some point a woman came in, holding a cockerel under her arm. In her rags and tatters, she looked just like any of those drunken women that inevitably turn up in novels set in port towns, where disgraced sea captains live on, passing themselves off – without knowing what they're talking about – as Lord Jims. Universal Lord Jims, as it were, who all have some act of cowardice or maritime crime on their conscience, which they expiate by continuing to exist head down in a barrel.'

'Like a kind of Diogenes with a bad conscience! Very true,' the Poet Criminologist exclaims with delight.

'Kindly don't interrupt any more. You were saying that a woman holding a cockerel . . .'

'Speaking of Lord Jim, did you know that there's a woman at Hyères, a very hot-shot literary expert, who has, she claims, discovered the actual sources for Lord Jim, that perfect symbol of guilt of whom increasingly faint traces seem to keep turning up in a great many rather mediocre novels,' says the Poet Criminologist.

'And in some very fine ones too,' says the Literary Expert. 'The Consul's *guilt*!'

'Are you referring to the two German submariners burned alive in the boiler of the disguised freighter that Geoffrey Firmin was in command of during the war?'

'That's right. Any literary work of real merit is almost inevitably generated by an earlier work of merit. So much so that a good reader is delighted to recognize this affiliation. One can even say, more precisely, that every work of merit is a critique of an earlier work of merit. *Anna Karenina* is clearly a critique of *Madame Bovary*, an admiring and, let's say, even friendly response . . .'

'So, what about this woman holding a cockerel under her arm, who comes into the *cantina* in the new port of Pals?'

'The woman sat down at our table and, letting go of the cockerel that she kept on a string tied round its claw, she asked old Knigh whether he needed her services "today". "You know I always need you! Here, have a drink!" And laying a fistful of banknotes on the table he told her to continue from where she'd got to the other day "in the future novel of my life", as he said, rather sarcastically. Thereupon the woman with the cockerel began to tell him some terrible things, by interpreting the pecking of the cockerel to which she threw some grain.'

'What do you mean by terrible?' says the Investigator.

VII

'She was quite simply in the process of warning him of a family tragedy . . .'

'What?' the Investigator and the Poet Criminologist say in unison.

'Those were her exact words: *a family tragedy.*'

'You're interpreting . . . or some kind of recent memory is replacing the older one. Otherwise why wouldn't you have told us this sooner?'

'Wait! Wait! Not everything can come at once. There are lots of pointers in my thesis. How tempting it is to read certain events with hindsight. Karl Knigh was constantly consulting clairvoyants and seers. Whether among the gypsies, in Granada; or in New York, where he took me along to some strange seances with an Indian Bengali; or even in Berlin, visiting a woman whose entire family had disappeared, so she said, somewhere in the wilds of the Mongolian steppe, from where she received certain *messages*.'

'Really? And the woman with the cockerel?'

'She drank one glass after another, and occasionally attempted to kick out at her cockerel. Knigh kept pouring her more. And she talked. A little later, as we were staggering back to the house where Lotte Knigh was waiting for us, he made quite an astonishing comment: "Would you believe it," he said, "that vile woman dictates to me what I'm writing at the moment? That old Parca weaves the destinies, as it were, of those I talk about in the latest book that I'm working on." He wasn't drunk, although he was certainly very much under the influence of the wine, as I was. I find it quite difficult now to distinguish between my memories and my impressions.'

'It's clear that Knigh was trying to mislead you,' says the Poet Criminologist. 'Nothing of what he said to you can be taken seriously since it was his intention to sabotage your thesis or to leave you floundering at least.'

'That's exactly what I think,' says the Literary Expert, 'and

I'm counting on my reading of the manuscripts to distinguish between drunkenness and the true facts. In that respect Karl Knigh's writings seem quite surprising – knowing both his modesty and immodesty. Just as we arrived in front of his house in the port of Pals, he stopped, and squeezing my arm so hard that it hurt, he said to me, "I'm going to tell you a secret on condition that it doesn't appear in your thesis. Promise?"

' "Promise!" I said, aware that our conversation was ever so slightly over-oiled with wine.'

'Well? Well? What was the secret?' says the Investigator impatiently.

'Well, the strange confession that he made was this: "It's my ambition – and this will be my final book, there'll be no going back on that – to bring together fiction and reality." And when I expressed surprise, he added, "You see, in the end life and the written word become indistinguishable for me. You'll tell me: every text eventually drowns its author" – he used the word *drowns* – " in the pit previously dug and inundated by his own writings." '

'Wait a moment, please,' the Investigator cuts in. 'Just a little while ago you were hesitating between *next* book and *last* book, unable, you told us, to be really sure of the term used by Karl Knigh. And yet it's essential for us to know. You said *next*, then *last*, then *final*. Try seriously to search your memory.'

'You being an investigator and I a criminologist, we both know that there's no such thing as reliable memory. Ten people may have witnessed the same event and when they give their account of it they seem to be talking about ten different events in ten different places at times that don't correspond at all.'

'In any case I can tell you this: Knigh was a tired man. "I'm tired of everything. It's time to invert the hour glass," he told me some time later. "Whether the sand runs in one direction or another is no longer important to me, since my life is no longer represented by that stricture, that impossible knot to untie, and which I shall have to cut through." Wait, that's not all,' continues the Literary Expert. 'Striking the ground with his walking stick several times, Knigh then spoke with anger and scorn of those authors who "confine themselves to carrying out the suicide they announced more or less explicitly in their last book". That's what he said to me in Granada, which is where we were and where he'd insisted on taking me himself.'

'Everything you've just told us,' says the Investigator, 'is highly significant, and in my view reinforces a very unsavoury impression: that Karl Knigh had *reasons* for drowning his whole family . . . along with himself. To invert the hour glass, as he put it, once and for all, without confining himself to suicide.'

'And do you know why Knigh dragged me off to Granada?' continues the Literary Expert, regardless of the Investigator's interruption. 'He couldn't bear the idea that I might meet Julius without him. He wanted to be there. With us. I suppose he hoped to create a climate between Julius and myself. To set us before each other in the way that he wanted. Julius had been living in Granada for years, in the poorer part of town, among the gypsies, and it was there that Julius and I had agreed to meet. "Come on," Karl Knigh said to me, "we'll give him a surprise." As soon as we arrived he took me to a smoky *cantina* where several guitarists punctuated their playing with barbaric cries. There he was, in a corner – Karl pointed him out to me from a distance. Imagine my surprise. The two brothers were disagreeably alike. Especially at first glance. Afterwards all kinds of little differences became apparent, to Julius's advantage, of course, since I was prejudiced and had for a long time been a devotee of his writing. Julius looked up, and seeing his brother, he smiled without showing pleasure or annoyance. He wiped his thick, badly trimmed moustache bedewed with the wine that he had just knocked back.

'"Sit down, brother, and let's have a drink."

'"Gladly," said Karl Knigh, and he sat on the bench, right up close to Julius with his arm round his shoulder.

'I didn't say anything, almost moved . . . no, not almost, deeply moved, I have to admit, by these two old fellows, clasping each other by the shoulder, cheek to cheek. They looked like twins, so strong was the impression each of them gave of being pressed against a very slightly deforming mirror. I'm not exaggerating, I assure you. Except that one of them seemed too well groomed, too pale and as if powdered, whereas the other's face looked ravaged and at the same time there was great calmness in it.'

'Well,' the Investigator suddenly says, 'I have to leave you. If you like, shall we all three meet up again at the end of the day at my office in the Maritime Affairs Department?'

'I'm very fond of my old friend the Investigator,' says the Poet Criminologist, on being left on his own with the Literary Expert. 'He's a wounded man. We've known each other since we were teenagers, and it so happens that we got married on the same day. We were glad to celebrate our happiness with a joint wedding. But then, several years ago now, his wife insisted that they separate. From one day to the next, and for some reason that escapes me, she wanted to live *uncomfortably*, she told him. And indeed, it led to a *separated non-separation*, as my friend the Investigator describes his relations with his wife. They meet constantly, and spend every night together. You notice how hurriedly he left us. That's how it is. There are times when he has only one thing on his mind: to run off and join her, in a square, or at a small hotel in the port where she lives, or at some supposedly anonymous restaurant where people pretend not to know them. For everyone here knows what's going on, and is amused by this curious passion that seems able to survive only by deluding itself that it's unknown to the world. They sometimes sit for hours side by side on a rock on the seashore. Sometimes they go off in a sailing boat and don't return till after dark. They spend their time seeing each other, but *in precarious circumstances*, my friend the Investigator said to me. "There's no question of our living together again," he told me, "she absolutely refuses to." And, you know, I understand them. No family, no children, no responsibilities, the illusion of being alone in the world!

'If you like, I'll accompany you back to the hotel, where I'll leave you to get on with your deciphering. Come on, if we go through the shipyards, we'll get to your hotel more quickly. This is where the successive *Uranus*es were built, the last of which immediately acquired the reputation of being the most magnificent of modern cabin cruisers. In fact, look, you can see its shiny white superstructure rising above the low-built houses in the port. When you think that they were willing to live on board together, and not only to do so for the length of time it took for a cruise, but also to write during that time! We have to assume that this Knigh family did nothing but write, just as others do nothing but talk, or keep relentlessly gazing at the sun, in the hope even of blinding themselves.'

'You're right,' says the Literary Expert. 'By writing so much, they blinded themselves. They no longer saw life outside themselves, but within themselves. And it's within themselves, in that kind of subterranean world, that they eventually all crossed paths. In any case, that's my impression from the little I've already managed to deduce from the manuscripts in my possession.'

'Ducasse said these fine words: "The phenomenon passes. I seek laws." And it certainly seems that, in this family, writing had the status of inexorable and quasi-religious law.'

'Exactly! They all lived in submission to the dictates of writing. That would explain the fascination they had for each other, such that they were willing to be confined together at sea in that shiny thing out there, glinting in dry dock.'

' "The *Uranus* is no ordinary yacht," I said to my friend the Investigator when we boarded it for the first time, that terrible day when the coastguard found it drifting out at sea, with not a soul left on board. You can't imagine the impression created by an empty yacht, containing no other sign of humanity but that kind of husk of a living person that is an unfinished manuscript. But before I leave you to your reading task,' says the Poet Criminologist, 'would you sit down with me for a few moments on this bench looking out to sea, and tell me how that meeting in Granada with Julius and Karl ended?'

'For those two elderly brothers,' says the Literary Expert, 'the death of their childhood was interminable. Although Julius was the elder, Karl was obviously "the successful man", the one who'd managed to arrogate the "right of seniority", which he did from the moment he came into this world, all equipped with this "right" that by some inexplicable infant self-confidence he'd usurped. "I emerged from the same womb as Julius fully armed, whereas Julius, who was actually the elder, in a way started out unwarily," said Karl Knigh, when we were alone again after leaving Julius. Dawn slowly brought into view the Generalife gardens above us and the Nevada mountain range, pink and pale blue in the distance. "Julius was born the victim of his future whatever it might be. He was infinitely more talented than me, and I'd even say more of a *genius* . . . taking the word *genius*, of course, with the irony it deserves when used at daybreak after spending all night drinking in a seedy bar in Granada, with an impossible brother and a clever young literary expert. If you'd rather put it this way," Karl continued, "Julius is a born genius, whereas I became one! I persisted, singlemindedly, decade after decade, in listening to the voice that dictated to me."

'I'll tell you later,' the Literary Expert says to the Poet Criminologist, 'whose voice it was that Karl was talking about. As you'll see, it's of the utmost importance.

'"Yes, I persisted," Karl Knigh reiterated, "whereas Julius on the other hand played around, overconfident of his *genius*. Being creative, my brother Julius has always maintained, is above all a matter of surprising yourself. Every book in progress, Julius has always told me, is a total departure from the previous one. That's what my older brother, now my junior, has always said," Karl Knigh concluded, as we made our way back to the Washington Irving Hotel.'

'The one where Lowry puts up Geoffrey?'

'Precisely.'

'Julius's remarks, as reported by Karl, remind me of Flaubert when, sick of all the fuss caused by *Madame Bovary*, he angrily called his next book *Salaam Bo!* An ironic and bitter *Farewell Bovary*, as it were.'

'To give a writer such a hard time for a few corset laces hissing like snakes! But actually, it was Flaubert's homosexuality, his disguised homosexuality, that the public prosecutor and those who sought his downfall detected in the author's identification with Emma. I'm now summarizing for you a thesis by a colleague of mine that I met at a conference on "The Great Suicide Victims in Literature", where Emma Bovary and Anna Karenina were top of the list.'

'And what about Julius in the *cantina* in Granada? You were saying that you were with him until dawn?'

'"Guess what, Julius. I've brought along someone who tremendously admires your books," Karl Knigh said. "He's come a long way to meet you. Did you hear that, Julius? This clever young man who's writing a thesis admires you. He admires your writing — everything you've written, without exception. He considers you an *unclassifiable* writer."

'Silence from Julius. At some point he looked up and winked at me. He observed Karl with amusement in his eyes. "So you're here?" Then he was silent. From time to time he said, "Let's drink!" And we drank. "So you're here, my *big* little brother! And why are you wasting your time writing a thesis? What are you going to write in your thesis? Quotations? Quotations are old clothes too impregnated with someone else's sweat. You may quote that in your thesis! In my *big* little brother's books you'll find enough for heaps of quotations!"

'"Ah, Julius, ah, Julius!"

'"There you are! Every time we meet, Karl demands my silence. Karl needs calm gazes on him. Gazes that lay his doubts to rest. And the more his writing's praised, the less he accepts my gaze on him."

'"Ah, Julius, Julius!" Karl sighed again, without conviction.

'"I'm the thorn in the fingertip of the man lying on a rose-petal."

'"Julius! Don't forget, this man with a thesis to write is making a mental note of everything we say."

'"Well, let him! Let's drink and take notes! Since you can't have a thesis without quotations, I'm going to provide you with a double quotation, one, I regret, that I'm not the happy author of: *Remember the man who was asked why he took such trouble practising a skill that few people could appreciate: 'I'm content with a few,' he replied. 'I'm content with one. I'm content with none.'"*

'That cast a chill. Karl scowled. And from that moment on, Julius was in charge of the situation. He ordered another bottle and some fried octopus. He ate and drank, glancing at his brother Karl Knigh with an exaggeratedly loving gaze.'

VIII

'For me, that was the beginning of a fascinating relationship,' the Literary Expert goes on. 'The following night I went alone to the *cantina* in the gypsy quarter of Granada. There was Julius, in the same place, as if he'd spent not only all night there but all day as well. He seemed to have been sitting in the same place for days, months, years. The guitarists were playing away furiously, and from time to time one of them would get up to come and drink the glass of wine that Julius held out to him. There was nothing picturesque about it. Around him, everything assumed a prosaic ordinariness. Julius was *unfair*. He wasn't one to sublimate, you understand, he'd no use for transcendentalism. "I shall never forgive Time," he said to me, "for the fact that I wasn't born four hundred years earlier. What's four hundred years to Time? Nothing! And to me, Julius Knigh, it would have been sheer joy. Imagine breathing the same air as Montaigne! Reading over his shoulder his song of love for La Boétie! To read, as he was penning them, the quotations from ancient authors with which his *Essays* are almost casually punctuated. Yes, I know! I'm saying exactly the opposite of what I was saying to you last night! I hate quotations . . . and I love them. How to make sense of that contradiction? But quite simply, by considering who's using them. Certain words are sublime, coming from some people, and the same words are inexplicably offensive coming from others. It's also true of reading texts. I bet that Karl was constantly hiding behind myths. Ah, you see! But how does Karl use them? To what purpose? Myths can't be used as a support for *good* quotations."'

'I like that!' says the Poet Criminologist. 'I like that very much.'

'But wait! This marks the beginning of a very strange confession. I was planning to tell you about it later, when I'd made more progress in examining Julius's manuscripts, having so far got just an inkling of their complicated links not only with Karl's manuscripts but with those of the whole family, and above all with a fact of reality that for more than half a century has never ceased to torment these two elderly writers. Something very serious happened between Karl and Julius. I daren't suspect what. If my future reading were to confirm this suspicion, it could be that we might have here the true motive, the violent, delayed motive, for the *Uranus* tragedy.'

'Stop torturing my curiosity!' exclaims the Poet Criminologist.

'I'm no less curious than you are, believe me,' says the Literary Expert, staring out at the still sea in front of them. 'As on the previous night, Julius ordered fried fish and those terribly greasy fritters they make in Spain, in those *cantinas* that I detest. "Enough of bookish myths!" Julius declared. "There's nothing more instructive than myths if you want to penetrate the tensions that serve to bind any family whatsoever. Family histories are of no interest if you don't keep uppermost in mind the myths which are their true foundations. All the years of our adolescence, Karl, and I . . . and our younger brother Arno . . ."

'He left a long pause,' the Literary Expert continues, 'then, resuming, he said, "Has Karl spoken to you about Arno? Of course not! I shan't go into *details* of his death now. Who will ever know what happened? In any case, there was Karl, there was me, and above all there was our very young brother Arno. Remember this: of the three of us, Arno was the one who was to have written what neither Karl — whatever he may say — nor I have succeeded in writing. If Arno still survives somewhere, if what he was to have written lives on anywhere, it's in Rosa and Kurt's writing that we should look. In Kurt and Rosa! Yes, there's that same youthfulness in them, that elegance of inutility, that pure pleasure in writing!"

'That's what Julius said to me,' the Literary Expert continues. 'Then he began to ramble on about his adolescence, from which he couldn't "recover", he said. "I'm a casualty of my adolescence. My adolescence is a serious illness from which I shall never recover. Arno was a complete adolescent when he died. As for Karl, he killed his own adolescence within him; he's spent a lifetime killing it. Myself, I've become an incurable invalid. Through all the years of our adolescence, the three of us immersed ourselves in myths. We youngsters were very good on myths. On every human group that we decided to observe, we applied the grid of myths, not without some irony, and, believe it or not, it worked *divinely*. Of the three of us, Karl turned out well, as they say; let's forget about me; and as for Arno, sadly . . . or happily perhaps, he didn't survive beyond seventeen, an age when you still believe there's a meaning. Arno was Arno, and we, Karl and I, positively adored him. Can you imagine, we called ourselves Mino, Rhadamante and Sarpedon. We were the offspring of Europa and Zeus. Poor Europa, abandoned by Zeus, who managed to get herself married to Asterios!

' "So, is the young literary expert fascinated?" Julius suddenly said to me, filling my glass with that almost saccharine red-black wine that you find in the countryside round Granada. He was making fun of me now: "Don't miss anything I tell you. Take careful note of everything. Drink and listen. We're working on your thesis. I'm collaborating with you. We're adding to it! So let me tell you that the Knigh family writes at the dictation of a ghost. Believe it or not, the ghost of Arno is there, leaning over the shoulder of every member of the Knigh literary family. Although he's been dead for nearly fifty years now, Arno Knigh's heart still beats in all of us. When you meet Kurt and Rosa, you say to yourself that they are, together they constitute, they give form to, the ghost of our young brother Arno, whom we killed. And I mean killed, Karl . . . *and* I." '

'Wait! Wait!' exclaims the Poet Criminologist. 'What did he mean by "Karl *and* I"?'

'Glancing through their incomplete manuscripts, that's to say Karl's and Julius's, has given me an idea that I can't reveal right now. In my thesis I mentioned the death of the young brother of these two elderly writers, when they themselves were still young. I developed the idea – rather too sentimental, I admit – of both Karl and Julius writing their respective works and dedicating them to their deceased young brother. I stressed the fact that they felt both proud and ashamed of having continued to write after his premature death, which – so I believed when I wrote my thesis – explained that "we killed him", which Julius admitted with such terrible bluntness in the *cantina* below the Generalife gardens in bloom.'

'And you really think it's possible to establish a connection between that unexplained event dating back half a century and the mystery of the *Uranus*? Tell me at least what young Arno died of.'

'It seems that no one's ever known for sure.'

'Well, well, another mystery? You're joking?'

'It would indeed seem like a joke if it weren't documented, as I was able to ascertain when gathering the *solid* foundations, as it were, on which I was intending to build my thesis about the Knigh literary family. At the time, it caused quite a stir, as they say. Two brothers from a good local family questioned at length by the police and only reluctantly released. What really happened? No one has ever been able to give a satisfactory answer. How did Arno die? One morning he was found dead, close to his two brothers. It was alleged that all three of them had tried to commit suicide and only the youngest succeeded where the other two failed. It was also alleged that the two elder brothers had helped the younger one to die. After consulting practically all the contemporary newspapers reports of this macabre incident, I had to give up any attempt to form an opinion. Having failed to get anything out of Julius or Karl on the subject, nothing specific at least, I tried with no greater success to question Kurt, then Rosa, then Franz when I spent several days with him in Hamburg. Only Gustav Zhorn claimed to know a lot about this "crime", this "murder", this "devastating deadly game", this "appalling result of a bet such as only young people from good families, by definition irresponsible young people, are capable of dreaming up for themselves". The tone alone smacked of slander. It was painful for Rosa and Kurt. The death of their father's and uncle's younger brother was supposed to remain in the dark corner to which it had been relegated. It was one of those, I'd say, indispensable family secrets. Every family has its own. They are indeed rooted in myth, as Julius so pertinently remarked, in Granada. And as it so happens,' the Literary Expert goes on, 'those allusions to the myth of the three brothers Mino, Rhadamante and Sarpedon throw a very fascinating light on the mystery of the *Uranus*.'

'What Julius said about the family might also be said of criminology. Every family brings together an unconscious knowledge of the great myths. The *best* crimes are latent within the bosom of the family, where everything, from cannibalism to the darkest taboo, is committed – albeit virtually, let's say, most of the time. Family members murder each other a thousand times a year, there's continual rape – not for one moment does the child escape this secret history that forms the bedrock of the family.'

'Anyway, I think I've got to the bottom . . . almost . . . of this secret in the two Knigh brothers' interrelated manuscripts. Numerous allusions, in Julius's writings especially, pointed me in a direction that hadn't for one moment occurred to me at the time I was writing my thesis.'

'So what happened?'

'As I was telling you, Arno was found lying on his bed, in the room next door to the rooms of his two brothers. His heart-beat had stopped and the autopsy proved that he must have died around midnight. A few details caught the investigators' attention. Arno's boots were muddy. And his cape – like all young dandies of their age, the three brothers wore those capes called coachman's capes – was also splattered with the same mud, and furthermore it turned out to have a tear in it, on the lower left-hand side. Young Arno's hands, particularly his fingernails, were also caked with this mud. Obviously whatever it was had happened outside, and not in that bedroom. The young man had died out of doors and someone had carried him back to his bed. Who? The two older brothers, of course. But it so happened that the two brothers were found half-dead, except that they'd been drugged with very powerful sleeping-pills. Their boots were also stained with the same mud as their young brother's.'

'And then what?'

'And then nothing!'

'Stop playing games with me. What do you mean, nothing?'

'Nothing, I tell you. No, wait! After the case was closed, in some remote part of the grounds of the Knigh family home, servants found a rusty sword muddied up to the hilt with traces of the same mud as on the three brothers' boots. But the law dismissed this vexing object, leaving the mystery complete.'

'And what do you conclude? You think you've penetrated this mystery?'

'Almost. I happened to come across references, in Karl's and Julius's unfinished manuscripts, to an identical writing project.'

'You mean, the two old Knighs intended to write the same . . .'

'Yes, the same story.'

'And in this duplicate writing project, you think . . .'

'Yes, I think I've almost identified . . . almost found the key.'

'Tell me!' implores the Poet Criminologist. 'What is this duplicate writing project?'

'It's about a strange bet. A young man takes up a bet to go and plant his sword into the grave of a friend, buried that same day. A cheerful gang accompanies him to the gates of the cemetery. Naturally, it's midnight. The young man goes off, making his way between the tombs, and his companions wait for him with increasing anxiety. Finally, at daybreak, since he still hasn't come back, they in turn enter the cemetery and find him dead, kneeling on the still-fresh grave.'

'Dead? How come?'

'Dead of fright. He's quite simply planted his sword, inadvertently, through the flap of his cape. When he stands up he feels that he's held back. Overcome with fright, he dies on the spot.'

'And you think that Arno Knigh's death had something to do with this duplicate writing project?'

'Relying on various other clues, I've reason to believe so.

But what's especially fascinating is how each of the two old Knigh brothers tackles this theme that's both literary and so deeply personal – assuming, of course, that my intuition in making this connection is correct. Julius recounts the events with even more restraint than I have in relating them to you. It's all there: the mud; the coat – not a cape; the sword pulled out from some ridiculous panoply which the young man in a spirit of derision goes to plant in the grave of a friend, buried that same day. The attack of fright. The seizure . . . Karl, on the other hand, constructs his story in a completely different vein. Of course, there are two young swells. Of course, they fight each other in a duel. One of them's killed. He's buried. On the very night of the burial, "the murderer, intoxicated with arrogance", takes up a bet to go and plant the loser's sword in the still-fresh grave. As a kind of provocative homage, as it were, in the manner of Don Giovanni. And like Don Giovanni, he dies screaming with horror when he thinks he's being pulled underground by the dead man's hand. There you have all the difference between the two brothers.'

'That would have been a good ending for Conrad's *The Duel*. But what significance can a duel have today? It's a pity the two old Knighs didn't have time to see their projects through to the end.'

'As far as Karl Knigh is concerned, it could be said that it was *already written*. With Julius, it's another matter. What would he have made of this eternal drama? Julius destroyed *stories*. His writing was an acid; in a way it corroded *stories*, and it was to this game of cruel destruction that he invited you, you understand? He operated in public view, before witnesses. He managed to extend the illusionism of writing to get you to share his madness. A bit like Borges, when the multiple layers reveal themselves, one by one, and the *story* breaks up into as many facets as the human mind can encompass. That was Julius! As for Karl Knigh, although he's always desperately claimed myths as his authority, his *stories* have never succeeded in being anything but the same old *story* endlessly written and rewritten by the thousands upon thousands of passing *story*-tellers. Except that in Karl Knigh, there was a persistent guilt, a gnawing guilt. And this guilt consumed him right up to the very last second ... if the marks found on the hull of the *Uranus* are actually the marks I take them to be. Julius's disclosure regarding the mythological names adopted by the three brothers shows how much they wanted to place themselves in true perspective with regard to the family lie. The next day I managed to continue that conversation with Julius – still without Karl Knigh – in the same *cantina* where I'd seen him on the two previous nights.

'He told me: "My brother and I only talk to each other now because of the superabounding emptiness left within us by the death of our young brother Arno. We used to call him Sarpedon – he who flees, who's kept out, as Sarpedon was from Crete, roaming the seas all the way to Caria, where Anax, son of Uranus, ruled. Sarpedon-Arno who mysteriously died! Ever since, I've been outliving my time," Julius said. "Karl, too. Ever since, I've been waiting. What for? Nothing! Karl, too, is waiting. I know what it is that Karl's waiting for, and it frightens me. I also know what I'm waiting for, but that doesn't frighten me. After Arno's death, Karl and I committed suicide. Our suicide was reversed. Ever since, we've been dying a slow death, and that's been going on for the past fifty years. Karl has become the 'great' Karl Knigh, and what have I become? Karl survives by convincing himself that *he is Arno*. That surprises the young literary expert? And yet that's how it is! It's not Karl Knigh who writes Karl Knigh's works, but Arno Knigh who dictates to Karl Knigh the works of Arno-Karl Knigh. That's what my brother believes. 'The day that Arno's ghost decides his oeuvre is complete,' Karl told me, when we were sailing aboard the *Uranus*, 'is the day I shall reset the hour-glass and we'll all pass over to the other side where he awaits us. It's preordained: not only must you and I die together, at the same time, but I've been warned through mysterious channels that all who bear the name of Knigh are to die as mysteriously as Arno died.' That's what madness Karl's life is," said Julius,' concludes the Literary Expert, sitting next to the Poet Criminologist, looking out to sea.

'Look! There, do you see?' says the Poet Criminologist,

pointing to a sailing boat slipping out of the harbour channel. 'Those two little heads belong to the Maritime Affairs Investigator and his beloved wife. That's why he left us in such a great hurry. She was expecting him. They'd arranged to meet. With what sad longing I watch that diminishing white sail on its way out to sea! Nearly every day they take advantage of the autumn mildness to leave Earth, as it were, together, for the afternoon, abandoning the rest of us mortals to our painful duty . . . But did you hear what you've just said to me? *All who bear the name of Knigh must die!*' cries the Poet Criminologist. 'Everything points to old Knigh, then!'

'Wait, wait. Everything points to him and also everything clears him. So many other clues of equal weight awaken some amazing suspicions no less unexpected! Speaking of which, it's time to return to those manuscripts.'

'And I must leave you,' says the Poet Criminologist. 'I'm reluctant to go. I have to forget our investigation for a few hours and suspend my cheerfulness to descend into the damp and airless cellar of my real life. Would you like to meet up at the end of the day in my friend the Investigator's office, or would you rather I came to fetch you at your hotel and we all three dined together at the Yacht Club?'

IX

Some time later, shortly before dusk, the Maritime Affairs Investigator knocks at the Literary Expert's door.

'I'm by myself. My friend the Poet Criminologist will join us a little later at the Yacht Club. I know that he left you rather abruptly just a while ago, but you'll forgive him once I've told you the reason. For the last few years now, that man has been living with a tragedy difficult to cope with. He and his wife, I should say, for they constantly take it turn to deal with this tragedy. Their child has a muscle-wasting disease. At first there was no particular sign to make them suspect this terrible misfortune. The child was splendid. Something wasn't right, but the child was truly splendid! What was wrong? Neither my friend the Poet Criminologist nor his wife could have said. Something wasn't right, that was all! Things weren't as they should have been. The child crawled, and didn't stand up. If he was on his back he couldn't turn on to his stomach, and if he was on his stomach he couldn't turn on to his back.

'"Your child," the pediatricians told them, "will certainly never walk, certainly won't live long, will never talk, will recognize you but without ever understanding where he is, who he's with, and why. You ought to put him into a special home before you get attached to him and he gets attached to you, like a young animal."

'"I want to keep him," said my friend the Poet Criminologist's wife. And she did. At first the child was quite attractive and strangely normal-looking, in view of his hopeless condition ... except that he couldn't talk, still couldn't stand, crawled with increasing difficulty, and made cow-like noises or moaned. They gave him a very poignant name to which the child seemed more or less to respond. And indeed, as predicted, they became inordinately attached to him, the way you do become attached to someone whose need of you is urgent. I'd even go so far as to say that his weakness made them find a primitive, almost animal strength in themselves.

Their home became a real retreat, the roof not only a roof but also a kind of protective lid that was utterly heart-rending. Still, my friend was lucky enough to be called out constantly to solve criminological problems or mysteries, such as the mystery of the *Uranus*, which has always allowed him to escape, without too much of a bad conscience, the protective enclave that he and his wife ended up erecting not only around their child but also around themselves, in their affliction with this destroyed and destructive child, do you understand?

'Happily, I might say, there are many crimes in the outside world, which is very lucky for my friend the Poet Criminologist. Otherwise, how would he escape that distressing tranquillity where only the child exists, with its continual moans, its soft and terribly upsetting cow-like noises, like the anguished protests of young calves snatched from under their mother's belly? In fact the child did gradually assume the lost and gentle look of a young calf, and even its milky complexion was always a little damp and smelt like that of a young animal much licked by its mother. And indeed his mother was constantly caressing him, comforting him, holding him close as if he were still part of her own flesh, and she was meant to go on carrying him, *within her* as you might say, never to become a carefree woman again, the footloose, light-hearted woman my friend had known and loved. As the years have gone by, she's acquired an expression at once blissful, yes, truly blissful, and of such sadness that to see what's in the depths of her eyes makes your blood run cold, as they say.

'I'll tell you something else. I don't like to talk about my personal life, but at this point I have to admit that this tragedy at such close hand brought about another, which I would describe as the symmetrical opposite. Did I tell you that at one of the receptions held at the Yacht Club by Karl Knigh for the launch of the latest *Uranus*, I was there with my young wife? From whom I'm now separated, without being really separated. I've always been very much in love with her. I say always, because I've been in love with her since childhood. And believe me, she's always been in love with me. The Poet

Criminologist and I have been inseparable friends since we were young. Combining love and friendship, we all four decided to get married on the same day. This double wedding delighted our wives, and was fun for us too, especially as we were practically never apart, being called on, on the one hand or the other, to deal with some unsolved crime or shipwreck. And suddenly disaster strikes! Not immediately, no! It's deferred. Our friends' wonderful child, to whom my wife and I naturally became the happy godparents, turns out to have a muscle-wasting disease. Believe it or not, the effect of this awful discovery was doubly devastating: our friends were not the only victims . . . my wife suddenly tells me that she can't go on living with me *as normal*.

'"No," she told me one morning, "I can't go on living with you *as normal*. I love you, it's impossible for you to know how much, my beloved, but I shall never again be able to live with you *as normal*." That's what she told me after hearing the diagnosis that left no hope for the child of our close friends . . . that left no hope for our close friends. And you won't believe this, she immediately gathered up her personal belongings and went off to live in the hotel.

'"I want to go on loving you," she said, "I want us to love each other without being under any obligation or constraint."

'And it's turned out the way she wanted. I'm more in love with my wife than ever, and she's more my wife now than ever. She sends for me – and I come running! I feel like seeing her – and I go rushing off to her! You smile? Go ahead and smile. After a certain age love is ridiculous. That sort of love, anyway. But forget what I've just told you.'

The Investigator takes a few indecisive steps among the piles of manuscripts cluttering the bedroom floor.

'I see,' he says, 'that you seem to have made considerable progress in sorting through this overwhelming mass of papers. My friend the Poet Criminologist will be joining us in a moment. "I'll contrive to free myself, without fail," he assured me. He told me that on the seashore earlier he listened to you with intense curiosity. "From what the Literary Expert has revealed," he told me, "too many suspicions are falling on

Karl Knigh, when in my view it's the almost over-transparent personality of Julius Knigh that we ought to be examining." My friend the Criminologist has put me in the picture about the "almost too elegant" circumstances, as he described them, of the death of the two elderly writers' brother.'

'But I repeat, nothing's certain,' says the Literary Expert.

'That's just the point: this *nothing's certain* makes me think *it could be so.*

'Since I left your friend the Poet Criminologist, I've changed my opinion three times. On returning to this room, which has become a kind of literary graveyard of the Knigh family, I broached, dipped into, flicked through three different manuscripts. And each time I found myself confronted with a different facet of this dazzling diamond, as it were, constituted by all these violent collective deaths. Here's Lotte Knigh's journal. Here are a few extremely disturbing poems of Kurt on the "desire to be condemned".'

'I don't understand. What desire to be condemned?'

'Fragments of some very fine poems in which Kurt maintains that humanity wishes to be condemned to the *eternal flames* rather than dissolve into Nothingness.'

'So what?' says the Maritime Affairs Investigator, beginning to lose patience.

'Well, this desire to be condemned, for damnation actually, expressed in verse, reveals unusual exasperation, a need to believe, and therefore to provoke, to go to the limit of whatever's worst. Listen to this:

> 'Overwhelming evidence of iniquity
> Man marked by forged steel
> The bone-penetrating blade meting out
> Salutary torture to torment
> Necessary though futile lucidity
> Like the Obscure Presence not of flesh
> Ape-like shadow demoniacal sign
> Wrested from aeons of leaping flame.

'Wait, wait!

> 'Demon God it's not the trial that matters
> Eternal damnation's what we want!
> Go on, cast us into hell!
> Welcome its volcanic torments
> Yield us to our terror
> Iniquity! We're proud to name it
> Crave responsibility for the "filthy beast"
> Deny the supposed error of our ways.

'Wait!

> 'Accepted that we're at fault
> Don't save us in deafness to our prayers
> Hey! God! Pass sentence on us
> No spiritualism on our wickedness impinge
> Cast no shadow on us lure us not
> Promise no lost Paradise Your wrath
> A malediction on us to bring torments
> Hell flames Lethe all into the abyss!'

'I'm sorry,' says the Investigator, 'I don't see anything here bearing any resemblance to a motive or, if you prefer, a promise to drown his entire family along with himself.'

'Wait! That's not all! This time, look at the lines. I don't mean read them, but look at them, let your eyes caress them, as it were.

> 'All blasted devoured consumed by the Devil
> Limbs roasted in red-hot iron pincers Ah!
> Long live Hell! Unite us damned in eternal
>   torment of the flesh
> Digging lances foul clots perpetually
> Rupturing our veins in perpetual retribution
> Oh, we aren't sufficiently wicked?
> Wax wroth, Spirit, chastise us sufficiently
> Now, just how wicked would you have us be?
> Exercise your prerogative to play the tyrant!
> Down into the abyss send us hurtling!'

'Well? No, I don't see,' says the Maritime Affairs Investigator, getting increasingly irritable.

'Nothing leaps out at you, as they say, really nothing?'

'No, really nothing, I assure you.'

'Wax wroth?'

'What about it?'

'You don't find it an unusual turn of phrase, to say the least.'

'Poetic affectation, no? That often most irritating poetic licence, no?'

'Not at all. It's there to tell us something: to draw our attention to a very disturbing acrostic. Now read it!'

'It sends shivers down my spine,' exclaims the Investigator. 'All drowned.'

'Ah!'

'But here we have the guilty party!'

'Personally I don't think so. I've found other acrostics in the poetic fragments Kurt had accumulated. For the moment I prefer to leave them aside. I must first of all compare them with several texts left by Julius, including this one, which was clearly written with the aid of a mirror, like the texts of Leonardo da Vinci. I've deciphered a few pages – it's a fairly unsettling exercise. One thing for sure that emerges from this oddity: Julius was not the man you were led to believe from what you saw and heard of him. These texts in reverse handwriting are among the most frightening, the most terribly diabolical ever to have been written about jealousy. If these cryptic texts are to be believed, Julius was a man destroyed by jealousy. Ever since childhood. His backward-written words are horrible words. Almost *untranslatable* into normal writing. Julius! The fascinating Julius who so won me over in Granada! A man so indifferent, it seemed, to everything but his misanthropy! That said, all this means absolutely nothing, and doesn't make Julius an exterminating angel. That he should have wished one way or another for the extinction of the whole Knigh family is a possibility, coming from this old bachelor *with nothing to lose*, not even himself since he didn't really care about anything or anybody.

'Yet some of the remarks Karl Knigh made about him at the time I was researching my thesis are now haunting me. These remarks are associated for me with the Generalife gardens in bloom and especially the Lions Courtyard where Karl Knigh liked to stroll with me. "I know that at night you go stealing into the gypsy quarter where Julius spends his life getting drunk. You needn't fear," Karl Knigh said to me as we sat on the edge of the fountain in the Court of Lions, "don't let it bother you, I'm not jealous of Julius. Julius is jealous of me but I'm not at all jealous of Julius."

'Naturally his insistence made me assume the opposite. What is Everyman always jealous of? Of anyone who's got something when he has nothing, and of anyone who has nothing when he's got something. Julius had convinced me by his extremely winning attitude that there was nothing more he wanted. That he was indifferent, as Diogenes appeared to be, since he'd lost what people call *self-respect*, that's to say all sense of shame. Julius seemed to have reached a point where he was beyond all shame. Nothing to hide, nothing to wish for . . . "except death", he told me, as the ultimate appeasement. Appeasement! How could I have suspected at the time what this word perhaps meant to Julius? His backward-written pages, of which I have so far deciphered only fragments, cast some light on this "appeasement" for which Julius seemed so eager.'

X

A little while later the three of them are once again seated at table in the Yacht Club, the Poet Criminologist having been filled in on the Literary Expert's strange discoveries.

'Well?' says the Poet Criminologist when they had ordered a lavish seafood platter.

'Do you really want to pursue the subject while we're eating?' says the Literary Expert.

'It depends. As much as I'd be yawning with boredom in the case of a *story* – and I've always found Karl Knigh's interminable books terribly boring – our investigation into the hidden lives of this same Karl Knigh and the other members of his family fascinates me. Facts are one thing and the way they're lived another. The life of every "great man" – whether he's truly great or only in social terms – reveals a certain private terror. There's the biological progress of the human animal in all its remarkable banality, and then on this foundation of banality, consisting of marriage, children, the possibilities of exercising power over the greatest possible number of others, a kind of tumour develops, made of vanity, pride, and perpetually unsatisfied desires, called the 'epic quality' of certain individuals. These individuals use the same, let's say trivial, materials as everyone else, but somehow they transcend them. Some exploit the spirit of the age; these make excellent strategists of immediate "greatness". Others, like Julius, build up their lives like scaffolding . . . or rather make a scaffold of their lives, if I understand correctly.'

'That's absolutely right, that's exactly the way it is with Julius,' exclaims the Literary Expert. 'In fact, all his life Julius has been baring his neck for the blade, which has come down on him over and over again. And from these repeated failures and injuries he has been able to draw a mysterious venom, a horrible and beautiful sap. Yes, Julius's writings have a beauty of the kind that you said certain crimes had. Their brilliance lies in a sheer inventiveness that's not of this world, something in the nature of some strange fragment of the future that turns up too soon in the present. While Karl's career has never interested me, the anti-career that is Julius's life has always fascinated me. As do the anti-careers of Rosa, Kurt and Franz, especially with an awareness of the extremely delicate thread linking them to Julius's genuine "greatness".'

'Come now!' says the Investigator. 'The important thing is not the aesthetic development of all their respective bodies of works, but the relation between their compilation of works and the mystery of the *Uranus*.'

'But surely if there is a mystery,' says the Poet Criminologist, 'it has to be read as some obscure footnote added to both their works and the lives of all of them. And I welcome the discovery our friend the Literary Expert has recently made, among the papers left by Julius Knigh, of texts he wrote backwards, confessing in the simplest of cryptograms to his jealousy – his hidden sickness. Now we need know what exactly Julius was jealous of? Probably not his brother Karl's success?'

'Of course not,' says the Literary Expert.

'Or Karl Knigh's love life or family life.'

'Not really.'

'Or the enormous sums of money Karl Knigh's books earned.'

'No! Julius lived on nothing, as they say, or so little . . .'

'What then? Could he have been jealous of the jealousy he aroused in Karl Knigh? Jealous in a way because he didn't feel jealous?'

'More of your tiresome paradoxes,' says the Investigator.

'Not at all,' says the Poet Criminologist. 'We're always jealous of the other.' Turning to the Literary Expert, he says, 'Remember *The Beast in the Jungle*? What's the beast's secret? Jealousy, of course. Clearly, no ordinary jealousy, yet fundamental. What happens? The "beast" moves through the jungle of James's text all his life, thinking he's living, feeling, without *knowing* of his indifference, until the day when the woman, the beast's friend and companion, suddenly dies.'

'True,' says the Literary Expert, 'there's no finer metaphor.'

'Yes, there he is, the "beast" that is this man, incapable of receiving or giving love, standing bewildered at his friend's graveside, and he doesn't really know what he's lost. He feels that he's lost something, not someone. Something. And he's bewildered because he can't grasp what it is he's lost, at the graveside of the woman who was his attentive confidante ... and above all so discreet in her love that the man had never suspected it. But then he notices at a grave close by ...'

'A stranger weeping, is that it?'

'Yes, weeping! And all at once James's jungle man – the "beast" – realizes that he's jealous of this grief. Jealous of the tears of this stranger at the next grave,' cries the Poet Criminologist. 'In fact, jealousy and envy are often confused. A person can be jealous, without being envious, of someone who experiences strong emotion, an emotion that gives the impression of living intensely. But in the case of the Knigh brothers, do you think that Karl was secretly jealous of Julius's failures? Wanted to be able to experience what Julius experienced in that imposing solitude that everyone talked of with respectful unease? Was Julius, for Karl, the "beast" beside him? Or conversely, was Karl, for Julius, the "beast" beside him? Was it Julius who was jealous – as he would seem to be confessing in those pages written in reverse handwriting – of something Karl had? But what?'

'One night in the *cantina* in Granada Julius surprised me with a strange comment he made, not about his literary failures – he didn't think he had failed in literary terms; on the contrary, even in his heart of hearts he felt great certainty regarding the quality of his literary output – no, what he told me concerned Failure per se, as it were. Julius told me, "I certainly don't want to get anywhere,"' the Literary Expert continues, '"I don't want to reach any goal, I don't want any goal, managing to reach any kind of goal, for me, would be as terrible as death, do you understand? I want to live with failure. Failure is as necessary to me as this wine is, even more so. This isn't a pose," he added, seeing me smile in spite of myself. "No, failure is more necessary to me than air. What I dread is praise. I don't want to be praised or not praised. I don't want to be anything! Nothing must confine me in any way whatsoever."'

'In the light of what he wrote in reverse handwriting, his remarks are terrible, and were he still alive, we'd have every reason to charge him with responsibility for the *Uranus* tragedy.'

'That remains to be seen . . .' the Literary Expert goes on. 'If we take into consideration what he also said to me: "I want to remain socially unformed. I feel constant nostalgia for the state of adolescence. I want to remain adolescent."'

'But exactly. Isn't pulling up the ladder an adolescent prank? Julius can't resist the pleasure of giving fright. He climbs up the ladder and from the deck of the *Uranus* laughs along with those down in the water who don't take Uncle Julius's practical joke seriously. Nor does Uncle Julius take his practical joke seriously. But after a while, watching his brother pant for breath and begin to panic as his strength gradually drains, Julius feels such happiness, such a sense of appeasement that he extends the torture beyond the limits of his brother's endurance. The others start to hold Karl up in the water, while shouting at Julius. They're tired. They, too, feel exhausted. And old Karl Knigh is getting terribly heavy . . .'

'And you think that seeing his brother . . .'

'Yes, seeing the "great" Karl Knigh in a position of extreme weakness, swallowing bucketfuls of water and getting frightfully out of breath, Julius couldn't resist the appeal of the irretrievable.'

'You mean that he then jumped in among the other swimmers?'

'Out of high-spirits, yes! Adolescent high spirits. He made the leap – dare I say? – laughing.'

'So he's the one who turned the hour-glass?'

'Wasn't it tempting?' says the Poet Criminologist, turning suddenly serious, and continuing under his breath: 'How tempting it must be to turn the hour-glass once and for all!'

'Except that, even after it's turned over, the sand inside remains just the same, nevertheless.'

'You're right,' continues the Poet Criminologist, becoming

increasingly agitated. 'But what about the illusion. The illusion of deliverance. The same illusion that the person responsible for the *Uranus* tragedy, whoever it might have been, contented himself with, as a motive for his action. What is action? It is the outcome of a long, very long, secret journey. The same's true in criminology. A crime is simply the point you reach after an intolerable chain of suffering. The only way out. The appeasement that Julius speaks of in his writings. I've met criminals, some very great criminals on that famous Death Row. They nearly always acknowledged a sense of boundless appeasement, like a severing of all their nerves, at having put an end to their suffering by their crime. If you asked them what particular suffering they were talking about, they would reply: "Suffering – with a capital S." They had been suffering and now they weren't suffering any more! In some confused way they were already living their death. You see, for them, crime was often no more than a detour on the road to their own death.'

'I can accept that a person might kill himself, but to choose to die and expect your nearest and dearest to accompany you seems to me the most dreadful example of cowardice,' says the Maritime Affairs Investigator, gazing fixedly at the Poet Criminologist. 'No, there are no "beautiful" crimes, any more than there are justifiable suicides – unless physical suffering compels.'

'Apollinaire said more or less the same thing,' the Literary Expert interposes.

'That famous phrase!' exclaims the Poet Criminologist, laughing inappropriately. "Spare me any physical suffering, the moral suffering I can deal with."'

'That's it!'

'And he died under the surgeon's trepan.'

'Enough digressions,' says the Investigator, beginning to lose patience.

'You're right, enough digressions!' says the Poet Criminologist, still laughing. 'When we came to the table, our friend the Literary Expert was recalling the Generalife gardens where for several days he went strolling with Karl Knigh, whereas at night it was with Julius that he spent his time in the *cantina,* a description of whose charms we're grateful to have been spared. Karl and Julius, like day and night! When he talks about one of them, in some ways it's the other he describes by reflection. It is these reflections that interest us. These writings, like the echo perceived by bats, being accurate only if the reflections succeed in charting round what cannot be spoken of. Similarly, among the finds at Pompeii are lava impressions of people surprised in their sleep by the eruption close on two thousand years ago. Gassed by the poisonous fumes and immediately covered by the shower of hot ashes, many citizens of Herculancum and Pompeii were cast in a mould of these ashes that rain and weather eventually transformed into a kind of cement as hard as basalt. Two thousand years of silence and stillness, of slow decomposition, and finally nothing remained of the organic matter of the creatures trapped inside this basalt matrix, until the day when some archaeologists with enough of the artist in them, I'd say, had the sublime idea of injecting plaster into these concavities of creatures, these human hollows sleeping a sleep whose absent presence is literally of unbearable violence.'

'I see what you're getting at,' says the Literary Expert. 'Expressing the inexpressible by talking *round* it. Isn't that what you mean? You're thinking of Rilke and that woman he talks of . . .'

'Exactly! The one whose admirers could only talk of her *circumscriptively*, leaving her a blank, says Rilke.'

'Which immediately calls to mind that famous phrase of Wittgenstein only too often quoted: *What we cannot speak about* . . . But is it not precisely in order to talk round, and thereby contrive to encompass the unutterable, that speech has been so indispensable to man. Wittgenstein's phrase, quoted promiscuously by every Tom, Dick and Harry, means quite the opposite, that what cannot be uttered is an invitation to *the game of circumscriptive language,* that lasso of words by which the ineffable prey is encircled, then captured.'

"Don't forget," Julius said to me, "you who are planning to write about the Knighs, that Karl is nothing without Julius, and Julius would obviously not be Julius if Karl didn't exist. By existing my brother gave me the desire not to exist. Whereas he became the author Karl Knigh, I was not the author Julius Knigh. Whereas he decides to settle down in a place he can call home, as they say, I continue to live alone, without a home. He gets married. I don't. And believe it or not, by evidently not loving the woman we knew as Belle, by giving concrete form to this non-love in the shape of one, two, three children, Karl put Julius in a total amorous impasse, since of course Julius never in his whole life dreamt of any other woman but Belle."

'That's what Julius himself confessed to me, at night in the *cantina* in the gypsy quarter of Granada. While during the day, up in the Generalife gardens, Karl talked to me about Julius, trying to find out what Julius could possibly have said about him the night before. You can imagine how very satisfying it was for me, researching my thesis, to be caught between the two elderly brothers' sparring.

'Last night I jotted down in this notebook some very strange phrases that I found in Karl Knigh's unfinished manuscript: *Tristan's ecstatic nihilism. Nirvana complex. All romanticism's fascination with death. What power great enough to match its dark spell? Is love the magic remedy whose power could make everything dubious and destructive become life-serving? But how hard it must be to learn the language of love! What reservations must be overcome, what favours granted?*

'These are marginal notes, which occur throughout his manuscripts. Later on I also found these words hastily scrawled on a corner of a page: *I haven't lived. I've written. I've not done anything that hasn't been transformed into writing. Disastrous absurdity! Will I at least die well?* Then he had crossed out several words – the most important of course! And further on: *Death is an enigma that we must if possible render even more . . .* here the word *enigmatic* was badly crossed out and replaced by *problematic*. But what I didn't want to talk to you about so soon,' says the Literary Expert, lighting a cigar, 'is a suspicion that has rapidly become a certainty: Karl Knigh's unfinished manuscript is not solely penned by him.'

'What?' exclaim the Investigator and the Poet Criminologist, startled.

'At first you don't realize what's disturbing you in your reading. But gradually it becomes obvious that a hand other than his own has made additions, inserted remarks, often acerbic, always intelligent and neatly written. "Well, well," I said to myself, "why would Knigh change his handwriting when reading over what he'd written?" I was rather puzzled for a while, then a little later, opening Lotte Knigh's journal at random, I recognized the handwriting in the margin.'

'You think he gave her his manuscript to read and she made comments on it? A fairly common practice,' says the Poet Criminologist. 'Remember *Ada*, for instance.'

'Yes, but there Nabokov was once again showing off, as they say.'

'You may be right, but what writer isn't *playful*?'

'I don't think that Karl Knigh was being *playful* with his young wife Lotte.'

'What then?'

'She was apparently contriving to tell him, in the margins of his manuscripts, what she needed to tell him and he refused to listen to in real life. But what disturbed me more is that Lotte's journal, on the other hand, is dotted with little sketches and bizarre signs indisputably drawn by Karl Knigh.'

'You're the one who's being *playful*. You're having us on, now!'

'Not at all! And in my opinion what Knigh drew in the margins of his young wife's journal had a far more worrying significance. In any case these sketches and annotations, which I shouldn't have mentioned to you so soon, show that a fierce and wordless dialogue was being conducted between Karl and Lotte. He'd speckle his wife's journal with his horrible little drawings. She'd respond with some caustic comment in the corner of a page of the "great" man's manuscript. He'd come back, at night, I assume, and draw another horrible little image – which I know was taught to him by a Bengali guru he used to consult in New York, as I've already told you – and she'd make some other caustic comment in her neat firm handwriting . . . and he . . .'

'What's this?' says the Investigator. 'You're not going to tell me that old Knigh was casting spells on his young wife?'

'We'll see. But I believe there's reason to think so.'

'Don't you think it more likely that Knigh was amusing himself with these graffitti, as indeed Vladimir Nabokov amused himself, apparently, by drawing tiny graffitti on the patterned wallpaper decorating the rooms of the luxury Swiss hotel suite where he lived with his wife at the end of his life,' says the Poet Criminologist. 'This scribbling mania affects nearly all criminals. One leaves one's mark. In writing too, of course. By the way, you remember that paper criminal Humbert Humbert, *drowning* his wife on that boating trip!'

'Let's get back to Granada, shall we?' says the Investigator. 'You were saying that the two old Knigh brothers made parallel confessions of the utmost importance.'

'Yes, indeed, Karl Knigh confided a great deal in the young literary researcher that I was then. Was it because he knew that at night I was being told things by his brother Julius? Did they both experience a kind of jubilation in raising the stakes, Karl outmatching Julius, and Julius outmatching Karl, with the stranger who was eager to note everything down scrupulously? My good will and naivety at the time must have encouraged these two old writers to pursue their covert battle on the blank page of my future thesis. At one point, when Karl and I happened to be up at the top of the Generalife gardens, I pointed out to him that it was there, in that very same place, that Malcolm Lowry had met his wife who later became the 'pathetic and brave' Yvonne of his novel. "All women are pathetic and brave," said Karl Knigh testily. "My wife Lotte is pathetic and brave, my first wife Belle was pathetic and brave, but however pathetic and brave they may be, they can't help dying. When they're only childless pathetic brave women, like Lotte, of course it's dreadful if they die, but think how much less dreadful than if they leave three children behind. A mother has no right to die prematurely," he said, "a mother is guilty of great cowardice by dying prematurely. My first wife

Belle was pathetic and brave, but far too delicate to live, and at the same time strong enough to have lumbered me with three children. That's nature," he said, beheading several flowers with his walking stick, "it creates wombs strong enough to produce three offspring in rapid succession, and at the same time forgets that a mother has no right to die leaving a writer on the threshold of his career with three kids to bring up! Nature might just as well carry off her three children too, if it's so improvident, if it's stupid enough to let their mother die in childbirth. I took Belle's death as an outrage. I self-centredly took it as the most intolerable outrage. Along comes Franz, and she dies! Not straightaway, no! She dies without taking her eyes off the child that killed her. Is it possible to feel so much love for your murderer? 'Be brave,' I told her, 'overcome your tiredness, you've no right to leave me on my own with the three children you've *given* me. I'm a writer. The children are yours. You must live. And I must write!'"'

'You know, there's some truth in that cry, as it were, of old Karl Knigh,' the Poet Criminologist cuts in. 'What man is capable of taking on responsibility for the child *given* to him by the woman? In what way does the child *really* belong to him? I keep asking myself that question. The woman's child belongs to the woman. The man is there to give support to the woman, to supplement the pathetic bravery – as you were saying – of the woman. But that responsibility he cannot take on.'

The Poet Criminologist falls silent for a few moments, then laughs with embarrassment.

'This selfishness of writers,' the Literary Expert resumes, 'reminds me of Dostoyevsky giving birth to *Notes from the Underground* in the room where his wife lay dying. He wrote to his brother: *Every day there's a moment when we expect her death. Her suffering is terrible. Sometimes I think it's going to be rubbish, but nonetheless I write, I write furiously; I don't know what the result will be. Another thing: I fear that my wife's death is near; THEN AN INTERRUPTION IN WORK WILL BE UNAVOIDABLE. If it weren't for this interruption, I'm sure I could finish.*'

XI

'A propos of the rampant egotism typical of most writers,' says the Poet Criminologist, 'while they're bringing us a third coffee, I'd like to quote an example of a particularly disturbing case. A rather little-known text by an author I'm slightly familiar with, having read some of his books and in particular some of his poems – dedicated to his wife – deals with an incident that he presents as a true story. Sometimes he tells it in the first person, sometimes in the third person – as if now and again grief and horror prevented him from completely accepting the reality he's attempting to embrace. In a moment, if you don't mind, I'll recite you a short poem about Alban Berg's music, written by this author by way of an ending, it would seem, to the text I'm talking about. So, this writer has been living for forty years with a woman with whom he's extraordinarily in love. What's exceptional is that she's just as extraordinarily in love with him. The relationship between them is something quite rare – and it's this rareness of sentiment that inspires numerous texts published by this writer. They love each other passionately. And what's remarkable is that this passion is so exclusive, of such joyful freshness that nothing, it seems, has ever cast a shadow over the almost infinite number of days and nights they've lived together. But then one day the writer inserts in one of his autobiographical books several pieces of writing by his wife. We were speaking just now of *talking round*. When we can't say what we'd like to say, the only thing left is to talk *round* it – that's what he tried to do. Suffering from a kind of excess of passion that literally paralyses him, he says, and maintaining that not at any time has he achieved by literary means a *true* rendering of this woman who so fills his life, he ventured to include in this book, in which he was attempting to depict, to capture, if you prefer, all those years that he'd lived with her, some of the things that in fact she'd written. By this device, which he considered elegant, bold and amusing, he bound her even more closely to himself and his work, of which she'd always been the inspiration and often the heroine. Unfortunately, among the texts borrowed from his wife was an account of one of her early memories. It concerned a young musician that she'd fallen in love with as a young girl, and very soon lost touch with. This happened a few years before she met the writer and before their passion for each other turned them into twins of a kind, possessed of two minds and two sensibilities of extraordinary closeness. The fierceness of this passion so absorbs them that the young woman – later his wife – retains nothing of this girlhood love but a sweet and distant fondness. No matter how many years, then decades, fly by, their present always retains its vigour, its continual freshness. Time's passed but they've scarcely noticed. Therein, perhaps, lies the reason for this autobiographical book and perhaps, too, the reason that prompted the unwise author to mingle his wife's prose, so limpid in style, with his own.

'But then, by an inconceivable quirk of Fate, the book in which these writings are inserted falls into the hands of a man in the terminal stages of a horrible illness. He reads the text by the writer's wife. He recognizes himself in it. He recognizes his young admirer of long ago. It comes as such a shock to him that he thinks he's been sent a declaration of love which has skipped the years to reach him there, on his death-bed, just before he ceases to be. He immediately writes to the author's wife to let her know of his inevitable death sentence and above all to tell her that neither has he ever forgotten her. She's thunderstruck by this letter. So is the author. A letter of terrible shamelessness in which the stranger of today, the former young musician, describes his illness with unbearable crudeness. Anyway, that's more or less what this short work, which the author *couldn't not write,* is about. And that's not all! On one page of this short work describing the impact of what his wife had written, and giving an account of the letter received in response, are two very dense paragraphs that occupied my thoughts a great deal. At one point the writer thinks his wife is on the brink of taking a train to go to the bedside of the stranger whose call, though not explicitly made, is there between them, like an obsession. The writer is walking with his wife when he *lives through* the experience, more vivid than a dream, of his wife leaving, of her absence, of time passing without her. She's with the dying man, whom she doesn't recognize but who, on the basis of that text of such freshness, of so long ago, by the young girl of long ago, expects to turn back the clock, yes, to invert the hour-glass. The writer imagines it all, while she walks beside him, apparently carefree and cheerful, at the water's edge, on the quayside of an Italian town. And the writer's grief is such that he has to stop himself from falling to the ground and not moving any more. It's this grief of the imagination that I liked in the writer's short text, and above all the admission of his rampant egotism.'

'Wait,' the Maritime Affairs Investigator cuts in, 'did she go to the dying man, or not?'

'No.'

'She stayed with the writer?'

'Yes. A little while later came news of the death of this ghost who'd briefly reappeared, bringing to an end this sad and brittle story.'

'I'd like to know,' says the Literary Expert, 'if the writer at least got a novel out that imagined abandonment?'

'No, he didn't!'

'So he didn't do anything with it? Literarily, I mean?'

'Apparently not. But a short time afterwards, however, he wrote a curious poem about friendship, love and death . . .

>   How I would strike the sun if it insulted me
>   With the frenzy of a living god
>   With my lacerated body and (if it exists) bleeding soul
>   The one poured into the other
>   Incensing me to raving madness
>   With all the fury and hatred gathered
>   Upon me by infuriated humanity at slaughter
>
>   I feel just as blinded but by a gentle frenzy
>   When deciphering pure music

Of Vienna as it was
ADSCHBERG – AEBE -ABABERG
rnol – oen – r – nton – w – rn -lnr
So were those three friends playfully transcribed into notes
Thus dedicated to their 'Esteemed maestro on his fiftieth
   birthday'

In Friendship – Love – World
The three movements of the Concerto entitled
Friendship: Nucleus gathered round Sch
Love: music for mAtHilDE (late beloved of Sch)
World: "Death's dark silence
Mingled with Life's brilliant splendour" – wrote Alban – to
   his friend
Schoen-Berg
La soh re mi AHDE – musical motive

Dawn reapers advancing side by side lost in thought
Behind their blades swishing through the wet grass
Dear friends I remember you in analogical sadness
By what anagrammatic music of your past lives
Could I here encode (rhythmic symbolism
Of numeric esotericism undecodable
Except by instruments of musical speech) the intolerable
   absence.

Deep in sadness this morning
ArnolD SCHoenBErG – Anton wEBErn – AlBAn BErG
Playing in these chords close to my love
Together mourning the loss of all our fellow lives
Friendship – Love . . . World
But in what World?
ADSCHBEG – AEBE – ABABEG

'There,' the Poet Criminologist concludes. 'The title of that poem is 'Jealousy of Music'. It was accompanied by a fragment of the score written on the anagram ADSCHBEG, AEBE, ABABEG – that is, Schoenberg, Webern, Berg.'

'Let's get back to the *Uranus*,' says the Investigator. 'You were talking about Karl, about the birth of his three children, and the death of his wife Belle. It seems that slowly, by routes obviously less direct but reliable, we were getting closer, perhaps closer than we think, to our mystery.'

'How strange,' says the Poet Criminologist, 'that every passenger on the *Uranus* apparently had good personal reasons for making the leap. I mean that by taking to the point of absurdity all the given facts, it's possible to imagine that, without having conferred, they all jumped together spontaneously.'

'You want us to believe in a collective leap, dictated by some crazy logic, crystallizing, in one single, almost instinctive action, the diversity of propositions that each member of the Knigh family represented?' says the Investigator, clearly irritated. 'According to you, there's no secret then, but something in the nature of a biological mystery, such as can be observed in insects, for instance?'

'Or in those American lemmings whose sudden mass suicide is recorded once or twice in a century. Having come together from all points of the compass, these little animals that tend to be homebodies by nature are suddenly seized with frenetic excitement. They set off and all of them without exception make their way towards the Pacific coast, where high cliffs form a kind of wall of no return. You see them in their millions rushing headlong into the sea, and wilfully drowning themselves. What's the signal? What biological process is acting on these hordes of little animals? Why all together?'

'Steady on! If we start to look to the inexplicable for an explanation, we'd better give up our investigation right now. We might just as well take into consideration the countless hypotheses that the mathematical games of lunatics' logic have to offer us. So what about Granada?' says the Investigator, turning to the Literary Expert. 'Can we get back to that, if you don't mind?'

'Gladly. So we strolled a great deal, Karl Knigh and I, round the Generalife gardens in bloom. "I'm extremely fond of the Court of Lions," Karl Knigh told me. "That may not be original, but I myself am not an original person."'

'*I myself* ! Did you hear that? *I myself am not an original person!*' exclaims the Poet Criminologist. 'Doesn't that *I myself* go and throw his whole family over board?'

'Let him go on, let him go on!' says the Maritime Affairs Investigator.

'Indeed,' the Literary Expert continues, 'Karl Knigh always stressed the fact that he was not an "eccentric", he said, "as are my children, on whom my brother had a deplorable influence from their very earliest youth." So over a period of several days we strolled round the gardens in bloom and Karl Knigh in a way dictated to me the thesis he wanted me not to write. "I'm a terribly wounded man," he told me when we were in the Princess's apartments.

'He would occasionally stop in one of the little alcoves to observe the countryside through a slit window. "This landscape pacifies me, as the great beach of Pals pacifies me, and the Sierra Nevada pacifies me, and the water you see flowing down the slopes of these gardens, this snow water of a slightly soapy colour, like jade, also pacifies me. Yes, I'm at peace here, far from my family, and at the same time not far from Julius whom I dread to the point of not being easy unless I know he's close at hand, near enough for some of the mysterious resources in my possession to be effective. Julius and I are locked together. When I'm at Pals, I wish he were there too. Just as I seek him out in Granada, where he lives in the district of squalid *cantina*s and dark blind-alleys. He likes the darkness of blind alleys. He avoids me and I avoid him. Sometimes at night I go down to one or other of the *cantina*s where I know he'll be so drunk he won't recognize me. I sit with him and watch him. He doesn't say anything. He's drunk and he doesn't say anything. I don't say anything either. We both remain silent and sometimes we sit there face to face till dawn, without exchanging a word. And so we measure our closeness and the terrifying distance that separates us since the death of our young brother Arno.

'"Then I leave him and rush off to an old gypsy who lives below the spur of the Generalife gardens. She lives somewhere down there, surrounded by cats and chickens, in a kind of hen-house. Like the woman with the cockerel in Pals, she reads all the dreadful things gathering in upon me, all the dreadful things inscribed long ago in some illegible word penned by Destiny.

'"Do you know that in Greece they used to chain statues to their seats to prevent them from escaping?" Karl Knigh went on, suddenly switching to a subject that seemed to have nothing to do with what he had just been saying. I listened,' says the Literary Expert, 'I listened and made mental notes. "At Argos, the statue of Hera was chained to the gold and ivory throne on which she sat,' Knigh went on, 'because for a city to lose the statue of its god or goddess meant losing its divine protection. Do you know who Hera was, young literary expert? Hera was the mother of Ares, Hephaistos and Hebe. Zeus had these three children by Hera, just as I had three children by Belle. These children were engendered by Zeus when Hera touched a certain flower. You see the significance of this? Those three children were born by parthenogenesis. Hera conceived three children. She *gave* herself her three children. Wait! Her son Hephaistos, not wanting to believe in this fatherless conception, abducted his mother and imprisoned her in a mechanical chair with folding arms that most cruelly gripped those placed in it. He kept his mother Hera imprisoned like this until she swore by the river Styx that she wasn't lying and that he and his brother and sister were indeed parthenogenetic children. Hera in Greek means Protectress.

'"So, you see, when Belle died it was impossible for me to provide protection for her three children. Those children weren't mine but Belle's. Why did I not chain her to life?

Why did I not have that mechanical chair to prevent her from dying! That's what I said to myself on my way back from the cemetery. It's impossible to have three children and devote yourself to literature, I told myself, it's impossible to live in a house where the lack of Belle's presence oppresses me and prevents me from concentrating. I locked myself up in my study and remained there for several days, thinking and smoking, and eating nothing. I could hear my . . . Belle's children running along the corridors and up and down the staircases of the big empty house, and if I'd been able to turn the hourglass, I assure you I'd have done it, as fathers in Antiquity jealously guarded the right to do so. Tomorrow, perhaps, I'll reveal to you what role Julius played in all this. And to what extent my imagination, on the basis of nothing, began to attribute to him all kinds of misdeeds, both in his rather too eloquent silences with Belle, when she was expecting Franz, as well as afterwards when Belle's three children were orphans."

'That's how,' says the Literary Expert, 'I gradually came to realize what a deeply deranged man old Karl Knigh was, because of Julius. And every time he had to explain his bizarre behaviour, it was to the font of myths that he'd go running to seek refuge. I've saved up numerous examples to give you when I've made more progress in reading and comparing the different manuscripts. However, from the little I've managed to grasp of them, very few things seem to add up, as they say, between what Karl Knigh told me when I was gathering material for my future thesis and the fragments of texts that I glanced through last night and this afternoon. There's a remarkable discrepancy between what Karl Knigh said and what he wrote.'

'But it's in those very discrepancies, those kind of faultlines, that the solution perhaps resides,' says the Poet Criminologist. 'In every investigation it's absolutely essential to adopt a position at a slight remove from the *normal* view one would be tempted to take of the problem in hand. What fascinates us about the mystery of the *Uranus* is the means of approach that by an extraordinary fluke has been placed in our hands. And this means of approach is you: not only are you well acquainted with all of the Knighs but you've also interpreted them in your thesis.'

'Since being called in by you and visiting the deserted *Uranus*, I've become full of doubt. I was for a long time an assured literary expert, and now I'm unsure. The pile of manuscripts you've saddled me with weighs so heavily on my conscience it's deprived me of my good conscience. And what's a literary expert deprived of his good conscience? These days, behind a writer's every word lurks a literary expert. Behind a writer's every comma, a literary expert has made his nest. What use is a literary expert if not to track down, in the full confidence of his own good conscience, the guilty conscience of every good writer?

'Though I'm a literary expert to the very core of my being, I'm beginning to loathe literary experts, yes, I loathe myself! Since the tragic demise of the Knigh family, I loathe my thesis, and the thought of having to immerse myself every night for the foreseeable future in the mountain of papers left aboard the *Uranus* plunges me into deep dejection. It's too late now. *All I am* is an expert on the Knigh literary family! I've devoted years of my life to writing this thesis. I've practically not lived in order to dedicate myself to this work, and now this work is entirely called into question. If you only knew what lurks in those manuscripts piled up in my bedroom! All the material I had on the Knigh family suddenly devalued, like a currency. I'm a literary expert who's crashed. It's enough to make you blow your brains out, I assure you.

'You laugh? I was laughing about it, too, on my own last night in the midst of these maniacal handwritten remnants. I've already mentioned to you, I think, a literary expert who's made a special study on the subject of *Why Lord Jim?* She's spent her whole life proving that Joseph Conrad, who had been living at Hyères, in France, fled the town because of some ridiculous story of a broken engagement. And according to this literary expert, it was in order to escape a sense of guilt, extraordinarily exaggerated by the prevailing climate of puritanism, that the young sailor Joseph Conrad threw himself into writing, miraculously transforming himself into

Conrad the writer. Hence, according to this same literary expert, the parallel with Lord Jim and his unfailing sense of guilt. Lord Jim, who deserts the ship filled with pilgrims, who out of cowardice abandons on the high seas the ship for which he was responsible, is supposed to be young Conrad running away from love. That, according to this researcher, is the origin of this seminal novel without which there would be no Faulkner, no Lowry, no literature on themes of disintegration, such as that of Julius Knigh or Rosa Zhorn-Knigh.'

'But suppose we get back to Karl Knigh, the birth of his three children, and the death of his first wife Belle?' says the Maritime Affairs Investigator, losing patience.

XII

'So, going from one brother to the other, from Julius to Karl and Karl to Julius,' the Literary Expert goes on, 'I began to realize that, of the two of them, the one who was a wreck was not the one you would have assumed. Julius had within him an elemental force – as we say of the elements – serving one of the most complex of minds. And by a kind of inverse symmetry, you had the immense weakness of Karl, the universally respected author, who seemingly presented an exterior suited to the world and who, beneath that exterior, could only keep himself together by relying on the predictions of all kinds of "diviners", such as the woman with the cockerel in Pals, or the witch in Granada, or the Bengali in New York. And when he didn't have them within immediate reach, it was in myths that he found the certainties that he lacked.

' "You know why Julius unwittingly chose to stay and write in Granada?" Karl Knigh asked me. "It's because Hera holds in her hand a pomegranate (*granada* in Spanish) and a cuckoo: the cuckoo bird, and the fruit whose flesh resembles the human cortex. Julius doesn't know that I know, yes, everything! The cuckoo lays its eggs in the nest of an unsuspecting bird. As for the pomegranate, it was offered to man by woman to send him tumbling into the abyss of his own intelligence. Hera claimed to have given herself her three children, by touching a certain flower. But I know! What's true of the pomegranate is also true of the fate that Hera offers to one who succeeds in deceiving Zeus. I'm the sad hero of my own life," Karl Knigh lamented later, when we were strolling in the Court of Lions in the Generalife gardens. "I'm a hero stupidly turned into a monument by my books and for my stance as a vigilant humanist, a man crushed by an admiration that's too massive, you understand, a deadly admiration."

'Karl Knigh left a long pause, no doubt imagining that I was going to protest a completely different kind of admiration from the one he was criticizing. But I continued to walk beside him in silence. At last he said, "Every new book is a rock that I heave against the pull of admiration. I heave it, haunted by all those bright eyes that are waiting."

'"You think people are waiting for your books to roll over you and crush you?" I replied, laughing.

'"No, on the contrary, what crushes and shrivels me up is the idea of all those readers eager for their literary rations. Just thinking about it brings the heavy rock of my writing down upon me! And you won't believe this: I envy Julius whose books don't have that importance, or if you prefer, aren't awaited as mine are. What can I do when the rock of the work-in-progress is too heavy and occasionally impossible to heave? I come rushing here, to Granada, to see the old gypsy woman with her cats, or off to New York, to visit that blind Bengali whose clairvoyance is the most lucid, most acute of all. That's how the *spirits* participate in my work. Arno, especially, guides my hand and substitutes for my own thought! I've all kinds of secret practices for getting down to writing.

'"Don't smile, young literary expert," Karl Knigh said to me,' the Literary Expert goes on, '"those are my medications against the great pain of writing. Do you know what *hero* means in Greek? As the word suggests, the *hero* was the sacred king, sacrificed to the goddess Hera, whose body remained under the earth, his soul having flown off to a paradise located behind the north wind. Well, the way you see me now, old and tired, with these bags under my eyes and this tobacco-stained moustache, I am that sacrificed king. Belle not only abandoned me, but the three children settled on my body are cuckoos who, the very day after their mother died, began to devour me. I was a father devoured by Belle's three children. Kurt devoured me. Rosa devoured me. Franz devoured me even more than the other two because he killed his mother on his arrival among us. They all devoured and devoured me. Devoured by three young children while your readers are also devouring you! Devoured, too, by the symposiums on this or that book of mine or on all my books. Devoured by the bloodsucking press. Devoured by machines that steal your image. Devoured by the obligation of humanism. And meanwhile, look at Julius! Ignored! I, devoured! He, ignored! And I was the widow of Hera," Karl Knigh went on, "the sacrificed king devoured by his children. The cuckoo perched on Hera's wrist – she was represented in this way by the Greeks – symbolized the duplicity of her love life. The pomegranate and the cuckoo. The human cortex and song! But what love did I get from Belle? Three growing children who, the better to devour their father, begin to write even before they can draw! *Normal* children do drawings and *offer* you their drawings as they *offer* you their excrement – for which they are loudly congratulated. No such messes from Belle's three abandoned children! Oh no! Pages of writing! All three practically born writing! Born with an inexplicable sense of syntax. And the more I withdrew and buried myself in my own work, the more Julius became the replacement father to these three cuckoos settled in my house.

‘ "They're born writers, Julius told me, handing me a page by Kurt and a page by Rosa.

‘ "There's no such thing as a born writer, I replied. In music perhaps, there may be born musicians, but in literature, no! Did you dictate to them or guide their hands? I asked him.

‘ "I assure you, Karl, he said, it was *our* children who wrote these texts!' That *our* infuriated me, and I drove Julius out of the house. Wasn't it absurd? Making a mess, being noisy – that's the realm of normal children! A child's born crying and making a mess. A bit of a musician, if you will; a bit of a painter, if you will. But verbal expression – of what? Of complexity? No, what father would put up with such little monsters in his house?

‘ "Since you're preparing to write this thesis," Karl Knigh also said to me,' the Literary Expert went on in the Yacht Club restaurant, "since you won't give up," Karl Knigh insisted, "you'll have to get Julius to show you the very first writings by the children that Belle left us to cope with wrote. That *us* surprises you? Well, let me tell you that Julius craftily took my place in the affection of these children that a Danish 'au pair' kept confined to the top of the house in which silence was strictly enforced. Try to get from Julius the first texts by Rosa, Kurt, or Franz! You know what I hope," Karl Knigh went on to say as we were strolling in the Court of Lions, "is that once you've gathered the spoils on me and my family, you'll give up. I shall overwhelm you with material and so your thesis will smother you and smother itself."'

'Indeed, there was good reason to give up,' the Poet Criminologist breaks in.

'Believe me, I would have done, if he hadn't challenged me as if he wanted to provoke me into not letting go. "And besides, what proof is there that I'm not lying to you? What does Julius have to say for himself? And what proof have you that he's not lying to you either? Why shouldn't we all lie, to confuse you, to make you unable to reconcile all the nonsense we may be telling you?" There he was, getting all worked up, and suddenly coming to a halt on the path, beneath the wisteria and roses, he drew several weird signs in the sand with his walking-stick.'

'The same as you assume the others to be?'

'Yes, no doubt the same as those you found on the hull of the *Uranus*. "You see these signs," he said to me. "They're terrible signs. I have only to write them, on water, sand or in the air, to be protected from those who wish me harm. If I want, I can stop you, I can paralyse your thinking. Thanks to certain symbols, I can save myself from a desperate situation when others couldn't."'

'You're giving us a portrait, here, of a man incapable of distinguishing reality from the irrational. Why would a guy like that, having got them all into the water, not reckon on these symbols to get him out of trouble? You know, things difficult to believe have happened in my family!'

'As a matter of fact, he spoke to me several times about levitation, in connection with his Bengali. He also believed in contacts with an entire population of spirits living on a different plane. "You see this crowd," he said to me in New York, when we were on our way to visit the blind Bengali, "all these people jostling us on this pavement are nothing compared with the invisible crowd we're surrounded by . . . just as modern physics has recently proved that we only perceive a tiny part of the matter of which the universe is formed." I listened to him, while saying to myself, how can any sensible man come out with such drivel. Of course I kept silent.'

'But it's often the most sensible men who believe in spirits as well as angels. Victor Hugo, the materialist Hugo, went in for table-turning in the bosom of his family. Not only did he believe in rapping spirits but he obeyed their orders,' says the Poet Criminologist. 'And, you know, I, too, would like to believe in them! There are tasks in life that, to accomplish, you'd wish for the help and support of these unexplained forces. Balzac as well believed in spirits. His text on Swedenborg and his *Heavenly Arcana* would encourage you to appeal to angels.'

'Things have happened in my family,' says the Investigator, 'that are very . . .'

'Wait, there are more surprises yet to come,' says the Literary Expert, laughing.

'It's getting late,' says the Maritime Affairs Investigator. 'Come on, let's drop by my office. You must see the photos of the signs found on the hull of the *Uranus*. Then we'll leave you to your study of the manuscripts.'

'After what you've told us about Karl Knigh and the trust he placed in those who purported to help him overcome his fears, I've no doubt the signs in the blown-up photos are the same,' says the Poet Criminologist as all three of them make their way down towards the boat yards in the port.

Having studied the enlargements for a long time, the Literary Expert finally says, 'These are certainly the signs that Karl Knigh surrounded himself with. And these are also the signs, with a few variations, that I found in the margins of Lotte Knigh's journal.'

'So, according to you, no one but him could have drawn such symbols on the water-line of the *Uranus*?'

'I can guarantee it. Karl Knigh told me on the flight to New York, where he was anxious I should accompany him, "Personally I'd prefer you to drop this thesis project, but if you're still really set on it, well, it's absolutely essential that my blind Bengali should lay hands on you. He must also make certain signs over you, without which none of what you're preparing to write about me and my family would be valid. Your thesis must take into account the hidden part of my writing as well as other members of my family's writings, because Arno is within us, and it is at his dictation that all we Knighs write."'

'He also told me,' says the Literary Expert, examining the photographs by the light of the desk-lamp, 'that "great books are those in which humanity scarcely dares to look at itself. They're vast stuffy caverns in the form of dark mirrors. Great books are crushing rocks. Lesser books are to be sat upon, on aeroplanes, trains, or wherever, but great books that represent humanity weigh on you with the weight of the earth. These books are tellurian, real sweat-boxes. That's why, continually heaving the rock of the work in progress, I keep on attempting the great sweat-box book. And I intend to finish off all literary experts like you with my last great sweat-box book." And it was then that he came out with several terrible remarks that I can not recall without a sense of unease. "I plan to write a great sweat-box book about a family of human rats and the terrifying multiplication of these literary human rats with relations beyond number. Everything will be apparently respectable, well-balanced, reassuring, but what's happening beneath the surface will be appalling. It'll be an oceanic book, and it will end under the sea."'

'Are you sure of the words old Knigh used? Knowing what became of them all, are you certain you're not allowing yourself to be influenced?'

'That story of human rats is not the kind of thing you invent,' says the Poet Criminologist. 'Whether it was Karl Knigh or one or other of the passengers of *Uranus*, it meant storing up a fair amount of scorn and loathing for mankind to want this mass drowning.'

'But what I haven't told you,' the Literary Expert goes on, 'is that Knigh was planning to write this book under a pseudonym. Having achieved almost universal fame, he wanted to be read without preconceptions, as if he were an unknown author that no one had ever heard anything about.'

'The height of arrogance.'

'Yes, no doubt, but also the need to have what you don't have. I think that the old writer coming up against the immensity of his success felt a kind of nostalgia for innocence ... or obscurity? To be Julius in some small way ... and himself. To be himself ... and his children. To be him ... and also that which he's not. It's like that with certain authors: as they get older, instead of clarifying their work, they make it opaque. You've only to see the state of his last manuscript. Unlike Julius whose last writings are of morbid though disguised lucidity. In any case,' concludes the Literary Expert, laying down the photographic enlargements, 'I can assure you, these signs definitely belong to Karl Knigh. The oblique light that made it possible to photograph them shows them up perfectly.'

XIII

Having left the Maritime Affairs Investigator in his office, the Poet Criminologist accompanies the Literary Expert to his hotel.

'I'm extremely disturbed by what you've just told us. Everything points to Karl Knigh and at the same time I'm convinced he's innocent of this mass drowning. Now that we're alone, tell me honestly: do you think it's possible that Karl Knigh's guilty?'

'I honestly don't think he's guilty.'

'Ah, I'm pleased to hear it. The trails seem to me so confused! If I look to the classics of criminology, only the clear trail should lead us to enlightenment. It's always been the way with criminals: they invariably blur trails not by obscuring them but on the contrary by overclarifying them. The classic criminologists and investigators are like those ramblers on their return from a hike over glaciers. They tell you they haven't seen anything but the perpetual whiteness of great torrents of forever frozen water. May I come into your room for a moment?

'I'd like you to know how much of a consolation to me this investigation and its surprises are. I don't know why, your presence allays the despondency I feel in living. Your way of releasing to us little by little all this information on the Knigh family somehow raises me above myself and my terrible problems. I like hearing you talk about the Knighs. The way you bring them so much to life through your words makes me temporarily forget the personal tragedy that oppresses my days and nights and my wife's days and nights.

'May I share a confidence with you? One freely given. A confidence to which I ask you not to react. Not to seek consoling words. If I embarrass you, tell me, and I'll be off straightaway. My excessively serious tone puts you on the defensive? I'd be put on the defensive if I were to be cornered in my bedroom by a criminologist such as myself, especially if he announced some terrible confidence with so many precautionary remarks.

'What is the tragedy of the *Uranus* beside some other secret tragedies? What are those drowning hours beside the years of drowning and despair that some people suffer? Do you think there's any crueller torment than to be afflicted through your nearest and dearest, as they say? If the mystery of the *Uranus* affords us a glimpse of what cannot be expressed in writing, of the unimaginable, what's to be said of the person stuck on Charon's boat for years and years? We sail the Styx daily, my wife, my child and I! I don't know why, the mystery of the *Uranus* keeps taking me back to our days and nights of suffering.

'That the doomed Knigh family should scratch the unforgiving hull, weep, cry out in terror, that its members should assist and then thrust each other aside, try in vain to hoist one or other of them on to the deserted deck, then attempt to climb on top of each other, and in the end, knowing they're doomed, let themselves drown from exhaustion – what is that beside the daily spectacle of a child whose muscles are destroyed? My child, you understand! Do you realize what torture life is for my wife? What torture I have to suffer, while appearing outwardly cheerful and full of energy? The *Uranus* must have represented a white enamelled hell to those who wore down their fingernails on the hull till they were bleeding. But for my wife, especially, life is a high-security hell just as white and enamelled, believe me, and it's been that way for years without end! The literary family's torment lasted no more than forty-eight hours for the stronger of them, seven or eight for the weaker ones. And I imagine that Karl and Julius, seeing the situation for what it was, must have let themselves drown as soon as they realized it was useless to struggle. And I ask you, a complete stranger to me, should I struggle or should I let myself drown, taking my wife and child with me?

'No. Whatever you do, don't answer. I'm sorry I lost control of myself. Tomorrow or the next day, I'd like to give you some of my secret poems to read. What is poetry if not the selected memory of woes that cannot be spoken of? We are the sum of sufferings.'

'Your friend the Investigator told me . . .'

'He's my only friend, too close a friend for me to be able to confide in him as I have just confided in you.'

'He . . .'

'Please! Not another word on the subject! At times, I find the universal mystery so overwhelming that everything else, except this mystery, seems unreal. The inexplicable mystery is the only contender for being a reality. The mystery, however elusive it might be, precisely because of its elusiveness, *is* more graspable than God or even the universe, of which we have no assurance that they really exist. And I tell myself that Oscar Wilde or Borges, for instance, with the wittiness of each, would no doubt offer us a very special literary *game* on the reason for this empty *Uranus* whose scratched hull suggests that the smooth and insuperable wall will remain insuperable for ever. Let me stay with you just another moment, sitting on this bed buried under all these manuscripts. Then I'll be off, to where a completely different kind of questioning awaits me. Carry on talking about the Knighs. Save me a while longer from my own darkness!'

'Gladly,' says the Literary Expert in embarrassment.

'I know that after sharing this confidence with you – and I thank you for having received it without trying to console me – it may be difficult for you to go on. And yet you can't imagine how eager I am to know. Who was Gustav Zhorn? Who was Kurt? And Rosa, who was she? And Franz, and Lotte – you've said nothing about them yet. Did Karl Knigh not talk about them?'

'Knowing that they were all to appear in my thesis, the old writer of course took the precaution of preparing me. He particularly loathed Gustav Zhorn, "that failed actor". "I know you're to meet him," he said to me on the flight taking us to the United States, "he'll seduce you just as he seduced Kurt, then Rosa, whom he married, also marrying Kurt through her. 'Don't forget, I'm their father,' I told Zhorn on the day of this weird three-way wedding, 'whatever happens, Kurt and Rosa are my children.' And can you believe it, this fiendish lover of my two children replied in that mocking tone of voice which not for one moment does he ever abandon, 'But *I* love them!' Seeing how much he was annoying me, he kept on insisting, 'I love Kurt and I love Rosa, and they love me too. Since Kurt and Rosa were in love with each other even before I met them, I couldn't help but fall in love with them. I love your children more than you've ever loved them!' That's what he dared to tell me." Our plane was now approaching New York, whose luminous haze was visible in the distance.'

'And having met him, did you include Zhorn in your thesis?'

'Not really, but certain information that he gave me, after I made the acquaintance of this extremely charming man, was useful to me. He spoke of his relationship with Kurt and Rosa in terms so provocative that even today, when there's greater freedom of morality in words than in the actual intimacy of unconventional relationships perhaps, Zhorn's jubilatory indiscretion managed to be shocking. And yet what's left to reveal about the practices of carnal love? What could possibly surprise us today?

'It was fascinating to witness at close quarters the life of that trio – as all three of them allowed me to. I stayed for a while in their house in the suburbs of Vienna. There was a very strong current that flowed between Kurt and Rosa. I've no doubt that they'd carried over from childhood a kind of twinship in which they enclosed themselves, and that this twinship, which was both sensual and sentimental, was something that Zhorn envied as an indivisible whole. By marrying Rosa, he may perhaps have wedded, above all, the anger of Karl Knigh, who was *disturbed* by this triple union. Yet, I assure you, Karl Knigh was not an easy man to disturb on such matters. Did he not talk freely about myths? About mythological cannibalism, about mythological incest? Was he not the modern writer whose every reference invariably went back to Greece? "Zhorn," he told me, "married Kurt and not Rosa, although it was apparently Rosa that he married. This guy Zhorn acts like a burglar who enters his victims' homes without breaking in. Rosa is the pass-key that this crafty burglar managed to get hold of,"' says the Literary Expert reporting Karl Knigh's words to the Poet Criminologist, sitting on the bed, among the manuscripts, in the quiet hotel room.

'Was old Knigh implying that by marrying Rosa it was the Knigh family this guy Zhorn was entering without breaking in?'

'Absolutely! Knigh was at the centre of everything. Everything converged on him, so he thought in his intolerable self-obsession. The plane was circling over New York and now kept us suspended above an endless spiral of waiting. "Yes, until that ill-fated day when Gustav Zhorn penetrated our midst, it had never bothered anyone apart from Julius whether or not I loved the children that Belle had left me with. No one at all! And least of all, my children, I'm sure! What use would they have had for the affection of a man so deeply buried in his writing, a man obsessed by his writing and the shadows linked to his writing?

' "Through Belle's death, my children are twice-born, like triple-guised Dionysus who was called twice-born or child of the double door," Karl Knigh went on. "Although I've always kept them at a distance, my children are twice-born: of Belle, and also of me, against my will. After Zeus betrayed Hera with Semele the Moon, Hera treacherously urged Semele to demand of Zeus that he remain faithful, to her at least, whose changing aspect must, she thought, suffice to gratify his every desire. But Zeus refused and lovely Semele denied him her bed. Then in a rage he appeared in the form of thunder and lightning – and so she was consumed. But Hermes saved the triple-faced child, Dionysus, that Semele was carrying. As he was not yet in the sixth month of gestation, Hermes cunningly sewed him into Zeus's thigh, so that he could continue to be carried for the remaining months. When he came to term, Hermes delivered Dionysus. Likewise were my three children, as it were, sewn into my thigh," Karl Knigh continued to complain. "I carried that heavy burden for years. They fed on my substance. They devoured me from within. And believe it or not, it was Julius who took it into his head to deliver them, when he decided they'd come to term." That's what Karl Knigh told me as we finally landed in New York.'

'You could almost understand this complaint of Karl Knigh,' says the Poet Criminologist. 'But what's Semele got to do with it?'

'If I had to interpret some of the notes in Julius's papers that happen to have caught my eye, the inescapable conclusion is that — although they never discussed it between them — all their lives the two brothers played a game of disputing paternity of the three Knigh children. In my opinion, knowing Karl and his rather perverse habit of distorting myths, it would seem that in his mind Hera and Semele were one and the same woman. Except that one of them actually shared his bed, and the other, only in fantasy it seems, that of Julius. But what empty dreams Julius must have entertained in his solitude!'

'You mean that Karl Knigh mischievously enjoyed believing what deep down he clearly didn't believe?'

'Yes, I think so. By this ploy Karl Knigh managed to forgive himself his refusal to assume the paternity of his own children.'

'And according to you, Julius willingly took on this role?'

'Yes.'

XIV

Having spent the whole night reading through the Knigh family manuscripts, the Literary Expert has just fallen asleep, exhausted, among the pages littering his bed.

'I hope this isn't an unpleasant surprise,' says the Investigator, waking the Literary Expert in his untidy room. 'I was waiting for you in my office, but seeing that you didn't come, I took the liberty of coming over to you. My dear friend the Poet Criminologist is to join us here. I see that you didn't even undress and that you were overcome by sleep in the middle of reading. So? Anything new?'

'A fair amount!' says the Literary Expert with a yawn.

'Allow me to sit on the corner of the bed. May I put this pile of manuscripts next to that one?'

'Mind,' says the Literary Expert. 'Those are Rosa Zhorn-Knigh's writings. A quite remarkable series of texts, of rare literary density. While reading some of those pages last night, I said to myself that all too often women's writing has not only been underestimated but deliberately pillaged and rewritten by men.'

'What man understands anything about women!' sighs the Maritime Affairs Investigator.

'Especially when they write! Although, actually in those pages there, on which you've just rested your elbow, Rosa shows great sureness of style and of thought: "When the day comes," she writes, "like you, Virginia, my sister, I shan't hesitate to enter the water, with my pockets filled with stones!"'

'Enter the water! Her pockets filled with stones!'

'Wait! That's not all! Further on, in those pages you see there, she portrays an old man who has such a terrible obsession with signs that he can't lift a finger or take a step without drawing, either mentally or physically, sequences of signs that eventually bury him in the labyrinth of his own making. She also describes the signet-ring this man wears. And I know the signet-ring she's talking about. Her father Karl Knigh wore one exactly the same. A jade seal, on which the same design as that found on the *Uranus*'s water-line was visible now and again when the ring was caught in an oblique ray of sunshine or light. When I asked old Knigh in Granada what these signs represented, he replied: "Remember Balthazar!"

'"Which Balthazar?" I asked.

'"The one in *The Quest of the Absolute*, of course!"'

'A very bad book!' breaks in the Poet Criminologist, appearing in the bedroom.

'I don't agree with you,' says the Literary Expert, moving aside some manuscripts so that the Poet Criminologist can sit down. 'What author has not attempted his *Faust*? And do you know that for Baudelaire this *Faust* of Balzac's was superior to . . .'

'Please, let's get back to that ring and to what you were saying about Rosa. To enter the water with her pockets filled with stones – isn't that throwing the ladder overboard? Do you think she had any reason for wanting to wipe out her whole family? Have you found any clue in her writings, any mental instability?'

'What kind of stability could you hope to find in anyone who writes?' says the Literary Expert.

'So you think that none of them . . .'

'None of them was mentally stable, that's for sure.'

'But Zhorn didn't write, to my knowledge.'

'He may not have written, but I have proof here, in this manuscript in particular, that he intervened in the margins of his wife's writings, as well as those of Kurt.'

'You mean, we have a mirror phenomenon. On one side, Lotte Knight intervening in old Karl Knigh's manuscripts, and on the other, Gustav intervening in Rosa's and Kurt's manuscripts?' says the Investigator.

'Yes, I've various evidence for it.'

'And what about Julius and Franz in all this?'

'Oh, Franz is a completely different kettle of fish! I'll tell you about him later. I visited him several times in Hamburg. He was the gentlest, most intelligent young man, and perhaps the most inventive of the lot. His research on the senses is certainly among the most important ever attempted. And the fact that he used it as the basis for some philosophical publications places his work on a level of such originality that very few intellectuals can understand him. Franz has always been Julius's favourite. Just as much as Karl rejected this child whom he described as "his mother's murderer", Julius wanted to protect Franz and spare him the kind of remarks that Karl Knigh never ceased to heap on him from his very earliest years.

'But at the same time, even while he rejected his children, Karl Knigh was jealous of the very strong affection they had for Julius. And the older he got, he confessed to me, the more he regretted his inability to be just simply straightforward with his children. "It's Julius's fault for taken it into his head, immediately after Belle's death, to rescue them from me. He didn't have much trouble setting them against me. With astonishing persistency, knowing him, he imperceptibly influenced them. He took their writings seriously, to the point of encouraging them to publish too soon, with no concern for the name they were usurping. Already Julius was putting the name Knigh to his own, so unKnigh-like writings. That he should have tried to use my name to make one for himself was a very strange presumption. But then to encourage all my children to sign themselves Knigh! Furthermore, I'm going tell you something, on condition that on no account does it appear in your thesis. Promise?"

'"Promise!" I said, knowing that this was just so that it should appear in my thesis!

'"I've supported Julius all my life. I've helped him, so that it shouldn't be said that Karl Knigh let his brother die of hunger. I've regularly made over to him a substantial share of my income." We were back in Granada and he knew that every evening I went to join Julius in the *cantina* at the end of some blind-alley in the gypsy quarter. Was he hoping these words would get back to his brother? I think so.

'"Ah, let's not talk any more about my family! No! No! Let's not talk about them any more!" he exclaimed one morning. "I'm exhausted by so many Knighs clinging to my shirt-tails! As well as that Zhorn-Knigh by marriage, as they say, who's added to the burden that I have to carry! That marriage was just a method of blackmail. An outrage! You can't imagine the sums of money that Zhorn extorts from me by means that I shan't reveal to you. Since it's well known that men who've resolved to hate their fellow-men have to begin by hating themselves, I decided to go along with Zhorn's outrageousness. Not wanting to hate myself or to hate my children inordinately, I made the effort, believe it or not, of regularly inviting them on my yacht. Including Zhorn! It's an ordeal for all of us, but it's become a kind of maritime ritual that none of us shirks. Yes, and that includes Zhorn!" Karl Knigh insisted. "My yacht is a ship of fools. Shall I dare to confess to you that we enjoy hating each other at leisure?"

'That,' concludes the Literary Expert, 'is how Karl Knigh spoke of his family, and in particular of Zhorn, whose charm worked in an unexpected way on him.'

'And this charm, did you yourself experience it?'

'Yes, indeed! Zhorn was not of this world. He gave the impression of being in transit, of just stopping for a while, and curiously this way of behaving as if he were only there by chance, in passing, as if he belonged elsewhere in some region inaccessible to men, shrouded him with rarified mystery. I'm convinced that Karl Knigh saw in Zhorn a kind of semi-angelic, semi-fiendish ambassador from some intermediary plane. In any case that was what I thought I understood from his incoherent way of talking about him.'

'Let's play at imagining, shall we?' says the Poet Criminologist. 'Having met this Zhorn, you certainly formed an opinion of him?'

'No, not especially.'

'Well, let's say, you can at least place him, in the situation that concerns us?

'You mean, on the deck of the yacht while the others . . .'

'Exactly, while they thrash around in the water. Do you see him pulling up the ladder and then jumping in among the panic-stricken Knighs? Would you be able to find a motive for him? Would you have enough imagination to deliver him to us, bound hand and foot, as they say?'

'If we're to try to discover how he behaved, it's in his wife Rosa Zhorn-Knigh's literary efforts that we're likely to find the corresponding model. Have you read Casanova's *Memoirs*?'

'In part . . .'

'Like everyone else! His escape from the Leads – and people think they've read it all! Not only is it the most instructive book on the society of his day, but some pages on Voltaire or Catherine of Russia are among the most . . .'

'So, what about Zhorn? Enough digressions!' the Maritime Affairs Investigator says testily. 'Zhorn! Zhorn!'

'But it's Zhorn that we're talking about,' says the Literary Expert. 'There's a passage in Casanova's *Memoirs* that's, let's say, beyond the pale, worthy of the diabolical Marquis. It's the torture of Damien, the regicide. Casanova watches it, surrounded by his friends, from a balcony he has hired for the occasion. These are among the most appalling pages on the erotic effect on men as well as women of the sight of the wheel, the screams, the groans of the victim on the wheel, the sound of bones shattering beneath the blows of an iron bar, the blood, the retching, the defecation, and above all the infinite duration of such agony. This spectacle of prolonged death – nine hours of torture artistically measured out – so excites the spectators, male and female, that Casanova, very skilfully, makes you party to the liberties he gradually allows himself to take with a woman in front of him, squeezed against the crowded balcony. While the criminal on the wheel dies horribly, the author describes in detail how, mingling the horror with his enjoyment, he gives and takes pleasure . . . That's the fantasy you've elicited from my imagination,' concludes the Literary Expert with a laugh.

'Without going so far as to imagine that kind of identification of Zhorn with Casanova, do you really believe the lover of Rosa and Kurt was capable of getting pleasure out of watching the Knigh family drown?'

'You probably haven't read any of Rosa Zhorn-Knigh's stories?

'A few.'

'Haven't you noticed how many women writers choose themes of almost unbearable violence? The most terrible crimes in the entire history of literature have been *committed* by literary women. Often enough, even by sweet and kind old ladies. Why is that? Rosa Zhorn-Knigh wrote texts worthy of the most terrifying of those inspired Englishwomen who didn't shrink from any literary horror. One of her stories, as it so happens, features a diabolical couple who . . .'

'In criminology,' the Poet Criminologist cuts in, 'there are many *real-life* cases of diabolical couples, as they're called. Is there any need for literature to try to outdo fact? Don't you think this kind of horror one-upmanship in women's literature might derive from a lack of confidence, as with those English vicars' daughters inventing situations where terror provides the motive for writing.'

'You're thinking of Mary Wollstonecraft Shelley?'

'Of course! She invented the most frightening character in all of literature. Just imagine, that woman stitched together a kind of human patchwork made of bits and pieces stolen from corpses. Mary Shelley shared herself between Byron and Shelley. In a way Rosa Zhorn-Knigh was a sister of Mary the poet, involved with two men.'

'One of whom, incidentally, drowned off the coast of La Spezia.'

'Indeed! Rosa Zhorn-Knigh, Mary Shelley's present-day sister, in love . . . but with her own brother and a supposedly brilliant actor . . . to tell the truth, too intelligent a dandy to playact anywhere else but in real life. Every time I met Zhorn, not only was it always a different man I encountered but a different kind of man. Sometimes with long straight fair hair and a touch of nonchalance in his gestures and his bearing, sometimes with his head close-shaved, looking like a Prussian officer, sometimes with a moustache or beard . . . but always with flint in the depths of his eyes. And a carnivorous laugh.

Long restless hands with fingernails perhaps even more well-kept than a woman's.

'"So," he said to me, "you're a kind of literary sleuth?"

'"Yes, I am," I replied, playing up to his banter. "I'm investigating all the Knighs."

'"You know who I am?" he went on, baring his teeth rather than smiling, in a grin that I wouldn't allow myself to find extremely charming. Some guys are like that! Terribly dangerous, and that's why you're irresistibly drawn towards them. He was dangerously irresistible. He must have been dangerously irresistible since childhood. He knew he was attractive, it was obvious from his every gesture, from his entire behaviour.

'"Yes, you're Gustav Zhorn and I already know a lot about you."

'"To my discredit, no doubt?"

'"Mostly, yes. Karl Knigh has told me a good deal about you."

'"You mean, a good deal of bad."

'"Yes and no. He views you with anxiety and fascination."

'"Don't listen to Karl Knigh. The old man's losing his wits. If you're going to take what he says as a basis for writing a thesis about him, his children and his brother, you'd better disregard what all the rest of them tell you about each other."

'That was my first contact with the dangerous Gustav Zhorn,' says the Literary Expert.

XV

'You haven't answered my question,' says the Poet Criminologist.

'Let him go on,' says the Investigator. 'What an attractive culprit this Zhorn is!'

'That's almost certainly a good reason for ruling him out. Too many pluses in a criminological investigation always add up to zero. Unless . . .'

'Zhorn, you were saying!' the Investigator insists.

'At our first encounter Zhorn said to me, "Rosa and Kurt wanted me to be the one to see you at this initial meeting. You seem very young to be taking on such an ambitious thesis. What exactly do you want of Rosa and Kurt?"

'"I want them to talk about their books, their father, their uncle Julius and, where relevant, about Lotte Knigh . . . and why not about you, who bear the name of a great Swiss writer that died young?"

'"Ah, you're thinking of my namesake, the man from Mars! Who brings his cancer into literature. Where? In Switzerland! That little tumour wedged between France, Italy and Germany that so far no one has dared to remove. We did a play in Switzerland, yes, two hundred years after Rousseau's famous letter, we depraved the Genevans by giving them drama. They liked it! A very scathing play by Rosa. They didn't realize till the next day. But they'd already applauded. Kurt played himself, and so did I. That play was about *us*. We were bad. Kurt's too good a writer to be an actor. Like Artaud, too good a writer to devote himself to the theatre. A very bad playwright was Artaud. *Les Cenci*'s a dreadful play, completely devoid of cruelty despite his incredibly naive didactics. Brilliant writer, awful dramatist!" And so on. Zhorn kept talking, trying to get me to react. But I remained calm and smiling.'

'What he said about Artaud, especially with regard to *Les Cenci*, doesn't seem unreasonable,' the Poet Criminologist intervenes.

'I told you, this man was very intelligent, provocative, charming, very intuitive. He gave me the impression of some magnificent insect that searches for the exact spot to place its sting. He obviously wanted to make himself both loved and hated. He constantly blew hot and cold. He was walking a tightrope, you see. But I realized straightaway that it would only take one word . . . *the* word of an outsider to startle him and make him fall.'

'Do you really think our behaviour is so dependent on the way others see us?' says the Maritime Affairs Investigator, perturbed.

'I do,' says the Poet Criminologist, 'I firmly believe so.'

'You, my friend, who know all about my life and its complications,' the Investigator continues, addressing the Poet Criminologist, 'you who got married the same day as I did, do you think she couldn't bear the *outsider's gaze* on us? Could it be that marriage expelled us from the state of grace? Was she frightened that this grace would be lost? So, could the pseudo-separation that she insisted on be an act of love? Just now as I came through the port, I saw that she'd tied the red scarf on which we'd agreed as a signal to the balcony of her hotel room. For believe it or not,' says the Investigator, turning to the Literary Expert who out of discretion is pretending to read a page picked up at random from the bed, 'yes, believe it or not, her pursuit of the impromptu even extends to not telephoning me. She's determined not to be tied down. She possesses nothing more than one small suitcase that she keeps open as if she might have to take off at any moment. She's a delightful woman, you can't imagine how delightful! Even as a child she was, as a young girl yet more so perhaps, and as a woman more delightful still, I'd say. "Let's live in the present," she always says to me, "let's live for the moment." Do you think she's afraid of being awakened from her innocence? Could it be that she actually cares so much about *us*?'

'But that's what I keep telling you,' says the Poet Criminologist, shaking his friend by the shoulder a little.

'I'm sorry to have interrupted, with matters of a personal nature, what you were telling us about Gustav Zhorn,' the

Investigator says to the Literary Expert. 'But although I'm an extremely scrupulous investigator, never talking about myself, practically doing violence to myself to leave my personal problems aside, especially during an investigation as important as the one we're working on, to my shame I lost control of myself.'

'But you did the right thing,' says the Poet Criminologist. 'Speaking personally is a gift we make to those worthy of being our friends. Those who refuse it, often with suspicious ill humour, are at odds with themselves in general. But enough of that! How about going for a drink?'

'So,' resumes the Literary Expert, once the three of them are settled in their chosen corner in the Yacht Club, 'Gustav Zhorn could easily be suspected of having wiped out the Knigh family, as well as himself. A blend of languid calm and restrained potential criminality emanated from Zhorn. He would speak to you in a quiet voice that was extremely pleasant in its gentle modulations, and at the same time you might expect something like a sudden roar. His hands sometimes strangled the air, I assure you. Of course the first conversation I had with him skipped from Karl Knigh to Julius, then to Rosa, then Kurt, Franz and Lotte Knigh, then to him, him, him, obsessively going round the Knigh family to keep coming back to him, him! over and over again throughout that first hour I spent captivated by his charm. When we came to part, he said to me with a laugh that I'd passed my exam and if I wanted to come back at the same time the next day he promised me the meeting with Rosa and Kurt Knigh that I wanted.

'Gustav Zhorn was a kind of demonic angel, who had that desire in him which he kept hinting at in everything he said: to die spectacularly. "Death is our friend," he once told me, when I'd got to know him better and was questioning him about his wife Rosa Zhorn-Knigh's books. "Rosa writes about death and nothing else. The clock without hands has been set for us, once and for all. Yes, between Rosa, Kurt and myself, a pact has been made. We've made a pledge that when the day comes we'll die together joyfully."'

'When the day comes?'

'Wait, that's not all! At that time, there'd been an airplane crash. As it was plummeting to earth, a terrible conversation was recorded by the control tower. Do you remember, despite the co-pilot's desperate efforts, the plane disintegrated on impact. The pilot had found no better way to commit suicide than to take with him a good hundred or so passengers. "What a magnificent death!" Zhorn exclaimed. "What airline pilot hasn't felt the temptation to dive straight into the ocean?"

'I was already much better acquainted with all three of them. Zhorn and Kurt had come to the outskirts of Vienna ahead of Rosa. They'd agreed that I should watch the shooting of a film based on a work by Rosa Zhorn-Knigh, in order to enhance my thesis on the Knigh literary family with what's become an essential aspect of the written word's destiny. So much so that literature . . .'

'Faces certain death,' cuts in the Poet Criminologist with almost comic haste. 'Between too much commentary – forgive me, you being a literary expert – and adaptations, you have to admit that litera . . .'

'Never mind that!' says the Investigator, losing his temper. 'Enough digressions! What you were saying about death and especially about mass suicide decided by a single person seems to me a consideration of primary importance. To die spectacularly! That's a very powerful motive for engineering a mass suicide almost unique in the entire history of criminology, wouldn't you say?'

'Oh, there's no shortage of spectacular deaths of that kind in the history of humanity or the shorter history of criminology,' says the Poet Criminologist. 'Not to mention sects! Since the dawn of the world to the news stories of today, there's no counting the number of bodies! From what you say about Zhorn and the bonds of erotic complicity that kept all three of them firmly spliced, it shouldn't be difficult to work out an excellent solution to the mystery of the *Uranus*.'

'Assumptions aren't enough to wrap up an investigation,' says the Investigator. 'It's important that our friend the

Literary Expert should continue deciphering the manuscripts left in his room. Between what he remembers and the writings found in the *Uranus*'s cabins, he should be able to come up with, as it were, a third angle on the mystery. A third angle that would reveal to us the how, who and above all wherefore of that which we don't know what to describe as a crime? Mass suicide? Mass murder made to look like suicide by one, two or three suicide-murderers? An accident due to collective drunkenness? I even went so far as to imagine a fit of collective laughter that made them all fall overboard. You know how it is: you can't sleep and you turn things over in your mind . . . you speculate. I counted up to twenty-two possibilities. And what else did Gustav Zhorn tell you about this pact between him, Kurt and Rosa? Did he give any indication of how they were planning to put it into practice? If they ever were going to put it into practice? Assuming that Gustav Zhorn was actually telling the truth, and assuming also that it wasn't a matter of playing with words.'

'If you'd known Rosa and Kurt better . . .'

'I met them often and at different stages in their lives, since they made frequent appearances at the Yacht Club, every time their father launched a new *Uranus* or threw a party, as I was telling you. I even remember having seen Gustav Zhorn a few times.'

'So you saw all three of them together?'

'Yes, kind of international dandies – what better way to describe them?'

'There was something of that,' says the Literary Expert, 'but if you'd spent any time in close contact with the trio you'd have gone beyond that superficial assessment. Of course they liked to give an eccentric view of themselves. They cultivated not only their appearance but also the impact they made. And I assure you, when Gustav spoke of death, and how all three of them planned *to dally* with death, you wouldn't have doubted some of the things he said.'

'So you really think *all three of them could have brought about* this mass death, having decided that for them the time had come?'

'No, I don't think so. Knowing Kurt, I think that while playing along with Gustav Zhorn, who'd managed to establish a dangerous influence over him, he nonetheless wouldn't have agreed, in reality, to participate in the fulfilment of an idea thrown out as a provocation and a kind of aesthetic thrill. For, let's face it, this mass drowning remains absolutely aesthetic. The smooth, white, enamelled cabin cruiser lying in the blue sea, with nothing around it, no one left above or under the water, nothing, not even any bodies, just the merest suggestion of vague shadows slowly carried away by the strong submarine currents, like some funerary group caught in a final pose, surrounded by countless playful fish . . . That's the kind of image Zhorn could have elaborated for you with seductive ease — something that delighted Rosa and Kurt. They both loved Zhorn. With him they lost all critical spirit. So intelligent as they were, they seemed bewitched by the magnetism that emanated from this man of both physical and moral pliancy and elusiveness.'

XVI

'Wait! Wait!' says the Investigator. 'You really think that their dandyism, and the depraved aesthetic sensibility that it entails, could become sufficiently powerful motives to lead our three young people into this kind of transformation of their death into an art form?'

'Think of the theatricality of the lovely Lupe Velez's suicide, in Beverly Hills,' says the Poet Criminologist. 'Lupe Velez, who at the height of her beauty and fame took the decision to die at that very moment of her life that she considered unsurpassable. Never was a suicide better staged, more carefully prepared, more calmly planned. Her luxurious house filled with exotic flowers, the bed neither made nor unmade, soft lighting everywhere, nothing left to chance, down to the very last detail. Make-up assistants, hairdressers, and dressers busy themselves around the young woman. Finally she's left alone for the final rendezvous. She drinks the poison with champagne. And suddenly the whole edifice of death collapses: the mixture of poison and alcohol upsets the actress, who, overcome with nausea, rushes for the lavatory bowl in the bathroom, where she's found dead, her lovely face, which she'd taken so much trouble to prepare, a mess . . .'

'In the case of Zhorn, Rosa and Kurt, their exit would at least have had the advantage of leaving only a void to fill,' says the Literary Expert. 'Zhorn was *a lame devil*.'

'You're thinking of Lesage inspired by Velez de Guevara,' exclaims the Poet Criminologist.

'Let's be serious now. Don't you see how you're trying the patience of your friend the Investigator? Remember Diderot in *Jacques the Fatalist* amusing himself with the idea that he's annoying his reader: *If what I say annoys you, you should be even more annoyed by what I don't say*. But to get back to Zhorn, we mustn't forget that he was afflicted with terribly wounded pride, a moral lameness that you discovered as soon as you got to know him a little better. Arrogant Zhorn, intelligent, scathing Zhorn was a lame actor. Yes, he knew he was an undistinguished actor. Yet Rosa managed to get him a part in the film that was to start shooting in Vienna. And Zhorn was deeply humiliated by this. "Nothing can afford me greater amusement than to see how little my wife's recommendation counts for, since these people have found nothing better to offer me than a role of negligible importance," he told me,' the Literary Expert goes on.

'He tried to make a joke of it, but I realized from various comments, always supposedly made in jest, in his usual sarcastic tone, that he would never forgive us – not only Rosa but also Kurt, and myself as a witness to this setback – such a serious humiliation that put a definite end to his career as an actor. This wound for all to see, since the film would come out with Gustav Zhorn playing an undistinguished character in a small part, was for him "the last thrust of the dagger", he said laughing. This "treachery" allowed him to act out a bitter-sweet comedy with Rosa and the Knigh family. Zhorn became even more elusive, more seductive and dangerous. How could Kurt and Rosa not realize they were living with an enemy-lover? That watchful in their midst was an enemy in love with them?'

'Don't you think that the picture you paint of Zhorn and the way you emphasize his disappointments as an actor are in danger of distorting the objectivity we should adhere to as much as possible if we want to bring this investigation to a successful conclusion?' says the Investigator. 'By making him so plainly detestable, are you not setting us off on the wrong track? The way you describe him, he's *the one who could have done it* without a shadow of a doubt.'

'But I do think that if anyone *could have done it*, it was surely Zhorn.'

'So, we now have already two people who *could have done it*,' says the Poet Criminologist with a laugh. 'Bearing in mind the power of suggestion exercised by the seers that he seemed to obey without reflection, Karl Knigh *could have done it*. And Gustav Zhorn *could have done it*.'

'As far as Karl Knigh is concerned, I remember that the day

he took me to see his blind Bengali seer in New York, he said to me, "This man has the dates."

'"What dates?" I asked Karl Knigh,' says the Literary Expert.

'"The dates of death, everyone's death! The date of my death, the date of your death, the date of Julius's death, as well as that of my children and my wife Lotte. All my life I tried to obtain this date, for I'm impatient to rejoin my brother Arno to whom I've dedicated my success. I've always striven to achieve the absolute, but I've merely achieved success. Arno has been writing through me; I'm not responsible for anything. Nothing of what I've written is mine. And do you see this symbol engraved on my ring-stone, and which you were surprised to see me drawing in the sand at Pals or on the paths of the Alhambra, yes, this *yantra* that you see me drawing all around me comes from both the Cabala and from Melampus, grandson of Cretheus, who lived at Pylos in Messinia. He was the first mortal to receive the gift of prophesy. My blind Bengali is supposed to be the seventh of these true seers. Also bear in mind that Melampus was the first to add water to wine. Melampus understood the language of birds. His ears were purified by a nest of young serpents that he saved from death. Furthermore, Melampus was initiated in the language of insects. My blind Bengali also understands the language of insects and he obtains from worms or fish the dates on which they expect the arrival of those they are destined to consume."

'Karl Knigh also said to me,' the Literary Expert goes on, '"Look, do you not see this *yantra* on my forehead? Of course you're not an initiate. I know it's there, in the lines on my forehead, and that the Initiate who recognizes it will give me the answer that I'm finally to know as I breathe my last ."'

'He said, "As I breathe my last!"' exclaims the Investigator. 'He linked that symbol with the moment of his death?'

'He even said to me, "This symbol will open my brother Arno's tomb to me. One day I shall descend into that place where my brother Arno has preceded us, and on that day he'll see this *yantra* that I've worn all my life, to which he will add the complementary symbol that I've been seeking all my life. And I shall know that it was the symbol not of science or art or knowledge but of transit. Do you remember the Master of Ballantrae and his Indian, Secundra . . .'

'Wonderful book! The finest novel in the entire history of literature, Borges is supposed to have said,' exclaims the Poet Criminologist.

'Let's not place too much confidence in Borges's boundless generosity. How many novels has he not cited as the finest in all literature?' says the Literary Expert cheerfully.

'So?' says the Investigator impatiently.

'He spoke at length about the death, in the freezing cold, of Ballantrae, to whom Secundra had promised resurrection. "We can all survive our own burial. All we need to know is the sign the Cabala has bequeathed to us. You remember the woman with the cockerel at Pals? That woman's an abomination! She terrifies me. She, too, knows the date. She throws grain to her wretched cockerel and the cockerel pecks out a pattern of numbers. I could give you my date, I know it, both from my Bengali and from the women with the cockerel. Wouldn't it be amusing if your thesis correctly anticipated not only the date of my death but also that of all those you want to study, all the Knighs without exception, including Gustav Zhorn and even my wife Lotte?'

'And did he give you the date?' says the Investigator making a few notes in his notebook. 'The man was obviously deranged, but that doesn't prevent everything he said to you from being possible. What do we know about . . .'

'Wait!' the Poet Criminologist cuts in. 'I ask you to remain totally objective about these things. You're an investigator, I'm a criminologist. If our literary expert friend allowed himself to succumb to Karl Knigh's morbid charm, that's his affair. There's no shortage of stories about this famous date.'

'There are not just "stories",' says the Investigator. 'Some strange things have happened in my family that may be inexplicable but are absolutely genuine.'

'Were you there?' asks the Poet Criminologist.

'No, that's just the point. It was thanks to one of these

extraordinary phenomena which have convulsed my family that you see me here. Can you imagine, my mother, aged just nineteen at the time, was to travel by train to meet her fiancé – my future father. But then, on the night before her departure, she had a terrifying dream: a nun covered with blood appeared to her, shaking a finger at her, in a sad minatory way. My mother thought she'd better put off her journey.'

'And of course the train was derailed,' says the Poet Criminologist with a laugh.

'And of course the train was derailed. But wait! There were nuns on that train. Several of them were killed. My mother always maintained that it was one of them, who'd anticipated the date of her own death and had entered her dream in order to warn her.'

'So she not only knew her own date but knew that your future's mother date had not yet arrived!'

'You're an intolerable sceptic!' says the Investigator. 'There was another extraordinary phenomenon that happened in my family. Don't smile! On a train again, I'm afraid. Now, don't laugh! This time it was an uncle of mine who was told by a clairvoyant not to go on a journey. Since this journey was extremely important, his wife went instead. There was a very large amount of money at stake in this trip. So my aunt takes the seat by the window that my uncle has reserved. At one point she gets up and makes her way towards the restaurant car. There's a tremendous jolt. The train stops. Believe it or not, just as she left her seat a freight train carrying a load of tree trunks went past. By an amazing accident of chance, a log breaks free and, smashing into the passenger train, rams into the very place where my aunt should have been sitting.'

'Absurd,' says the Poet Criminologist, laughing.

'What's absurd?'

'Your railway stories. And I should like to know why you mentioned them?'

'They lend support in a way to what Karl Knigh said.'

'You didn't see either of these accidents?'

'With good reason, as I told you, they happened before I was born.'

'And you believe in them?'

'I want to.'

'Then we won't dissuade you. But bear in mind that those who want to believe are inevitably victims of this kind of phenomena. Remember the death of Karl and Julius's young brother. The sword planted in the grave.'

'Let's get back to the *Uranus* instead, if you don't mind?' says the Maritime Affairs Investigator. 'So Karl Knigh claimed to know not only his own date of death but all his relatives' dates of death.'

'That is indeed what he led me to believe.'

'Would he happen to have given you an exact date? And most importantly, do you believe that all these dates, which he claimed to know, coincided?'

'I see what you're getting at,' says the Poet Criminologist. 'You're suggesting that Knigh, relying on his seers' forecasts, managed to persuade his whole party to go for a swim out at sea. He then quickly climbed back on board, pulled up the ladder and immediately jumped in, abandoning his empty yacht, which is the way we found it when we came aboard.'

'That would be the most tempting solution.'

'At all events, the simplest, the least enigmatic. The most elegant, too.'

'Personally, I don't believe it's necessarily correct,' says the Literary Expert. 'In my opinion they all without exception must be suspected of having desired this mass drowning.'

'Although I'm a criminologist and therefore inclined to see crime sooner than accident or blunder,' says the Poet Criminologist, 'my first thought, when we took possession of the deserted *Uranus*, was of mass drunkenness. Everyone had a good deal to drink, a kind of merriment overcame every last member of this family . . .

'And acting on an absurd wager, everyone jumps in together.'

'I see rather a chain development, a . . . human phenomenon . . . All in together! At first, they think at least one of them's stayed aboard, and for a good joke is hiding. Then they count each other. They count again. All the sheep are in the water and the boat's empty, too high, smooth and white, like an insuperable iceberg.'

'In short, a fine image of humanity.'

'Too literary a metaphor, in my view,' says the Literary Expert. 'If I read that in a novel, I'd immediately throw the book away! Paradoxes of that kind about our common doom aren't worth a damn! Trust me, what I've glimpsed in the various manuscripts of the Knigh family leave much more subtle possibilities wide open.'

XVII

Exhausted by having stayed up the two previous nights, that evening the Literary Expert fell asleep without having had the strength to continue reading the manuscripts. On waking up, he sees that the day is already well advanced. With his cheek resting on a poem by Karl Knigh, his eyes still half closed, he listlessly reads these sixteen lines:

> My imagination murders and eats
> > as I know myself to be murdered
> Poetry with mirrors plays at the beautification
> > of naked flesh
> That as raw flesh is dying over millions of years
> > destined for the devoured
> Never quietened constantly intervening
> > placing me with those two
> Absurd paradox birth death
> > fracture of meaning dispels the illusion
> To the spinning remnants of lava ice gas
> > in search of a destiny
> Galaxies Worlds Universes of mine
> > attached to the biological instinct of my self
> The sublime perversions of my ravings
> > *blossom of sparks, TELL*

And so it was that the Literary Expert was found by the Poet Criminologist, still sprawled across the scattered mass of papers, holding Kurt's poem.

'My friend the Investigator and I came and knocked quietly at your door several times. Since you didn't stir, we refrained from disturbing you. I see that you've been reading all this time, and I admire your assiduousness. So? Anything new?

'Things are becoming clearer,' says the Literary Expert.

'I was barely able to sleep a wink last night. Believe it or not,

I felt almost ashamed at the idea of knowing you to be on your own in your little room, buried under this pile of unfinished literature that we've saddled you with.'

'Indeed, with so much to read last night, it was hard to know where to begin. At dawn I collapsed among the manuscripts . . . and now it's practically evening! Here, read these lines.'

'I don't see anything special about them,' says the Poet Criminologist. 'I don't deny the beauty of these lines, but what's the connection with our mystery? No acrostics. Apart from the words "murders" and "I know myself to be murdered" – no, I don't see anything special.'

'What about the *blossom of sparks*, *TELL*, taken from Mallarmé?'

'Well?'

'On the basis of that quotation, we could develop a second thesis on the Knigh literary family. And from one thesis to the next, we'd still be left with the unfinished . . . like these lines by Kurt Knigh ending inconclusively with that "blossom" of Mallarmé.'

'According to you, these verses . . .'

'Are unfinished. And as ever, when a thought can't find its own centre of gravity, along comes a quotation. In fact, this *blossom of sparks, TELL* reminds me of a conference on the Unfinished, which was held in Tokyo and which I attended in order to take advantage of the opportunity to travel, a trip that, as it turned out, offered no surprises. This conference was organized by "the great expert on the books that Valéry did not read all the way through". Just imagine: for more than half a century this man, a delightful old Japanese guy, scrupulously examined every book in Paul Valéry's library, noting the pages that had been cut and those that hadn't. "It's been scientifically demonstrated by me," said the old Japanese man of letters, "that Valéry would cut the first page, sometimes the second, and superstitiously the ninety-ninth page of the complimentary copies of books he received." Then, according to this Japanese literary expert, the author read the last page and almost always shut the book once and for all. That's how it was most of the time. Occasionally he leafed through a book, but it was rare that he went on to read a book in its entirety.

At this conference there was a German scholar who was also an expert on Paul Valéry – but only the elderly Valéry, of the last years. He'd spent his life identifying, by extremely sophisticated means, the tiny fingernail marks that Valéry left in the margins as he "dipped into" the books of his contemporaries. According to this German literary expert, some fingernail marks were clearly positive and others were distinctly critical. This reading of the great Valéry's fingernail marks gave us one of the most tremendous theses on the author of the notebooks. Not reading a book all the way through – that's what this thesis was about.'

'And indeed, why should anyone read a book all the way through?' says the Poet Criminologist.

'The difficulty today is that it's almost impossible to know whether a book's been read all the way through or merely dipped into, or barely opened. In the past nothing was simpler for an author, such as Karl Knigh, than to check whether his books had been read all the way through or not. To find out, all he needed to do was to go round the second-hand book dealers and leaf through the cut pages. But now that books are sold with their pages already cut . . .'

'It depends on who's reading . . . and what's being read. Honestly, have you ever read a book of Karl Knigh's all the way through?'

'Ah, awake at last!' says the Investigator, coming into the room. 'Well? Anything new?'

'Apparently,' says the Poet Criminologist. 'So far, we haven't yet broached the subject. Let's say, we were warming up to it. We were talking about various literary experts and their methods of tackling literary works.'

'But of all the literary experts I've met at various conferences and symposiums, it was an old Israeli researcher who taught me the most. For him, "in general those who read books all the way through are of rather weak intellect and sheeplike," he said. He maintained that when a book fell into the hands of a great mind, all that it could possibly bring to this great mind was at best a phrase, if not just a single word, and with this phrase or single word a free creative mind couldn't help but "build something else", as he put it. This Israeli researcher shared the subtlety of the ancient rabbis. "I'm an expert who hasn't written a thesis," he liked to say, "because all the great theses that contain any new thinking are unwritten theses." '

'Well,' the Maritime Affairs Investigator breaks in, 'shall we return to our Knighs? So, anything new on the subject?'

'I'm enchanted by what you've just told us about the researcher not working on a thesis,' says the Poet Criminologist. 'I'd like to discuss him again later with you. A propos of which, I'll tell you how a crime was solved, though no one ever managed to find the body or the murderer. A pure mystery.'

'Well, isn't that the case here? No bodies, no murderer! So, let's have some elucidation!' says the Investigator.

'Be careful!' says the Literary Expert. 'You've just knocked one of Lotte Knigh's notebooks to the ground. In fact, it's the last notebook of her journal.'

'Strange handwriting,' says the Investigator, picking up the notebook. 'Ah, so these are the drawings added in the margin by Karl Knight! They are indeed very similar to the marks found above the *Uranus*'s water-line.'

'This final notebook ends, you see, on a word with not just a line through it, but so furiously scored out that the pen-nib with which Lotte Knigh was writing made holes in the page as well as through the thickness of several pages underneath. We can never know what word the young woman wanted to hide. And the preceding words don't tell us anything. She'd only just begun the sentence, when she furiously crossed out, cancelled, obliterated . . . what? It would seem to be a name. In any case, there's nothing to rule out that assumption. As far as I'm concerned, if there was a name under all that crossing-out, the one I'd go for without hesitation is Franz . . .'

'Oh? Fancy that! Why?'

'You see the start of this sentence. Is it not leading up to a name that was favoured, wouldn't you say, in the mind of the woman who wrote these lines?'

'Oh?' the Investigator says again, darting puzzled glances at the Poet Criminologist.

'Yet it seems to me easy to deduce that here, under her crossings-out, was the only name in this family that mattered to her.'

'Oh, really? You mean?'

'Exactly! From the very first moment I met Lotte Knigh, I knew.'

'What?'

'That this young woman was unhappy. That her mind was on something else. "What's she doing with this old boy" I asked myself when I saw her sitting beside Karl Knigh. It was at Pals that I saw her for the first time.'

'"This is my young *companion*, Lotte," said Karl Knigh, using that expression with an irony that immediately made me think that a great deal of resentment had built up between them. You only had to observe Lotte Knigh's hands when her aged husband began talking about himself, his writings, his family, "all of whom are bent on writing, even Lotte, although she claims not to have put pen to paper since . . . since her aborted thesis on Karl Knigh, which she embarked on at Port-au-Prince six years ago, if I'm not mistaken."

'"Karl! No! Not that again!" Lotte said too calmly.

'Being the old writer's "companion" was visibly painful to that young woman. At the time I thought that she was actually just that, but I very quickly realized that the old man liked to use the term to avoid calling that young woman of mixed blood "my wife". "What could possibly have brought them together?" I immediately wondered. "What do they have in common? What do they see in each other?" I must admit, that light-skinned young black woman never ceased to amaze me, as she went about that big house in Pals. She wasn't beautiful, but she radiated a suppressed vitality so powerful that you expected this animal force to kick over the traces, and for nothing around her to resist this irrepressible violence. At the same time, she was attentive to Knigh's slightest gesture, treating him like an impotent old man – which he wasn't at all – as if she had to justify, before the gaze of some unknown outsider, her presence as a young animal constantly constrained by that disparity in age and vitality.

'"Lotte's a young female," Gustav Zhorn said to me. "What understanding of her does Karl have? See what havoc literary people like him can wreak on the children and grandchildren of slaves! And what understanding does this Lolotte have of her aged manufacturer of literature? The great writer makes a brief trip to Port-au-Prince, and the young female student, granddaughter of a slave, becomes enamoured of the idea of a thesis on this handsome old guy with a white mane and tired eyes, whose slightly husky voice awakens in her the congenital meekness of women of mixed ancestry who know on which side is the master's house. This girl imagines herself holding sway over old Knigh's mind, when it's over his declining senses, rather, that she exercises declining power. You've noticed how she hides demurely behind those big schoolmarmish glasses of hers, just as she conceals her sexuality, which I know to be wild. No, no! Don't believe what you seem to be thinking! Her big schoolmarmish glasses speak louder than a billboard: Lolotte has read a lot, Lolotte reads a huge amount, Lolotte will read! And apparently she pokes her nose into Karl's manuscripts and – big secret! – she herself writes. What? Who knows?"

'That's what Zhorn told me,' the Literary Expert goes on. 'On another occasion, Rosa spoke of Lotte, in Zhorn's presence, in completely different terms, claiming that she only agreed to see her father because of Lotte.

'"Lotte's my friend," she said. "Lotte makes my father's presence acceptable. Without Lotte, I would have refused to go on seeing him long ago. I like Lotte's intelligence, I like her clear view of what she sees around her. When I'm in a quandary about one thing or another, I call Lotte and I know what I should do."

'"That's typical of Rosa," Zhorn cut in, "valuing what you outclass. Not because it reflects well on you, oh no! Out of a certain existential shame. Rosa's ashamed of being Rosa

Knigh, especially in front of Lotte Knigh, because she feels a certain embarrassment on Lolotte Knigh's behalf for being the young woman that old Knigh picked up at the Dominican nuns' convent in Port-au-Prince."

'"There are no Dominican nuns in Port-au-Prince," Rosa corrected him.

'"Then in some native hut, or employment bureau."

'"You know very well that she was teaching literature in Quebec, and that she happened to be visiting her family when my father went to Port-au-Prince to give his talk."

'"Talk? Voodoo, yes! Don't trust Rosa," Zhorn added, "at least not as far as Lolotte's concerned. When Rosa likes someone, you can be sure of her total loyalty and total indulgence. You'll have proof of that when you talk about me in my absence. Believe me, you're off to a bad start with your thesis on the Knigh family! Ask Kurt what he thinks of Lolotte. Have you discussed Lolotte with Julius? And when you meet Franz, I warn you, be careful! And be careful, too, if you happen to mention Franz's name in front of Lolotte! As for Karl, the old father and husband, never mention the names of Franz and Lolotte together."'

'But what did you subsequently deduce from all these insinuations?' says the Investigator.

'About Lotte?'

'Yes, about Lotte Knigh. About Rosa from Lotte, about Gustav from Rosa, about Gustav from Franz, about Lotte from Franz, and so on. And what about Julius, how did he see Lotte? And what did Kurt have to say about her?'

'Kurt never understood what Lotte was doing among the Knighs. As for Franz, that's quite a story, as they say.'

'Hence your deduction regarding the scored-out word in Lotte's journal?'

'Hence my deduction.'

'And what place did you give it in your thesis, may one ask?'

Oh, the place it deserved, I think, as Lotte seemed to me then, at any rate.'

'That's to say, that since then?'

'Since then, I've read her journal, whose existence I didn't suspect at the time. And my opinion has evolved, especially over the course of the last two nights. On one occasion in particular, Lotte let me know that she wanted to meet me independently of Karl Knigh. This took place in Geneva.

' "I know that you've been to see Franz in Hamburg," she said to me without any preamble.

' "Yes, he's a very interesting person."

' "And you spent more than a week with him."

' "I did," I replied, amused that she already knew.'

'Wait,' the Investigator interrupts him, 'did you actually go to Hamburg to meet Franz?'

'Of course. Every thesis relies on the same principles as a police enquiry. And believe me, when Zhorn called me a literary sleuth, I wasn't at all offended. My thesis was based on definite facts, on irrefutable texts, on testimonies, on a whole host of details regarding the Knigh literary family, some of which were known only to myself. Franz welcomed me with unexpected generosity. When we got to know each other better, he . . .'

'Wait, not so fast,' the Investigator cuts in. 'Tell us more about Lotte Knigh. You were with her in Geneva. Let's stay with her in Geneva, if you don't mind?'

'Gladly. But I warn you: everything I'm going to tell you about Lotte must be perceived as being subject to a kind of fixed idea that she had. That young woman was completely obsessed with Franz, and if she wanted to meet me, it was to have the chance to talk about him and to hear someone else talk about him. In response to one urgent question, I said to her, "But how do you know that Franz and I capsized in the Elbe estuary?"

' "Franz and I telephone each other every day. I have a real . . . affection for Franz . . ." '

'What was that? You capsized with Franz Knigh in Hamburg?' the Investigator interrupts him again.

'Yes. Franz liked to go out in his little sailing-boat, especially when the sea turned green and the wind was getting up.'

'I understand that! For me too, the thrill of going out when there's a storm brewing is unparalleled. Together with the woman I told you about, we go for some utterly exhilarating sailing trips. There's nothing to equal the joy of *riding it out*. Of still being alive! What could be more exhilarating!'

'We'll discuss the pleasures of sailing later,' says the Poet Criminologist, 'let's stick to either Franz or Lotte, but without jumping from one to the other this time. We keep being unseated, if I might say so, as by the hangman's horse which at every gibbet along the way . . .'

'Fine, you've made your point!' says the Literary Expert, laughing. 'So let's stick to Lotte.

'"You know, I could be Franz's sister," Lotte went on. "Karl has always warned me against my excessive fondness for his children. 'I don't want my wife to show too much affection for Belle's children!' That's what Karl never stopped telling me after he *allowed me into his life*, as he puts it, without realizing that it was he who worked his way into my life and completely wrecked it. And now I can scarcely find a corner within me where I'm able to say to myself, 'You're in your own home here, Lotte!'"

'We were walking along the Jetée des Eaux-Vives, not far from Rousseau Island. Why did Lotte insist that we meet out in the open when it was snowing and she was shivering with cold? It suddenly struck me that this was not a professional interview for a literary researcher but more like a rendezvous of the kind that any unattached guy would wish to have with a young woman who made no secret of her disillusionment with regard to the man she'd agreed to marry despite the huge difference in age between them.

'"You know, she said to me, laughing through her tears, "in the end I can't stand his books any more. I thought I'd met and allowed myself to be loved by a great writer, when I was merely dazzled by the great man. Yes, I admired his name, above all I admired the admiration his name excited among my girlfriends, all young literary students like myself, dazzled by literary stars. And Karl was a literary star not only for me but especially for my girlfriends, and if I became Lotte Knigh it was undoubtedly to outshine them by grafting myself on to the object of their admiration. Well, I'm not going to bore you with the tritest of stories!" she added.

'"But you're not boring me," I replied,' the Literary Expert goes on, '"you can't possibly know how grateful I am to you for taking me into your confidence. Above all, don't worry, you've nothing to fear, not a word of this will appear in my thesis."

'"But on the contrary," she hotly protested, "quite the contrary, if my name's to appear in your thesis, I want, oh yes, I do . . ."

'She fell silent and I waited. What did she want with such vehemence? "What is it you want?" I asked in a gentle voice.

'"For you to tell the whole story about me! I'm against this global thesis that you're planning to write on the Knigh family, but if no one can stop you, then I want, oh yes, I do, I want you to tell all!"

'That's what Lotte Knigh told me while the snow fell on the Rhone below us, and snowflakes stuck to the young woman's huge spectacles. And I have to admit, she was not without a certain appeal.'

'I remember a rather intriguing woman at the Yacht Club,' says the Maritime Affairs Investigator. 'Whenever she appeared at old Knigh's parties, men behaved differently. It's not that they paid her too much attention, no, it was more subtle. How can I put it? They suddenly stood up straighter . . . I'm talking about the older ones, as if the fact that she'd married an old man, it has to be said, rejuvenated them, gave them a chance, who knows?'

'And for her part, she couldn't curb a certain attraction towards all that was young, fresh, not yet established. Literature was the snare, the lure with which old Knigh managed to seize the innocent "lover of literature", as he used to say of her.'

'But do you believe that all this gets us any further forward with our investigation?' the Poet Criminologist cuts in on them.

'Have no doubt about it,' says the Literary Expert. 'What I

learned from Lotte Knigh that day in Geneva, taken in conjunction now with the pages I've glanced at in her journal, makes me think that if there is a rational explanation for our mystery, perhaps it's in this young woman's irrational behaviour that we should look for one of the threads in this tapestry.'

'And so what did you learn?'

'That woman was waiting for something.'

'What do you mean?'

'She was yearning for "something that has to happen", she said. She also said, "This can't go on." And now, listen: at one point Lotte took out of her bag — it was my second meeting with her — she took out of her bag an envelope filled with banknotes. I was unable to judge what sum they represented as I've never seen so much money all at once.

'"You see these notes?" she said to me. "I pay him to manipulate Karl the way I please."

'"Who are you talking about?" I asked her.

'"The person he consults and without whom he can't do anything." We were in Paris. There, too, Karl had a clairvoyant — yet another one! This time a Persian. And that day she also told me some terrible things about Gustav Zhorn.'

'Ah, he's back again!' exclaims the Investigator.

'She seemed extremely hurt, bitter even.'

'Hurt? Bitter, you say? Strange woman! She pays a Persian clairvoyant to manipulate old Knigh from Paris. Then she's bitter and hurt with regard to Gustav Zhorn. And then there's Franz. I can't wait for you to finish deciphering her journal, as well as the symbols drawn by Karl Knigh in the margins.'

'That's just what I intend to do as soon as you've gone,' says the Literary Expert after they had dined at the Yacht Club.

XVIII

'What do you think of this literary expert?' the Investigator asks the Poet Criminologist, walking down towards the port.

'Does he worry you too? He seems like a very peculiar literary expert to me. The way he's just been talking about Lotte Knigh leaves me perplexed. His insinuations regarding Franz Knigh, about whom he's told us nothing yet, also arouse my suspicions.'

'Ah? What suspicions?'

'I fear his enjoyment.'

'I don't understand. What enjoyment are you talking about?'

'The pleasure to be had from being in a position of power. Don't you think that because we're hanging on his every word, as they say, we're letting him have it all too much his own way? I know it's the same with all literary experts, but this one is constantly playing on our curiosity. Besides, I'm convinced he has a theory. But precisely because he knows, he takes pleasure in keeping us in suspense. Holding back about Franz Knigh, for instance – don't you find that a little . . .'

'Absolutely.'

'Nothing about Rosa, and nothing about Kurt either, did you notice?'

'What do you think? Of course I noticed!'

'And you said nothing?'

'I was waiting for him to speak.'

'But you admit that he kept you waiting.'

'I do.'

'Should we press him about them? It's as though he's saving them up for some unexpected revelation. This holding back about them, the way he seems to be holding back about Franz, suggests that for some reason as yet unknown to us he's plumped for the three Knigh children . . . who supposedly decided to have done, once and for all, with their family, with everything to do with the Knighs ... and therefore with themselves.'

'But the motive?'

'As you well know, in criminology you must never seek the motive. People kill. And it's only afterwards that they find out why they've killed. With suicide, it's obviously more tricky. But when you ask some of those who survive why they attempted to kill themselves, they will either give you bogus reasons or tell you they don't know. My friend, let's sit down for a moment on this bench here, looking out to sea. I've a terrible confession to make. An intolerable confession: the only murder I can understand ...'

'Please, say no more. I detected your cry of anguish beneath your apparent cheerfulness a long while ago.'

'I'm at the end of my tether,' says the Poet Criminologist, continuing to stare out to sea. 'My wife has become so calm I feel she's waiting on me for the storm ... for murder, to put an end to it, once and for all. We can't take any more! We don't say anything to each other. We keep silent and we can't take any more. I'll be going home soon. Do you know what happens at home, in our house ... their house, I should say, if I wanted to be completely objective. I've been asking myself for years: has this really happened to me, to us? What did we do to make this happen to us, to us in particular? He moans all day long and hugs an old slipper. I know an old slipper's not very aesthetic. We did try a little soft toy, but he whimpered and whimpered so much that we gave him back his slipper. "The day your child doesn't want his slipper any more," the helper sent by the Institution told us, "the day when he loses interest in his slipper, will be the day ..."

'Forgive me! No, don't say anything. Let's sit where we are for a moment, watching the sea. What a welter of water-drops! Ah, there's mystery everywhere! Will I have the courage? With such suffering, such dreadful suffering still to come, I'm trying to find the courage! Now, there's a whole sub-continent that eludes criminology. No crime, or murder, or assassination. I imagine a kind of sleep within his sleep, a sweet dream, without distress. Who would worry about three absences? A kind of peacefulness, gentleness, some kind of drifting away, do you understand, without any fuss. But how?

'You see – no, don't say anything – you see, without this investigation to distract me, and I might even say amuse me, this sweet absence might have already befallen my wife, our child with his slipper, and myself. But, you see, there's curiosity. Curiosity sustains me. The mystery sustains me. Naturally, you must be thinking: there's no common measure between the slipper and the mystery of the *Uranus*. Well, don't you believe it! As long as there's any of hope of learning what, how, or why, I'll be there, at your side, feasting on the Literary Expert's words. Yes, curiosity! The same curiosity that a certain sultan's wife was able to rekindle night after night, with the fan of her words. Are we sustained by the words of the sultan's wife before this welter of water-drops?'

'I advise you not to go straight back home in your present state of mind. You'd better return to the Literary Expert, and urge him to explain in greater depth his reading of the manuscripts, especially those of the three Knigh children. There's going to be no avoiding that! You can pass the message on to him!'

'I've taken the liberty of coming back to bother you,' says the Poet Criminologist on re-entering the Literary Expert's room. 'As we were walking down towards the port together, my friend the Investigator expressed anxiety about the literary dispassion of your decipherment of the Knigh family manuscripts. "I'm quite happy for him to study them with a view eventually to getting the anti-thesis to his thesis out of them, but not now!" he told me to tell you. "If these manuscripts become the subject of a comparative critical thesis, that's his business, but afterwards, afterwards!" he kept insisting. "What our Literary Expert should be thinking about above all is that we have here a mystery, and a mystery is meant to be solved."

'Although the poet in me can't agree with him, because for me there must be mystery but it must never be solved, nevertheless, as a criminologist I'm obliged to act as my friend the Investigator's persuasive – but not persuaded – spokesman.

"I find absurd," I told him, "that story of the Sphinx being satisfied with the answer Oedipus is supposed to have given. Oedipus remained silent and that's why the Sphinx spared him. The fatuous reply attributed to him is just an apocryphal invention of some scribe who imagined himself to be imparting wit to Oedipus, when I know of nothing more dull than that riddle about the three ages of man."

'"You won't trick me with your paradoxes. I like them in themselves, but as far as the mystery of the *Uranus* is concerned, I swear it'll be resolved."

'"Although as a criminologist I agree with you about resolving the mystery," I replied, "the poet in me pleads for it to be left unresolved."

'If I've taken the liberty of coming back, it's for the very purpose of begging you not to take too much for granted. Remember the sultan's wife. Remember my embarrassing confession the other day. Bear in mind that every word you utter on the subject of the Knigh literary family holds me back, keeps me in suspense, stays me and distracts me. Just imagine, he now clutches an old slipper to his chest, day and night! Were it not for that old slipper that he hugs, moaning and whimpering if anyone tries to take it away from him, I would doubt his capacities of perception. Every word of yours about the Knigh family is as much of a necessity and distraction to me as my child's old slipper is to him. What would we do without all the old slippers that words are to us? Don't tell me to calm down. I am calm! Have no fear, I am calm. See! I am calm. Very, very calm. Look, I'm calmer than the sea. Reassure me, tell me that you don't mind my bothering you like this. Another moment and I'll be off. I'm expected. I'm desperately expected.'

'But you're not bothering me at all,' says the Literary Expert, 'on the contrary, I'm very . . .'

'No! You won't convince me that you're pleased to see me again five minutes after we've parted!'

'You see this notebook,' says the Literary Expert. 'In it are jotted down my initial conclusions about all these manuscripts lying scattered here. I was saying to myself while re-reading them: You can't stay on your own with all this! You must talk to somebody about it, otherwise this mass of written words is going to overwhelm you, drive you out of your mind. And I was sorry I'd asked you to leave. I should have kept you and your friend the Investigator with me.'

'You say that out of compassion.'

'Please, don't ever utter that word in front of me. What do we do? We help one another to survive. There's nothing more egotistical than to think of yourself as being necessary to other people. As far as the mystery of *Uranus* is concerned, I was wondering in fact whether, contrary to what we've been thinking till now, there might not have been some silly accident: one of them may have simply fallen overboard and then all the others simultaneously jumped in to save that person.'

'They weren't Chinese, as far as I know.'

'You're thinking of that ridiculous mass drowning when the ice broke on a Peking lake and to save one skater . . .'

'Exactly! Thousands of other skaters arrived in one great rush, suddenly breaking the entire surface of the frozen lake beneath their weight. At the time this act of solidarity drew immense admiration throughout the world. And yet, as is well known, whatever the pretext, any mass gathering inevitably turns out for the worst.'

' "It's impossible to be just without being human," a young poet proclaimed. And as Zhorn would cynically say: "Inhumanity is peculiar to mankind; let's leave humanity to dogs!" That's the height of disillusionment for you!'

'Exactly! For what's specifically human is indeed the loss of the species' protective inhibitions. Who would have dreamed of inventing the human science that is criminology if we were not these animals that have lost their inhibitions, and are capable, against every law of nature, of exterminating our own kind. Force of numbers leads us, just like insects, to *invent* for ourselves the worst abominations of their flawless system. The criminologist is a man who remains all his life professionally amazed. How? That's the question the criminologist asks himself when confronted with a "beautiful" crime, a crime that's, let's say, original. Not the insect carnage of past and future wars. No, I'm talking about the man standing in front of a mirror, who takes aim at the forehead of his own image. Sometimes there are cases of unspeakable necessity: man finds himself confronted with his human condition. Don't you believe that a person might kill what he loves, out of compassion?'

'Could I have been infected by Zhorn?' says the Literary Expert. 'Being in the company of that insufferable person introduced a kind of confusion in me. His sneer is inside me – I can hear it when words such as *redemption*, *love* and *compassion* are mentioned. Zhorn inverted these measures. And everyone he spent time with suffered the same infection. Imagine the Knigh family in the confined space of that yacht afloat on the ocean – how destructive that sneer must have been!'

'You think Zhorn worked on them in that confined space?'

'Look how even I was worked on by him, so much so that even today my thinking's clouded by it. Ethical? Aesthetic? Do these words have any meaning? I don't know how to use them any more. "Beware of Zhorn," Karl Knigh warned me. "He's a dangerous person. In real life the actor's dangerous, but on stage he's undistinguished. In real life his acting's inventive, on stage he identifies too closely with the roles he plays to be a good actor. He's dreadful! Beware of his playacting in everyday life," Karl Knigh insisted,' says the Literary Critic to the Poet Criminologist, '"beware of his susceptibility as a failed actor. On stage he's dreadful. In real life he's masterful. He's said to be handsome. I find him a disturbing presence."

'From when I first began my research, Karl Knigh warned me against Zhorn. I'd just contacted him and we were strolling along the beach at Pals. Every time he mentioned Zhorn's name, he would draw some symbols. Knigh later said to me, "You see these criss-crossing lines and this circle: not only do they ward off danger but they enable me to exert my influence, at a distance, on whomsoever I choose."

'He suddenly looked me in the face. "Are you really intending to meet them all?"

'"I'm obliged to by my thesis," I replied. "Only after I've met them all will I be able to start writing it."

' "And what about Zhorn? Do you really insist on making his acquaintance?"

' "Insofar as possible."

' "Beware. The man's destructive. I also advise you to beware of Julius. Don't give too much credit to his drunken ramblings. Don't believe anything!"

' "Don't worry," I replied, "I shan't believe anything, but I'll note everything." '

'An excellent response!'

'And I added, "Man listens, the researcher notes." On another occasion he said to me, "I assume I'm dealing with an honest researcher, with someone who's read *all* my books?"

' "Of course," I replied, although obviously lying.

' "And Julius's books?"

' "Naturally!"

' "And all of Rosa's, Kurt's and Franz's books?"

' "All of them."

' "Good, and you concluded that all these books were worthy of discussion, were worthy of this research you've just embarked on?"

' "Yes," I replied, "the Knighs' writings all overlap, complement, contradict and often conflict with each other. You're all laid bare in them, by one another."

' "What are you saying?" cried old Knigh.

' "If you'd been the only one of all the Knighs to write, there would have remained great dark areas unexplored, impenetrable zones. But where certain words are missing in your work, I find them in Julius's, and when they're missing in Julius's, it's in Kurt's work, or Rosa's, and even Franz's, that I can be sure of finding them. For me, your books form a single constellation in which everything advances together, an advancing army of complementary and contradictory words." That's what I said to Karl Knigh, aware of heightening his unease.

' "All lumped together, damn it!" he rebelled. "But I've no desire to be lumped together with the rest of my family. This fantasy of a literary family that unknowingly writes one sole book has a very unpleasant Borgesian whiff about it. And what is this supposedly unique book? This so-called constellation?"'

'Wait! Are you saying that the books separately produced by the Knigh family taken together would give us one single book?'

'If not a single book, let's say a reading that's complex, revealing, and in some respects unmerciful. Besides, what I've found in the manuscripts that you and the Maritime Affairs Investigator entrusted to me reinforces the intuitive idea I had of a literary constellation. There are black stars whose force of attraction diverts suns. Any scientific approach to a phenomenon must take into account the whole complex of phenomena. We must avoid compartmentalization as much as possible. While starting with apparently diverse facts, equations strive to find a global definition, and the same goes for literature. So, from the observation of diverse, though simultaneous, phenomena, a great many integral equations can be constructed that differ from each other only in the values given to the constants of integration.'

'Of course, I understand,' the Poet Criminologist interrupts him, 'then you only have to eliminate the constants by differentiation and so find a sole solution.'

'Exactly. What goes without saying is that there is no sole solution, no possible global vision, but our intellect needs to play with all the given facts in order to construct a coherent whole, a sole system, and that was the aim of my thesis on the Knigh family. I'm well aware that in practice there is no sole solution embracing every contemporary literary phenomenon; however, I stick to that which is measurable and, while knowing how debatable my means of investigation are, I want to overlook this debatability so as to avoid intellectual paralysis, in the belief that here in my first thesis, and in my future anti-thesis, all interactions will come together. What I've already found in these manuscripts invalidates my original work, and at the same time excites me with the possibilities that are opening up. In my thesis I sided with Julius, sometimes unjustly attacking Karl.'

'Wait a moment,' says the Poet Criminologist. 'Your thesis,

in which you analysed their works, as well as the multiple tensions that kept them indissolubly fettered to each other, was published while they were still alive?'

'Obviously.'

'What were their reactions?'

'Oh, apparently unanimous.'

'They all read it?'

'I think so.'

'Did they approve?'

'No. They must have all been disappointed. At least I suppose so, for I never got any sign of acknowledgement from them.'

'Unanimous silence?'

'Exactly.'

'Even from Julius?'

'Even from Julius. But I didn't expect any different.'

'You mean that even Julius had a higher opinion of himself than that . . .'

'Which I seemed to have of him in my thesis. I suppose so. He must have found unacceptable the parallel portraits I drew of him and Karl. Not the superficial portrait but the underlying portrait, as it were, of their two characters, which were so divergent and yet so close.'

'Another story of doubles?'

'Absolutely not! Enough of that! Literature's only too cluttered with them!'

'And what about theses, then?'

'Theses especially! It's an extremely oppressive legacy of the nineteenth century. Man and his double. The visible and the concealed. No, my thesis didn't present Julius as Karl's double. I was very careful to avoid it. It would have been too predictable. On the one hand, "the bourgeois"; on the other "the artist". On the one hand, the average individual, ordinary and strong; on the other, the man sick of being man, the divided self, the overintelligent intellectual. And then add to this duality their rivalry! How easy it would have been to show that relations between them became problematic, equivocal, fraught with ambivalent feelings because of this supposed duality. No, I avoided that trap! I didn't accuse the two brothers of the usual erotic relationship, thinking of Eros, of course, in the sense in which Socrates understood it.'

'You're referring to the insatiable Eros-Demon of the dialectical game?'

'Of course. That idea was far from my mind! In my opinion, the story of the two old Knigh brothers is the story of a third party. They, as it were, invested themselves entirely in this third party, who was their young dead brother. Through Arno, they ceased to exist. That's substantially what I argued in my thesis: when a dead person cannot die, when he's not allowed to die, when there's a sense of shame at being alive when the dead person is dead, then whoever feels that sense of shame is not fully alive. Julius was one of the living dead all his life, and nor did Karl ever manage to live other than by appropriating his dead young brother's ghost. That in substance was the argument of my thesis, with all the variations this theme of the absent person offered. And so, expanding in concentric circles, I extended the *presence* of the young dead brother to the next generation, analysing Karl Knigh's denial of paternity as a symptom of non-existence, of total vacuity to this presence of the absent brother, to the point of laying the blame on his own children, criminalizing them for being alive. Alongside that, I showed how Julius's denial of existence, and especially his wish that Karl's children should in a way cancel out their father, also derived from this fatal burden that never ceased to oppress him.'

'Did you really believe all that? And more importantly, do you still believe it?'

'Good question! I'm going to make a confession: my thesis very quickly closed in on itself. The Knigh family turned into matter, into a kind of malleable clay that I could do with not what I wanted but what my thesis required, do you understand? They all began to live on the abstract level of my thesis.'

'You mean that in writing about them you reduced them to nothing?'

'Exactly! All reduced to nothing! I didn't intend to speak of it so soon, but what I've found in the various papers you see lying here fills me with an apprehension difficult to acknowledge: could my thesis be responsible for the *Uranus* tragedy? That's what I'm beginning to wonder. Julius's reverse texts, which I'm deciphering with the aid of a mirror, like this, you see, clearly follow from what I wrote, and reveal what Julius might never have dared to reveal. There are some confessions so extreme they could only be cast in backward handwriting by him who felt the need to make them. With Karl Knigh too, the blend of that which is said and that which is signified by ideograms produces a form of expression in *language* rather than speech. In Lotte's papers, the tone seems to have changed since the publication of my thesis. Because her journal is dated, I've been able to establish some staggering coincidences. And with Rosa and Kurt, and even with Franz it seems, reading through some of their notes and additions . . .'

'Which your thesis . . .'

'I daren't swear to it yet. But it is possible . . .'

'That they were no longer able to write as before? Could it be that you'd *awakened* them?'

XIX

'Late as it is, I'm pleased to find you both still here,' says the Investigator.

'Ah, you've come at last! I was getting worried. So?' says the Poet Criminologist.

'I just called in on your wife at home to let her know. "Our investigation's progressing faster than we thought," I told her, so that she'd be patient. "It's possible we might even be kept late into the night."'

'And what did she say?'

'Don't worry, she took it very well.'

'Was he moaning, or asleep?'

'He was fast asleep on the carpet, with his cheek resting on his old slipper. So? Where have we got to?'

'We'd just lifted another corner of the veil,' says the Poet Criminologist, switching from anxiety to nervous cheerfulness. 'Can you imagine, our friend the Literary Expert is most surprisingly admitting his guilt.'

'Let's not exaggerate,' says the Literary Expert, laughing.

'According to him, his thesis in some sense *awakened* all those it dealt with.'

'Without going that far, I've come across certain evidence in the various manuscripts.'

'Let's imagine,' the Poet Criminologist goes on, 'let's surrender to the thrill of imagination: they all read our friend's thesis, and it became unbearable to them to be reduced to . . . not to be able to live any more without there looming in front of them at every moment their own spectre escaped from the pages of our friend the Literary Expert.'

'Now then!' says the Investigator. 'You're not going to tell us that in order to flee the spectres that sprang from our friend's thesis, they all threw themselves into the water?'

'That's part of what the *Uranus* mystery would allow us to imagine.'

'Let's be serious,' says the Investigator. 'Believe it or not, as

I was coming up the stairs, I said to myself, "What's this literary expert hiding from us?" You see, I'm being frank with you.'

'Oh, many things!' exclaims the Literary Expert, laughing. 'Let me tell you, it's very difficult for me not to succumb to romanticizing. These Knighs would encourage anyone to romanticize. Since my arrival I've done my utmost to refrain from romanticizing, do you understand. I strive to convey to you as soberly as possible, as things emerge, what I have reason to believe, what I know, what I remember, what I'm not sure of and am wary of, while thinking that certain deeds, certain words that I recall should be examined extremely closely. And at the same time I have to keep the literary scholar in me ever alert. Every literary scholar is a total neurotic. A born literary scholar – such as I am – will write you pages and pages out of nothing. So I'm wary of myself. Can you imagine, Flaubert's novella *A Simple Soul*, which is no more than thirty pages long, gave rise to a six-hundred-page thesis! Be smart enough, I told myself while writing my thesis, not to make the same mistake.

'And yet how could I not discuss the two old Knigh brothers' formative years? Especially as after the death of their young brother, a kind of morbid friendship, born of the secret that oppressed them, made them inseparable. For a while they wandered round Europe, eventually returning to settle down in the pretty town near the Swiss border where they were born. There, they decided to part, while continuing to live "under each other's eye", they told me. They each took an apartment,' the Literary Expert goes on, 'a bachelor flat, as close as possible to a café where the few intellectuals of that small provincial town – immortalized by the fact that Voltaire had lived near by – would congregate.

'Moreover, it was to this small Franco-Swiss town that I retired when the time came to write up my thesis on the Knigh family. And believe it or not, in the boarding-house where I stayed, I came across two sisters of the kind that exist in every little town in Europe, two sweet and jolly old spinsters. "Knigh! The Knigh brothers!" Their eyes blur with tears.

What's this? A charming provincial love story, kept quiet and discreet! These two old maids worshipped the Knigh brothers. The small Franco-Swiss town worshipped Karl Knigh, while the two sisters worshipped the two Knigh brothers – don't laugh! – one of them worshipped Karl, and the other, Julius. Apart from these two old maids no one remembered Julius. No one knew that in the overpowering shadow of "the great Karl Knigh" a second Knigh by the name of Julius had lived, been to school, spent many years writing and frequenting a certain little wood that one of the two sisters started telling me about with some emotion. Every day, when I went out for my daily walk, I would leave locked in a drawer of my work table the thesis I was writing. And of course . . .'

'Your two old maids read it?'

'Exactly. As soon as my back was turned, they fell on the manuscript and avidly read my work on the Knigh family.'

'And you behaved as if you didn't notice?'

'Don't you believe it! On the contrary, I behaved as if I had noticed but didn't say anything. As for the two old maids, the former sweethearts of the Knigh brothers, they contrived by means of subtle hints to slip into our conversations details about the Knighs, about their mother, their father, their young brother Arno, whom they worshipped and whose very first writings they claimed to have read. But the greater the flood of details, the more I suspected them of going too far.'

'You put me in mind of that one-hundred-and-twenty-year-old woman still alive today in the town of Arles. As she gets older and journalists from all over the world question her, she recalls a red-haired guy that people referred to as the Madman, who in her young days could be seen walking down the streets of Arles wearing a straw hat with frayed edges. The marvellous thing is that instead of losing her memory with age, in her case, too, the details come in abundance. Presumably, the interest aroused by these reminiscences stimulates in her this predilection for showing off that's so frequent in old folk who feel they've got an audience.'

'Exactly! The two old girls began to invent things. Nothing explicit, but innuendos, silences, shakes of the head, sudden sadnesses or sudden laughter. All this leaving an impression, or rather creating an impression . . .'

'Exactly like that one-hundred-and-twenty-year-old woman who suddenly remembers that one evening the red-haired man rather forced his attentions on her.'

'So the Knigh brothers settled down in the little Franco-Swiss town. Each with a place of his own, no more exchanging of manuscripts in the evening and writing comments in the margin. But it turns out that Mother Knigh is still alive, and she's there, keeping an eye on her two sons. She's old, authoritarian and demanding. Her life depends on her two "boys", for whom she has sacrificed everything: her charms, her smile, her jewels, she insists. In seclusion of the family house, she waits. She does nothing but wait for her two sons. In short, one day she's found dead. Having committed suicide in her big empty house.'

'Only natural,' says the Poet Criminologist.

'Sheer storybook logic. But what does she hold lovingly in her hands?'

'A photo of her son Arno, of course.'

'Right. How did you guess?'

'Oh, you know, in human conduct you have a few general principles, unvarying patterns of behaviour. In criminology, lives are nearly all fixed on rails, believe me.'

'So what?' says the Investigator. 'Where's this leading us? I don't see any sign of the *Uranus* on the horizon.'

'And yet!' says the Literary Expert. 'How did she commit suicide? Drowned in her bath, believe it or not, clutching the photo of her youngest son. It seems that the two brothers took this drowning as the starting signal on the race track. Their careers begin. They write. Both are published. However, both are haunted by the dead brother – dead twice over since their image of him now merges with that of their mother holding the photograph blurred by the water. Julius's books, being too bold and too challenging, only reach a small group of "initiates", while Karl's first work is an immediate success.'

'This is all quite normal so far. When does the first crack appear?' says the Investigator.

'Wait. Too proud, Julius starts to limit his social contacts. And there he is, drawn into being what his brother Karl is not and never can be – that's to say, like Ulysses: *Nobody*. In contrast, Karl breaks into literary life. He's to be seen everywhere. He's agreeable. Ingratiating.'

'So, you believe that this is the beginning of the path that will lead them to take the plunge from the deck of the *Uranus*?'

'Yes, there, in front of the bath where their drowned mother lay, clutching Arno's photo! The two brothers vowed to live *in place of* the deceased and once their works were completed to make an end of it at the same time. Look, read that with the aid of this little pocket-mirror. Those few sentences in Julius's reverse handwriting recall that vow. Moreover, they're his last words after they'd all set out on this final voyage.'

'You mean that all his life Julius had this vow ever present in his mind.'

'Absolutely.'

'And you think that he . . .'

' . . . might have pushed Karl overboard – is that what you mean?'

'You're the one who seems to think so, or to be inviting us to think so, at least,' says the Investigator.

'Very plausible!' exclaims the Poet Criminologist with excessive cheerfulness. 'Imagine old Karl coming out on deck at night . . .'

'Let me stop you there,' says the Investigator. 'When the *Uranus* was found adrift, its engines were turned off and everything suggested that the drama had taken place during the day.'

'I'm not saying they all went overboard at night. Let's imagine this: the *Uranus* was sailing at night and that evening Karl Knigh was on watch at the wheel while everyone else on board was asleep. At some point, with the yacht sailing on automatic pilot, its route well established, Karl goes out for a stroll on deck, where, as it so happens, Julius is lurking. Everyone else is asleep in the cabins. The two elderly brothers start to reminisce about the vow they made in their youth, and suddenly Julius grabs Karl, saying the moment has come, right there and then, for the night is beautiful and the leap easy to make under the stars. Karl Knigh struggles. Julius is drunk, as usual. In short, they fall overboard.'

'Let me stop you there,' says the Investigator. 'No matter what you think happened next, I can't see Karl Knigh drawing his famous signs on the *Uranus*'s hull in the middle of the night, while perhaps continuing to struggle in the water with his brother.'

'Those signs could very well have been etched by Karl Knigh before, long before – why not on the day the yacht was launched? Or any time that he rowed round his boat in a dinghy, or swam round it, completely undisturbed.'

'All right! Suppose the two old men are gone. What do you do about the others?'

'Morning comes, the old writers are gone! Karl Knigh and Julius are nowhere to be seen. The others search the boat. No sign of them! Imagine the shock. Then begins a classic process. In criminology it was identified ages ago, and has since been extremely well studied by successive generations of criminologists.'

'So? What is this process?' says the Investigator impatiently.

'It's *the desire to accompany*. You still see this primitive phenomenon manifesting itself in certain sects. The leader, or leaders, are accompanied in death.'

'Absurd! Plausible, but totally absurd,' says the Literary Expert. 'But wait, look at this pile of manuscripts. These are Franz Knigh's last writings. There are several important pages here regarding certain types of suggestion. According to Franz, after a very serious shock, and when the subject, or subjects, suddenly find themselves without their usual landmarks – and out there, on the open sea, all landmarks are gone – it doesn't take much "not only to make possible the possible, but to make possible the impossible," he said to me when I was with him, in a sailing-boat in fact, in the Elbe estuary during a terrible storm.'

'Ah, he's turned up at last!' says the Investigator. 'Who is this Franz Knigh?'

'How can I describe him?' says the Literary Expert. 'He was both a scientific researcher and a philosopher. At the time that I met him, he was working on a book now used as a reference by some philosophers. He argued in favour of returning to Diderot, of taking up Diderot's way of looking at the natural sciences.'

'You mean that we ought to take account of the latest discoveries in biology, physics, astronomy? That since *D'Alembert's Dream* or the *Treatise on the Blind*, philosophers have lost the path that Diderot so joyfully followed?'

'That is indeed, roughly, what I thought I understood of Franz's work. His last publication, *Eulogy of the Senses*, analysed a considerable number of senses as well as sight, hearing, touch and taste: the electric sense, the sense of heat and cold, the sense of ultrasound, of hunger, thirst, the hygrometric sense of bees, the fly's gyro compass . . .'

'Enough of that, if you don't mind! Too many details tire the brain. Let's stick to the facts. So, what about this Franz?' says the Investigator.

'I came into contact with Franz on several occasions. He was a withdrawn character, a loner, fascinated by the mysteries of nature, "fascinated by what no one knows," he would say, "the possibilities of human nature". I experienced some very strange moments when I was with him. He took me into the world of Alice. He lived in Hamburg and from his windows you could see large illuminated ships slip by. He didn't consider himself a writer. "Why do you want to lump us all together?" he asked me the first time we met. "Why a thesis on people as unalike as we are? A global thesis, you say? It doesn't make sense!" But after I explained my project to him in detail and he understood what I was trying to do, he agreed to support me, and I can say that I was able to win his friendship. I liked his sadness . . . his melancholy, to tell the truth . . . But look, dawn's breaking. I think that now it might be time for us to part. I must get on with reading the Knighs' manuscripts.'

'As for us, you're right, other duties call. We'll be looking forward to seeing you in my office tomorrow as soon as possible.'

XX

The next day, as agreed, the Literary Expert hurries down to the Maritime Affairs office. This time he has read a great deal.

'My friend the Poet Criminologist is to join us a little later on,' says the Investigator. 'After we left you at dawn, we were walking about for a long time, unable to tear ourselves apart. I accompanied him to his front door. Since he was reluctant to go in, we set off again for the boatyards, where the *Uranus* loomed up beneath the fading moon. As the tow tractor fitted with the iron ladder was still there, in position, we took it into our heads to climb aboard the yacht, still standing on the stocks. It's a strange feeling to be on dry land aboard such a stately vessel. My friend and I chatted for a long time, leaning over the rail, with the *Uranus*'s smooth white flank beneath us.

'You know, it's very much because of you that my friend hasn't succumbed to some dreadful deed? You distract him, you divert him from his dark thoughts, you make him cheerful, full of energy. This morning, as I joined the woman of my life in her hotel bedroom, I said to her: "This investigation is a last chance for our friend the Poet Criminologist. Our Literary Expert has a wonderfully beneficial effect on him. As our Literary Expert takes us into the heart of the Knigh family, our friend forgets himself, forgets the huge misfortune that is constantly destroying him. Here is he, intellectually cheerful again, excited, full of imagination and inventiveness. I love to see my friend with that suppressed smile on his lips, as if he were leaving you free to laugh or not at one of his clever jokes. Why did this friend, with such a gift for appreciating life in all its simplicity, have to endure such moral suffering?"

'That's what I said to my wife, whom I've spoken to you about, and without whom I don't think I could possibly appreciate life. Thanks to you too, she looks forward every evening to my slipping in beside her in the precarious little bed in her hotel. "So?" she eagerly prompts me. She rests her head on my shoulder and in the darkness I tell her, word for word, down to the smallest detail, what you've told us during the day. So, thanks to you and this mystery, she who was my wife, my daily companion, awaits me with delicious impatience. "So?" she says, and believe me, there's no happier man than I!

'As the *Uranus*'s superstructure was caught by the first rays of sunlight, my friend the Poet Criminologist said to me: "This mystery is more than a mystery. I hope the mystery of the *Uranus* will never be clarified. Just as I hope the Mystery in the depths of which we're immersed will never be clarified. Not to reach any objective," he said as we stood on the deck of the yacht that was sparkling with dew. "The word *objective* is absolutely detestable. For me," he insisted, "the greatest philosopher of all time is obviously the man from Elea: Zeno, sublime Zeno, whose arrow remains suspended for eternity between the archer and his target. The arrow flies but never reaches its objective. It flies. That's what I like! Flying, flying for all eternity. I want to be that suspended flying arrow that never reaches anything. Yes, that's what I want to be!" my friend the Poet Criminologist told me . . . and I saw that his eyes were filled with tears.

'If I'm telling you all this,' the Investigator concludes, 'it's to set your mind at rest with regard to your work of deciphering the manuscripts. Let's not rush things! You smile? That I should tell you not to rush? I, who am so impatient! Don't take any notice of my impatience. I'm bound to press you again, often, in spite of myself. It's in my nature, you understand? Unlike my friend, once I'm here, I'd like quickly to be there, and once I'm there, I'd quickly like to be here. That's why I hope the mystery's never resolved! "Despite your trying impatience," says my companion in separated inseparation, "I love you the way you are." She says that! So bear with me, accept my impatience.

'Ah, here's our friend the Poet Criminologist! I hear his voice. He seems distinctly less depressed.'

'I've just come from your hotel, thinking I'd find you still in your room,' the Poet Criminologist says cheerfully. 'I saw that there'd been serious disturbance of the papers. So?'

'A fair bit of news. This morning, after you left, I got deep into Rosa Zhorn-Knigh's manuscripts and a poem by Kurt, of which I want you first of all to read a few verses.'

20   So precise have surgical operations become
7   The scalpel dislodging eyes delicately slicing the heart
16   Or the red mound of liver that a hand will transplant

4   Dark blood-red pieces of quivering vitals
13   Live implants in implacable ninety-year-old recipients
42   From doomed young convicts the chance of immortality
10   Given to cold-eyed cold-hearted Chinese commissars

15   Vile uses of a wicked science in an age
      without blood laws
24   My regrets turn to burnings at the stake crimes
      dedicated to the Unknown
12   Kings butchered in matriarchal orgies during evenings
      of female libations
1   Lament the bygone era of Lycia's siren medusas
      slain by Bellerophon.
          ?

'Well?' says the Investigator. 'Is there some acrostic clue in that?'

'Not exactly,' says the Literary Expert, 'but there are three pretty frightening words hidden in this poem.'

'STO DLFG VMKL,' the Investigator reads out. 'No, I don't see it.'

'Yet concealed in these verses is a question fraught with significance.'

'Oh really? Explain! You know very well we're too stupid to work it out.'

'In the first verse is hidden the word *all*. In the second, *kill*. In the third, *Karl*. It's not a statement, but a question. Hence the question mark, which first intrigued me and in the end provided the key.'

'What key?' says the Poet Criminologist.

'To the hidden message. Give yourself time to think. Don't you notice anything strange about these three stanzas?'

'Not particularly.'

'Nothing surprises you?'

'Ah, yes! Wait! I think I've got it!' cries the Poet Criminologist.

'Could we get back to the *Uranus*?' says the Maritime Affairs Investigator.

'But this takes us back to the *Uranus* more than ever before. *All kill Karl*? But that's terrible! Who was he putting this question to, do you think?'

'To God, I imagine,' says the Literary Expert.

'Do you think God can count?'

'If Kurt was addressing God, he must have trusted Him to count to forty-two at least.'

'Stop playing games with me!' says the Investigator.

'But we're playing games with Kurt, don't you understand. Go on, count.'

'What am I supposed to count?'

'Look. Every line is preceded by a number. Count!'

'Let me tell you, I am cross with myself,' says the Investigator, laughing. 'You're right, I should have thought of it. So, according to you, Kurt put this question to *all*? *All kill Karl*?"'

'From Rosa's writings, I deduce some fairly remarkable things coming from a young woman. In her work too, I was able to find numbers suggesting the same kind of reading as in these stanzas by Kurt. It would seem that by means of these numbers scattered throughout their manuscripts brother and sister communicated questions and answers to each other.'

'Unless it was someone else?' says the Poet Criminologist.

'Zhorn? Yes! Zhorn secretly numbering their manuscripts so as to lead brother and sister to envisage, intellectually at least, taking action against their old tyrant of a father.'

'Those "siren medusas",' says the Poet Criminologist, 'that terrible image with which Kurt Knigh ends his poem enchants me. What did he expect of Rosa, of Lotte? Don't you find incredibly risqué in poetry that evocation of those old Chinese leaders using human transplants removed, before they're even dead, from young convicts sentenced to execution? While most poets today deal only with sun stone lavender air light, Kurt plunges into the surgical inferno, alone, without even a Virgil to accompany him. And what does he regret? The "laurel-chewing" dismemberers of kings!'

'When I was with him in Hamburg, Franz Knigh told me: "Although I'm the one who was rejected from birth, the supposed killer of my mother Belle, it was Kurt who was cruelly hurt by it. Kurt was a damaged child because of me – instead of me, if you will. Throughout his childhood I was his incurable wound. Kurt suffered on my behalf more than I suffered on my own account. And I may say that Kurt's suffering on my behalf was more painful to me than the suffering I'd have suffered in the normal course of events, since our father had placed the immeasurable burden of matricide on me. Throughout our childhood Kurt shouldered and carried this burden with which our father wished to crush me, and never shuffled it off. Rosa, too, united with Kurt to protect me from Father's resentment. All three of us huddled together day and night in order to resist, not to accept this terrifying burden that we sensed suspended above us, day and night. Believe it or not, Father used to call me Asclepius," said Franz, laughing,' continues the Literary Expert. ' "Why? 'You're horrible little Asclepius,' Father would say to me, 'the child thrown out on Mount Titthion by his mother, who was adopted, fed and protected by a dog, a goat and a kid.' Yes, that's what my father told me repeatedly during my childhood, using his knowledge of myths as an excuse not only to construct a lie but especially, by transforming them into animals, to debase as much as possible Rosa, Kurt and our uncle Julius, my sole supporters, my sole allies, my brother, sister and chosen father. One day when my father called me by this name stolen from myth, I responded: 'Later, like Asclepius, I shall have the gift of healing. In one hand I shall hold the healing serpent and in the other a sceptre, for despite your hateful temper, Zeus will have placed me among the stars.'

' "That a child of seven or eight years old should stand up to him, cleverly using his beloved myths, impressed our father

Karl Knigh. 'Besides,' I told him, my face lifted towards that giant carved in stone, 'besides, like Asclepius, I shall have the gift of bringing the dead back to life. I'll bring uncle Julius back to life for sure, but certainly not you!'" And believe it or not,' the Literary Expert goes on, 'Franz never wavered from the calling that in a way was dictated to him by his nickname.'

'What you say there is very true,' the Poet Criminologist cuts in. 'There are no innocent names or nicknames. At home I have a catalogue of names that have convulsed the world of criminology. All of them, or nearly all, are deeply rooted with terror in the collective memory. This catalogue was patiently compiled by a German criminologist . . .'

'Let him continue,' the Investigator interrupts him. 'So what happened to Franz?

'Well, Franz became what he'd been named in derision and spite by old Knigh, his father. "In one hand I seized the healing serpent and in the other the sceptre of philosophical enquiry," he told me when I was visiting him in Hamburg,' the Literary Expert goes on. '"Only the mysterious and the inexplicable seem worthy of interest to me," he also told me. "Father believes in symbols and transcendent powers, while I believe that before long I shall have found the means not of curing but of preventing all disease, and furthermore of bringing back to life some who are dead. Lazarus, the brother of Martha and Mary, who returned from extinction at Christ's merest intervention, ought not to be an exceptional case but the very model of the biologically commonplace. Cats are said to have nine lives; so have men, and perhaps many more. My research on the senses proves it. Without desiring immortality, we can envisage several deaths in our life and several rebirths. We're all a former chaos of cells. As with the universe, our cells have grouped together to form interdependent galaxies . . ."'

'Wait, wait,' the Investigator cuts in. 'I can assure you that in my family there have been several dead who've reawakened.'

'How do you expect to conduct an objective investigation when we have as investigator the most credulous of men?' says the Poet Criminologist. 'Franz Knigh may have had his theories...'

'I assure you that in my family...'

'For once, let me urge our Literary Expert to continue, and beg you not to interrupt him. What does it matter whether the dead rise again or not! Anyway, Lazarus didn't drown, as far as I know.'

'Oddly enough, Franz said to me: "The important thing isn't Lazarus's resurrection, but to establish scientifically what he died of." We were soaked through and shivering, on the deck of a naval despatch-boat in the Elbe estuary. The crew had wrapped us in army blankets and the captain scolded us like children for having gone out in a sailing-boat in such an exceptionally violent storm.

'"Knigh," he said all of a sudden as we were changing in his cabin, "as in the writer Knigh?"

'"I'm his son," Franz replied.

'"You know, I'm a devoted reader of his?"

'"I'm not," said Franz.

'"I read his books over and over again. I've read them, and reread them, at every latitude, in all weathers, in all seasons," he went on without noticing Franz's gesture of irritation. "In the absence of the writer himself, would you be kind enough to sign his latest novel for me?" And the despatch-boat captain actually took down from his bookcase Karl Knigh's latest fat novel.'

'But what happened to you? What were you doing on that despatch-boat?'

'Franz's sailing-boat had capsized in a squall.'

XXI

'How about returning in more detail to those experiments regarding our possibilities for resurrection?' says the Investigator.

'Well, I visited Franz Knigh at his home in Hamburg. At the time he was working on a book about bats in the imagination of children. At the back of his office, he'd placed several cages with fox-bats hanging upside down in them. In an adjacent room he'd had constructed a fairly sophisticated piece of apparatus, simple to describe. It took some thought, though! This apparatus served to test the sense of balance and especially the loss of this sense in subjects of the most socially integrated kind. This apparatus consisted of a moving cabin that could be tilted at will to either side of a central axle. Inside this cabin was a chair that also moved; it could be tilted on the same axle, but independently. "There is, as it were, a precise mathematics of the nerves," Franz assured me,' the Literary Expert goes on, '"alongside our sense of balance, our eye is continually checking our position in space, taking its bearings from the corners of rooms, houses, trees, all the lines that we're used to, such as the horizon, and a host of very precise points of reference. But," Franz went on to say to me in Hamburg, as we stood in front of this machine, "you must know, too, that there's no need to see for our sense of balance to function. You only have to lower your eyelids to realize that. Yet as soon as you open your eyes the internal sense of balance is reinforced. The reason I've had this machine built," Franz continued, turning on a light, "is in order to find out in what proportion each of these senses contributes to the impression of a vertical image. To elucidate this physical and philosophical problem, I've created a little anti-natural world, a little world where not only do the two types of senses not complement each other but they're in conflict," Franz Knigh explained,' says the Literary Expert.

'Very ingenious,' says the Poet Criminologist. 'The fact

is that in criminology such a machine could have been extremely useful. How, indeed, can you determine which senses participate in an 'excellent' crime, and which rebel against it? In other words: since we're a conglomeration of more or less disparate cells and organs, which of these organs, which of these conglomerations of cells take part in the crime or recoil from it? Suppose your liver, your heart and your eyes refuse to join in the action of your arm at the moment when it plunges in the knife. Your eyes close. Your liver secretes such an excess of bile that you spew up green foam. Your heart bucks, beats too fast and suddenly almost stops in terror and disgust. Basically, only your arm and your brain have acted. And what happens? This body of divers senses without unanimity, yes, this body as a whole is condemned. You know, a criminologist specializing in legal medicine invented an instrument called an optogram. From the dissection of the victim's eyeball and examination of its retina, he hoped to catch the image of the criminal photographed in that final moment.'

'We need one or more murderers yet to determine which parts of their body participated or not in the crime. We need more victims to dissect, to check their eyes for the photograph of the criminal or criminals,' says the Investigator, laughing. 'The mystery of the *Uranus*, however, offers only a disturbing emptiness. No one! Nothing! A pile of manuscripts, that's all!'

'But wait,' says the Poet Criminologist, 'let our Literary Expert finish. So what about this machine invented by Franz Knigh?'

'A sheer marvel of ingenuity,' the Literary Expert goes on. 'Imagine a small room constructed inside a box that can be tilted as necessary. Well, in the centre of this box there's also a moving chair fixed on an axle, which, as I said, can be tipped to one side or another. The subject is strapped into the chair. The box is plunged into darkness. Both the chair and the box are tilted, and then the light's turned on again. The conductor of the experiment slowly inclines the position of the chair until the subject says that he feels upright, because he's trusting the angles of the box. But he's nearly always wrong. Sometimes the subject is even inclined at an angle of thirty-five degrees. In extreme cases, it turns out that subjects believing themselves to be upright are inclined at an angle of fifty-five degrees. They respond most positively to the question: is this the position you're in when you're sitting at the table? Which means that they've trusted their eyes more than their internal sense of balance. Wait, wait. The marvellous thing is that once they close their eyes, they become aware that they're sitting at an angle. If they only trust their internal sense of gravity, they ask to return gradually, with perfect precision, to the perpendicular corresponding with reality.'

'Have you sat on this chair?' asks the Poet Criminologist. 'How's your sense of verticality?'

'May I be allowed not to answer that question?'

'Why not?'

'It would give you too much insight into my personality,' says the Literary Expert laughing with a certain embarrassment. 'You'll see why. By means of this very disturbing experiment as regards the ideas that we form about ourselves, Franz Knigh was able, he claimed, to calculate a personality constant. Unquestionably, there's a direct relation between the way in which the vertical is perceived and an individual's personality. Individuals can be classed into two categories: those who depend on what they see, and those who don't. Listen to this: those who don't depend on what they see are distinguished by an aptitude for resolving thorny problems, while in those who do — those who, despite a significant inclination of the chair in relation to the box representing a room, believe they're still sitting upright — this creative analytical faculty doesn't exist.'

'It would be curious to know which category each of us belongs to, and which of us therefore is most likely to be able to solve the mystery of the *Uranus*,' says the Investigator.

'But excuse me,' says the Literary Expert, 'that's not all. According to Franz, it would appear that those who don't depend on what they see are generally quite independent of those around them and of other people. "They're not readily classifiable in terms of the criteria established by society," said Franz, "they don't conform to custom or fashion, and in extreme cases they're pretty unsociable, misanthropic, individualist and wilful. By contrast, the gregarious type always takes account of the people around him or her, even in a purely physically manner. Women," he also said, "tend to be more dependent than men. Young children are entirely dependent on what they see. At about the age of eight there's a wakening individualism that develops more or less rapidly according to personality and education, reaching its maximum at about sixteen years of age. It remains at this level until the age of seventeen. Then something unexpected happens: for the great majority of adolescents the trend goes into reverse. The obligation to become integrated in an established order and hierarchy has its effect on the psyche. Only a very small percentage of young people continue to develop the tendency towards individualism and creativity," said Franz,' the Literary Expert concludes.

'And he wrote about this?'

'A terrifying book. "My father is a man with not a single sense left intact," Franz told me. "Despite what he believes, Uncle Julius must have reached more or less the same stage. Kurt and Rosa are obviously lost causes, especially having allowed a terrible destroyer of the senses into their lives. They're seared right to the soul by that pervert and I can assure you they'll all die in an accident. Put them in my machine and you'll see that not one of them can tell whether they're upright or at an angle."

' "What about Lotte?" I asked him, knowing that he would refuse to talk about her.

' "Put the entire Knigh family in a desperate plight, and we'll see which of them survive." '

'What?' exclaims the Investigator. 'You're sure you're not exaggerating?'

'I'm reporting word for word what Franz said to me in Hamburg, in front of his machine.'

'Excuse me,' says the Poet Criminologist, 'did he use the future tense or the conditional?'

'He didn't make it sound as if he was speaking hypothetically.'

'What are you trying to get at?' says the Investigator.

'As you well know, in order to impose their theories a lot of researchers don't hesitate to help nature along, as they say. Are we ourselves, whether we be investigators or criminologists, safe from the wish to falsify? In order to be recognized as being right, to establish our supposed perspicacity, are we not capable, more than anyone else, of falsifying the truth?' says the Poet Criminologist.

'You're right. How many innocent people have been condemned and even executed as victims of a disgraceful desire to be recognized as being right, on the part of an investigator who's not only intransigent but knowingly falsifies the evidence,' says the Investigator. 'There've been many times, I must admit, when even I have restrained myself from slipping in some false evidence when I couldn't find the proof I so ardently desired.'

'Indeed, so much evidence in the history of criminology has been criminally supplied by investigators who are not zealous, as they're too often said to be, but driven by the irresistible desire to be recognized as being right. And what you've just told us about Franz Knigh would suggest to me that he might be one of those people who, in order to prove a scientific point, would be capable of drowning their entire family.'

'Really now!' says the Investigator. 'You're not going to tell us that his machine condemns him!'

'A person capable of constructing this machine that the Literary Expert has just been telling us about, this machine for proving yourself right, seems to me a prime suspect. I see Franz Knigh as the misanthropic type, capable of no matter what criminal deed in order to prove that those who aren't misanthropic are simply the weak in society, kept by society with their heads under water, as it were,' says the Poet Criminologist.

'So, according to you, he takes advantage of a cruise organized by his father, when his whole family are gathered together, to put to the test those words of his: "and we'll see who survives"?'

'I can easily picture him in that role. Imagine him saying to himself: "If they were all swimming around the *Uranus* and I were to jump in after pulling up the ladder, I bet those of us who had kept our senses intact would surely survive.'

'A metaphor for the evolution of the species?'

'Exactly! What does Franz say to himself: "If life didn't founder at the first challenge, if it managed to overcome every obstacle, then what's the hull of a yacht, however smooth and enamelled it might be?" That's what Franz Knigh would have said to himself, if we name him the guilty man.'

'It's true that many dubious convictions have been made on assumptions just as fanciful.'

'Irony inevitably leads us to name as many guilty parties as there were passengers aboard the *Uranus*. It's a joy to find motivations for anything, in retrospect,' says the Literary Expert. 'Did not Stendhal say, when asked whether he made a plan before starting on a novel: "I make the plan afterwards"? So many of the most innovative novelists can only "make the plan afterwards". That's to say, they produce one, two, three and sometimes even as many as fifteen versions of the work in progress. As in painting, there are novelists who have second thoughts. Dostoyevsky, for instance. Did he not begin writing *Crime and Punishment* as the diary of a murderer? Then recast it as the murderer's confession written in the first person singular? And so on, from one plan made afterwards to another, until he came to the version that became the unsurpassable forerunner of . . .'

'No more digressions, please,' says the Investigator. 'As far as Franz Knigh is concerned, your fondness for the paradoxical is influencing both of you, and forcing us towards interpretations that are too literary and philosophical. I'm all for a little irony, but too much is reductive. Who exactly was this Franz Knigh? A scientist? A poet?'

'As in poetry, where you try to make the words fit a pattern, so too in the so-called exact sciences you try to make things fit. And if they don't fit naturally, you force them. But there's often a fundamental difference between the poet and the man of science: one of them's not serious, and the other is often too serious,' says the Poet Criminologist.

'Poetry is indeed something of a game,' says the Literary Expert, 'but let's not forget that every innovative science is also something of a game of surprise. Except that in poetry the game is a visual one and in science it's played out. By the way, you know that when Corneille was getting bored writing verse for his play *Horace*, to boost his enjoyment of writing, he amused himself by dreaming up a very irreverent acrostic – *fat arse*, apparently directed at the king.

'You're kidding.'

'Look at the text. Act II, scene 3. The contents of those seven lines demonstrate, moreover, what regard Corneille had for certain values.'

'What art carried to the sublime has not imposed joyful constraints on itself?'

'Let's get back to the *Uranus*, if you don't mind,' the Investigator implores them.

'And after all, what mystery is not a joyful constraint? So, what about Franz Knigh?'

'Well, I'm going to disappoint you. Franz was a person you couldn't suspect in the least.'

'Then it was him!' says the Criminologist, laughing.

XXII

'Franz Knigh said to me one day: "You know, water's an extraordinary liquid. We're children of the water cycle. It's possible that in the entire universe there's water in a liquid state only on earth." As I expressed surprise, he went on, "Any closer to the Sun, and the Earth would have been surrounded in nothing but steam; any further away and all its water would be frozen into ice. The margin for liquid water is frightfully narrow," Franz told me. "In the cosmos," he went on, "there's a vast amount of steam, just as there's a vast amount of ice, but liquid water surely exists nowhere else but here."'

'In other words, you can only drown on Earth.'

'Stop being sarcastic! "Liquid water is quite exceptional," said Franz, when I was with him in Hamburg. "Its presence on a planet requires utterly extraordinary conditions. These conditions are called: the water margin. This margin of liquid water is limited to a few degrees. It was Earth's good fortune to find itself situated in this narrow corridor in relation to the Sun." Hence, the condensation of water, as Kurt Knigh wrote in the first lines of poetry that you found pinned up in his cabin on the *Uranus*:

> On the secret clefts of Mother Earth he
>   showers rain in clear streams
> Grass flowers trees birds originate in the cavities.'

'So we're back to where we started!'

'I found those same lines in that unfinished manuscript by Franz, which you see there, on that chair. And I recall, now, with sadness that he liked to quote his elder brother Kurt's verses. Every morning, during my stay with him in Hamburg, we went out for long sailing trips. "On the water," he told me, "I think with an intensity I can't find anywhere else. Water is intelligence, memory, sublime precariousness. Water is life. So nothing's more desirable than to die in and by water."'

'You're sure of those words?' exclaims the Investigator.

'Absolutely. "Water is purifying," he said, his little sailing boat heeling dangerously as we sped towards the mouth of the river. 'What an absurdity that *Uranus* of Father's is! I hate that white enamelled floating palace – and he had to go and call it the *Uranus*, what's more. *Uranus*! The Sky god!"

'We were sailing past some enormous warships, sitting heavy and motionless in the water that nonetheless was beginning to break into foam. "They are the ships that represent my father," he said, pointing to those ironclad vessels the colour of lead. "Those guns are the exact equivalent of our father the "great" Karl Knigh's writing. His books are *great* heavy books, dealing with *great* subjects, of supposedly elevated thoughts, and all of the characters in those *great* books of his are detestable, as he has always been detestable to me, to Rosa, and to Kurt. They're the multiple facets of his detestable soul. While Julius's books have left a deep impression on me, our father's books have always left me cold, as they say. They're books that are absolutely determined to pass themselves off as books about love. Not real love, no, but Love! They claim to be full of Love. For whom? For what? No one knows. A love story is what the publishers of our father's books promise. But what kind of love? They don't know!" That's what Franz said to me on his little sailing boat as we passed the mighty warships anchored in the estuary,' the Literary Expert goes on.

'"One day," Franz continued, "I happened to find in my father's house the letters that were written by my mother, Belle, who died giving birth to me – yes, the letters my mother and father exchanged before any of us were born. My mother's letters were so overwhelmingly gloomy that I began to feel consoled about her death. To my great astonishment there was surprising kindness, tenderness and unimaginable love in my father's letters. Was it possible that Kurt, Rosa and I had been fathered by a Karl Knigh capable of tenderness, kindness and even love? How old was I when his letters came into my hands? Fifteen? Sixteen at most. Kurt and Rosa had already left home. I was soon to follow them. But these letters afforded me another view of my father, who hated himself for being my father, yes, hated himself for having begotten me. To tell the truth, as I know now, he never really loved my mother, Belle, but only the young girl in her that his brother Arno, who died in strange circumstances, had loved. He loved their love. He repleted himself with it. He thought he could keep it alive, as if Arno had bequeathed it to him. He though he loved Belle when in reality it was the woman Arno had loved that he strove to love. But that's not all," Franz told me, as he pulled away from the shore, heading out to sea,' the Literary Expert goes on, '"that's not all! There was Julius. And Julius was extraordinarily enamoured of Belle. Not of Belle and Arno. No, of Belle. Of Belle alone. The Julius you met in Granada is a Julius in love with Belle for the rest of his life, you see? And I'm sure now that of the two of them it was Julius that Belle really loved after Arno."'

'Now, this really is the height of romanticism!' says the Poet Criminologist, laughing.

'Oh, don't interrupt him, please! At last, a real love story!'

'A much more complicated one than you think!' continues the Literary Expert. 'Those love letters found by Franz, he learned many years later, were by both Karl and Julius.'

'How come? But the handwriting . . .'

'Was of course Karl's, but the sentiments, the words, the charm all came from Julius.'

'You mean, Julius dictated those letters?'

'Exactly. And this detail was something I came across last night in Lotte's journal. But to understand that, you need to know what kind of relationship there was between Franz Knigh and Lotte Knigh. But it's late. If you like . . .'

'We could go and have a drink at the Yacht Club,' the Poet Criminologist cheerfully cuts in, with the Investigator's approval, 'I was just going to suggest it myself.'

'So during my stay in Hamburg, Franz never stopped talking about his family, as if it was a relief to find someone he could unburden himself to,' continues the Literary Expert, now ensconced at the Yacht Club with the Poet Criminologist and the Investigator. ' "Our so-called father," Franz told me, "was just our father, whereas for Kurt, Rosa and myself, Julius was our *real* father, *our spiritual father*, as Kurt and Rosa called him before they were taken prisoner, if I can put it that way, by Gustav Zhorn, who managed to maintain his hold on them by leading them into the worst excesses."

' "But has Karl Knigh always consulted seers, as he confessed to me in Pals and Granada?" I asked Franz, preferring with untimely discretion to change the subject.'

'Wait!' says the Investigator. 'Can you tell us exactly what kind of excesses these were that Franz . . .'

'You mean, with regard to Kurt, Rosa and Gustav Zhorn?'

'Yes.'

'*Every* excess, if I'm not mistaken. Going to the furthest extreme. Losing themselves, seeking self-oblivion by every means, dying without quite dying. I think they tried all kinds of escapism, every drug possible and impossible. There was nothing Zhorn offered them that they refused, even to the point where they felt "the winds of death", Rosa told me one day in Vienna, when we were alone together, without Kurt and more importantly without Zhorn, of whom she was terribly afraid. Anyway, I asked Franz how long it was since his father had been so obsessed with consulting clairvoyants and seers. I told him about the woman with the cockerel in Pals, the gypsy in Granada, and the blind Bengali in New York. At the time I hadn't yet seen Karl Knigh in Berlin and Paris, where he also insisted on taking me to the clairvoyants of whom he was a devout visitor. "Our father has never undertaken anything whatsoever without consulting several of these dreadful characters," Franz told me. "One of them in particular, when we were children, had a terribly pernicious influence on him. Little by little, he *allowed* him to hate all three of us, and myself even more so, if that were possible. We were not supposed to write; by writing, this person claimed, we drew creative energy away from our father. We also had to be kept away from Julius, to whom, as children, then adolescents, then young adults, the three of us used to give what we'd written to read. This clairvoyant alleged that by his encouragement, Julius was trying to arm us against his brother Karl."'

'What do you mean by arm?' says the Investigator.

'Yes, Julius hoped that with the weapon of their writing the three children would succeed in overturning the oppressive statue of the great man. "Through our writing, we were to kill our father, you see?" Franz told me, changing tack and asking me to duck my head so that the boom didn't stun me,' the Literary Expert goes on.

'"The really dreadful thing," Franz went on to tell me, "is that this fortune-teller that my father obeyed was right. For Julius, we were indeed very delightful weapons that he handled with a great deal of intelligence and subtlety. For example, it was to Julius that Rosa owed her first published work. Here you have this very young girl by the name of Rosa Knigh publishing a quite extraordinary work. The daughter of the 'great' Knigh! What an event for those writers who covered literature! With what perverse pleasure they showered praise on Rosa! What was this work about? Love, as it happens. But what kind of love? An erotic love between brother and sister. A work like that would have burned with its author a few centuries ago; in the last century, burned and its author *killed* by slow degrees, in a prison-cell, or worse still, a convent, left to be stuck with pins by the nuns; no more than fifty years ago, still burned and its author *treated* in some luxury clinic; burned this time in a conflagration of praise and its author *exposed* . . ."'

'To the gaze of millions of avid spectators. We've got the point!' the Poet Criminologist interrupts him. 'So even your Franz wasted his time denouncing this practice that's no longer an issue?'

'At the time I was planning to write my thesis, it was still an issue. Today of course . . .'

'Go on, go on,' the Investigator says impatiently.

'"Ever prompted, encouraged and assured of her genius by uncle Julius, she publishes a second work just as unexpected of a young woman. A more opaque work of real literary beauty. I admire my sister Rosa," Franz told me, "no one writes the way she does today. There have been a few phenomenal cases like hers. Last deathly writings, a kind of literary intravenous drip . . ."'

'Oh, stop! Stop!' cries the Poet Criminologist. 'Not those words!'

'Dreadfully sorry,' says the Literary Expert.

'Forgive me,' the Poet Criminologist stammers. 'Some words are unbearable to use . . . there are some metaphors . . . But forgive me, it's my nerves . . . Truly, forgive me! Please, continue, nothing could be better for me.'

'Have a drink, my friend,' says the Investigator. 'So, what else did Franz Knigh tell you?'

'We were still on his little sailing boat, heeling dangerously, our backs soaked by the spray of the troughing waves. "Have you read my sister Rosa's books?" he shouted to me in the wind. "Yes, yes," I replied with an enthusiasm that made him laugh. "The reason I've undertaken this thesis is precisely in order to demonstrate that great literature does not necessarily lie with the "great" Karl Knigh," I was artless enough to shout back in the deafening wind of the storm, as Franz kept tacking in the attempt to return to the mouth of the estuary and reach the more sheltered roadstead as quickly as possible. The wind was freshening. The little sailing boat, heeling too far over, capsized in a gust, and we had to swim for it, struggling against the enormous waves to reach the side of one of the warships anchored in the harbour mouth. A rope ladder was lowered and . . .'

'What!' cries the Criminologist. 'After all that, we're back to . . .'

'Yes, indeed,' says the Literary Expert, laughing, 'to this dress rehearsal, as it were, a kind of prefiguration of the final sequence without a ladder . . .'

'A dress rehearsal, did you say? It's only in novels that this can't happen . . . *it happens*, as they say. An old trick to cause the novel to be forgotten in favour of "real life". Luckily, novelists today . . .'

'By novelists, you mean those who write in the hope of seeing their writings transformed to celluloid. Let's use a different term for the others . . . those who write . . . Don't tell me I'm old-fashioned . . . You must still believe in the written word, and above all in the word as *read,* to have invited me to join you in elucidating the mystery of the *Uranus.* Isn't it a funny sign of the times that the Knigh family writers should have all sunk without trace. Especially knowing what quantity of writings were on the *Uranus* . . . which didn't sink. Let's accept this fact, as we accept a musical overture to which the subsequent musical developments and variations hark back.'

'So you scaled the side of a naval despatch-boat by means of a rope ladder?' says the Investigator. 'If you don't mind, let's leave aside for the moment any games of comparison and their distractions, to concentrate more closely on the strange personality of Franz Knigh. I remember him very well when he used to come to the Yacht Club with the rest of his family. He was quite a timid and gentle boy, wasn't he? One day, on the occasion of the launching the last *Uranus,* his father asked him, not without irony, to explain to everyone there why the blood of mammals was red and not green "like that of snails", he said. I ought to explain that Lotte Knigh had just cut her finger slightly on one of those dreadful Yacht Club champagne glasses. Franz smiled and very charmingly gave us "the story of blood" in a few words. We were actually in here, except that the tables were all put together, running the whole length of the room, for the launch banquet. Franz got up and this is more or less what he said: "The adventure of blood starts in the ocean. Small quantities of oxygen are present in sea water. Living creatures seize on it . . . or rather," he said, still smiling, "imprison the water, as we can see with jellyfish, which carry around with them a little internal sea communicating with the ocean. In the worm this little internal sea is closed off, creating an environment that favours the production of oxygen-fixative metal pigments. Then circulation develops, to irrigate the entire complex of cells with this fluid, bearing memories of the ocean, that has become blood." As Franz Knigh tried to sit down again, Lotte asked him to go on. Needing no persuasion, he immediately continued with his little impromptu lecture. "There is a logic," he said, "to which the entire animal world conforms by the various means dictated in each case by circumstance, so that both contingency and necessity play their part. It was obviously necessary that blood should flow in our veins. But there was no reason why it had to be red. Our blood owes its colour to the fact that the oxygen dispersed round our bodies is done so in cells that carry haemoglobin, a protein that uses the fixative power of iron with which it is associated." And he concluded: "Of course other metals might have been used. Hence, the green blood of snails, based on copper." That, almost word for word, is the little impromptu lecture that Franz Knigh kindly gave us the day the *Uranus* was launched.'

'You couldn't have drawn a more accurate picture of Franz Knigh,' says the Literary Expert. '"Why isn't our blood green?" That absurd question sums him up perfectly.'

XXIII

Here they are the next day, all three of them, in the Literary Expert's room.

'You know,' says the Poet Criminologist, 'it seems that your reminiscences about the Knigh literary family are not only advancing our investigation, but also bringing a very unexpected peace where such peace was impossible until now. Believe it or not, when I go home, every evening, to distract the mother of our child a little I try to give her as faithful a rendering as possible of what you've said about the Knigh family.

' "Well?" she says as soon as I enter the place of anguish our home has gradually turned into.

' "Well," I say, "the Literary Expert has introduced us today to the *water margin*. And I suspect that something must have happened between Franz and Lotte which our Literary Expert is being a bit too evasive about." '

'Don't you believe it,' says the Literary Expert, 'not evasive, but rather unsure at the moment. However, I made considerable headway last night on the subject of Franz and Lotte Knigh. Her journal reveals a very strange love story.'

'Wait, before you go on, let me tell you how grateful I am. I want you to know that as I proceed to give a faithful account of your stories about this family, my wife remarks that the child seems to be taking an interest. I only have to mention Knigh, the Knigh literary family, and the child seems almost attentive. He suddenly forgets his old slipper and seems to be listening, I assure you. It's an inexplicable phenomenon, but it's definitely so: he listens, and keeps straining to listen and listen. I say, "Knigh literary family." And can you believe it, that child who's more likely to moan, begins to nod his head and smile in his own special way. Yesterday evening, after leaving you, I get home and he becomes all excited at seeing me and throws his slipper at me.

' "Talk to him," says my wife in a constricted voice, "go on, talk to him, you see how attentive he looks." Perhaps she's just imagining what for so many years she's longed for? And me too. Yet I assure you, that these past few days he's been reacting, and even more so yesterday evening when I spoke of the green blood of snails . . .

' "That poor Knigh family, disappearing so tragically, like that!" my wife said to me yesterday evening. "But in the end what proof of their death do you have?" she added in that calm and gentle tone of voice characteristic of her.

' "What?" I replied. "The scratches on the hull, the smears of blood, and the emptiness above all, the oppressive emptiness of the yacht, with its untouched lifeboats still in place . . ."

'So we went on talking, the child seeming to follow the words we uttered with something akin to intelligence. But I'm being ridiculous.'

'Not at all! Quite the contrary,' says the Literary Expert. 'If the mystery of the *Uranus* could only have some saving grace!'

'The same goes for me,' says the Investigator. 'Every evening someone asks me too: "Well?" So, my dear Literary Expert, you're a prisoner of these questions we face: "Well?" Allow me to ask you a question: "Well, what about Franz Knigh and Lotte?" '

'As I was saying to you yesterday, you couldn't draw a better picture of Franz than that of the person who explained "why our blood isn't green". He spent his whole time addressing problems whose wonderful absurdity inevitably led him to solutions that were themselves questions. He was in his element, dealing with these questions with consummate ease, as though suffused with intelligence. And when you mentioned Lotte Knigh, I didn't have time yesterday to tell you that if Franz had exiled himself to Hamburg, it was in order to achieve a necessary distance, a painful detachment so as to avoid carrying on with Lotte . . .'

'What great intuition women have! At the launch of the *Uranus*, my . . . companion . . . who was still my wife then . . . said to me: "What's going on, or not going on, between Franz Knigh and Lotte Knigh?" Since women see emotion everywhere, and are often excessively romantic, at the time I didn't attach any importance to this typically female interpretation of the glances and smiles exchanged between Lotte and this treacherous son. Now that all these people are dead and we mustn't overlook anything in order to discover the reason for such a tragedy, I'd like to ask you: in what terms did you deal with Lotte Knigh in your thesis?'

'She figured in my thesis, but wasn't given the place she'd merit today. Last night I discovered some curious details in her journal. That young woman was suffocating in this Knigh family. Moreover, I believe I'm right in thinking that the money she lavished on that "seer" in Paris was money she stole from old Karl, by falsifying certain accounts.'

'Ah! At last! At last!' the Poet Criminologist gleefully exclaims.

'At last what?'

'Money at last! Without money there's no romantic *realism*. That was until now the missing dimension, in my opinion. A young wife forges her old husband's signature to draw large sums of money that she rushes off with to a "seer". That's it, isn't it?'

'Absolutely! You remember, she showed me a large bundle of notes in Paris. "You think I'm neurotic?" she said. "Don't deny it. I am neurotic. I'm the neurotic wife of a neurotic old man surrounded by neurotic children. All of us are obviously sick people. Since you've embarked on this thesis on the Knigh family, I want to help you. You know, I myself began a study of the 'great' Karl, but that study was shelved in Port-au-Prince. The old man was quicker than me! And I said: yes. Which of us is to blame? Me, of course. And if I were writing the thesis that you're planning to write, this is what I would say about Lotte Knigh: 'Lotte Knigh is a very complicated young woman, so changeable in character that after spending an hour or two with her, you're no longer sure whom you've met.' Drop that sheepish look," she said to me, "and let me continue on the subject of this very foolish Lotte! 'Sexually unsatisfied. While he's running round just about all over the world chasing that very exacting phantom of his fame, Karl

Knigh has no idea that his Lotte is robbing him, buying his seers and much else besides . . ."'

'That's what Lotte confessed to me between tears and laughter in Paris,' says the Literary Expert. 'She was in an alarming state of nerves, smoking one cigarette after another, constantly rummaging in her bag, saying that time had overtaken her, fearing that I would go off and leave her . . . She was touching, I assure you, and almost beautiful.

'"Please," she suddenly begged me, "forget this thesis, don't write this thesis on the Knigh family! You've no right to!"

'"Don't worry," I told her, "on the contrary, a genuine thesis ought to be welcomed. Where there's too much celebrity, a serious study, a rigorous study . . ."

'She didn't let me finish, and cried with a despair that was out of all proportion: "But it's going to end up being the death of us all!"'

'What?' says the Investigator with a start. 'But what she said to you there is terribly fraught with significance!'

'Don't you believe it,' says the Literary Expert, 'nothing was more banal, more common with her. *Death* was the word that recurred most frequently in the desperate and at the same time oddly frivolous way she spoke.

'"Have you read Rosa's books?" she asked me.

'"Yes, all of them, I believe."

'"Have you noticed what place she gives death? Death never comes as a conclusion in her books, she never uses it as a literary solution. In Rosa Zhorn-Knigh's work death serves no purpose. It's there, omnipresent in its agreeable uselessness. There are few authors whose characters are burdened with such mortality. They're alive but at every sentence you feel they could suddenly die, for no reason, because they're mortal," Lotte said to me,' the Literary Expert goes on. '"With Rosa, with everything she wrote, the point of arrival is always set at the beginning. Nothing of hers can be read without knowing at every line that the drama of life is already over, every living being has already met with death, it's only after death that that being can live again in her writing. It's commonly thought that a text – like life – must be read by starting at the beginning, and so be apprehended by careful progress right up to the very last word. With Rosa, never! With her, the living are dead people restored to life for the duration of a book. In Haiti, we living mingle with the dead, giving them all kinds of familiar names. They're there, you can touch them, you speak to them, they live, dance and eat with us. Everything that Rosa writes is a bit like that. Rosa's world is a deconstructed world. Her books give rise to a subverted reading. Her texts and the lives within these texts of hers have this second sense. You can't really penetrate them unless you know what conclusion the crisis in which you're involved is leading up to. It's the same with places where terrible things have happened."'

'Your account of what Lotte said is very striking,' the Poet Criminologist breaks in. 'Believe it or not, having taken a certain dreadful decision, I was reading my life from a full stop set in the not too distant future. And then the mystery of the *Uranus* came along and disrupted this decision. Here I am now with no full stop from which to deconstruct my life, with no count-down, if you prefer. Do you think it's tolerable to live without knowing how it's all going to end? Is the mystery of life simply that? Not knowing? Until the *Uranus* was found drifting at sea, mysteriously empty of its occupants, I knew when the appointed moment would be. Since then, I've given myself reprieves, and the appointed moment escapes me. Without an appointed moment, how is one to live with a child, knowing how he will decline and what sufferings this decline will involve. What did I dream of before I became the person that I am? What did we dream of? Was I not inclined to set store by a human existence familiar with laughter from the cradle? Although a poet, did I not dream of the joys of banality? I read Tolstoy, Turgenev . . .'

'Oh, don't mention that dreadful Turgenev!' the Literary Expert exclaims, laughing.

'He was a friend of Flaubert.'

'Everybody's friend, the place man, the sycophant who hated Dostoyevsky.'

'Who returned the compliment.'

'The wolf cannot love the dog.'

'The dog is jealous of the wolf, as you well know.'

'Don't you believe it, the dog wants to remain a dog, the dog's a dog in his heart of hearts, but he wants you to think he's a wolf. He pretends to be a wolf! Look at the way Karl Knigh was jealous of Julius while at the same time . . .'

'Stop talking about literature, if you don't mind, and let's get back to Lotte and Franz Knigh,' says the Investigator.

'Just now, when I left home, as I was passing through the port,' says the Poet Criminologist, 'I stopped for a moment behind a child who was drawing.

'"What are you drawing, sonny?" I asked him.

'"God," he replied.

'Amazed by this answer coming from a child, I said to him, "And what's he like?"

'"I'll know when I've finished."

'That young philosopher beats us all hollow, don't you think?'

'What about Lotte and Franz?' the Investigator insists.

'Well! At one point she confessed to casting certain voodoo spells. Both for chasing devils away and summoning them. Such was Lotte's strangely contradictory character. Similarly, she spoke of Franz with a mixture of love and . . . not hatred but impatience. "I'll kill him!" she once cried. "I love him to death!" That's how she admitted her obsession with the younger of the Knigh sons.'

'And Franz himself?'

'He refused to utter Lotte's name. But here, in his writings found aboard the *Uranus*, everything suggests . . .'

'That he loved her?'

'Not at all! That he was afraid of her and somehow bewitched by her. He uses that word in a supposed fiction in one of his incomplete manuscripts, which reveals with almost embarrassing clarity his feelings . . . no, not feelings but his obsession with the excitement of his senses by this young woman. You see, unfortunately, his writing is indecipherable in places and the crossings-out so numerous that you can't tell if they're there to blot out certain words or to obscure them without actually erasing them. His others writings are as incoherent as his scientific and philosophical writings are clear and perfect in form. For Franz, Lotte was a sickness that he suffered – how better to describe it? To the point that he was unable to utter her name in a normal way.'

'Strange,' says the Investigator, 'from the sound of it, you seem to be talking about a completely different man. The Franz we saw at the Yacht Club, the one who told us about "the green blood of snails", was on the contrary extremely relaxed with his young "substitute" mother. At the banquet for the launch of the *Uranus* she even sat beside him, and there was nothing to suggest the least disquiet between them.'

'Yet Rosa, when speaking of Lotte and Franz, said to me: "Be careful, not a word about Lotte to Franz. He can't bear anyone talking about her. Franz has some strange secrets. Franz has always had strange secrets, since childhood. I'm sure that when you saw him in Hamburg he seemed straightforward to you, delightfully transparent."

' "Indeed," was my reply to Rosa,' says the Literary Expert, ' "I've rarely met anyone so uncomplicated, to the extent that I find it difficult to believe that he's really part of the Knigh family." '

'Rosa laughed and turned to Karl: "Did you hear that? Tell him how many times Franz almost killed himself when we were children."

' "Why talk about it" Karl said.

' "But on the contrary," Gustav Zhorn intervened, "it's always very amusing to speak ill of Franz. I know, Kurt won't have a word said against his little Franz, but he forgets that little Franz isn't little Franz any more. Franz is cunning, Franz is elusive. He's the greatest mass of secrets you're ever likely to encounter, and I think that if you manage to see through him, he'll provide you with some very valuable material for your thesis." '

'And did you find out these secrets?'

'A few.'

'Well?'

'The principal one goes back to the very night that Karl

Knigh married Lotte. "Just imagine," Zhorn said to me, "on the very night that he married Lolotte, old Knigh couldn't find her anywhere. No one had seen the bride. If only this had happened on dry land at least, it's likely that everyone would have drawn a veil of discretion over the matter. After all, why should a young woman a third of the age of her old husband have to answer to anybody! Disappeared! But the whole Knigh family was aboard the *Uranus* – I don't remember which ... the first, or the second? It doesn't make much difference," said Gustav Zhorn in his usual supercilious tone of voice. Rosa and Kurt tried to interrupt the actor, but their discomfort seemed only to excite him.

'"Do you know the island of Reunion, that volcano that sticks out of the Indian Ocean, with its Piton des Neiges and its coves all named after saints? Why did old Knigh insist on celebrating his sunset wedding on Reunion? Of course the whole family was there: Franz, Julius, Rosa and Kurt, as well as me."

'"That's enough!" Kurt broke in.

'"But we promised to lend a hand to this young researcher. There shouldn't be anything left in the dark, especially not one of the essential parts of our great man's life. There'll soon be a time, and it's not far off now, when Lotte's going to become a much sought-after woman. When a young girl fills the place left vacant in the shadow of a great man, it's only to be expected that she'll make a suitable widow for a good half-century after his death. Haven't you noticed with what lucidity great men choose a very young girl as their last spouse? That way, they die with their minds set at rest. Nothing's more effective than a young widow for keeping afloat a relatively undistinguished body of work like that of *our old father*, Knigh. You know," Zhorn went on,' says the Literary Expert, '"Lolotte was originally a young researcher like you? Ah, you knew that! Nothing like a researcher to keep the flame alight when there's a shortage of fuel. I bet that for more than half a century Lolotte will be able to produce a supply of unpublished ..."

' "Gustav!" Rosa shouted. "You're appalling! You must stop at once!"

' "All right, let's stop. So, marriage. We'll pass no comment. Marriage between Karl Knigh and Lolotte, the young black researcher whose skin's too pale. What happens? Once she's married, she disappears. The *Uranus* is anchored in one of those little coves dedicated to one of the many saints who protect the coast of that little mound always ready to vomit up its lava. Fancy that! No sign of Lotte, and no sign of Franz. On the very first evening! There's a search of the yacht. The bride's disappeared as well as the groom's younger son. No! Kurt! Rosa! Let me have my say!" Zhorn suddenly cried. "If you don't like my version, you can correct it, but afterwards."

' "Don't listen to him," Rosa begged me.

' "Nothing very dreadful, after all. On her wedding night, Lolotte eloped with young Franz Knigh. Usually the bride's the one that gets carried off. Well, for once, in this case, it was the bride herself who eloped, drawing in her wake the old husband's youngest son." '

'Do you believe this story?' says the Investigator.

'At the time I had my doubts, especially as Rosa and Kurt seemed even more astonished than I was, as if this was the first time they'd heard of these events – which nevertheless took place, more or less, but not as Zhorn recounted them. It's true that Lotte was no sooner married to the great man than she . . .'

'Realized her mistake? Nothing more commonplace. Only Chekhov managed to transcend that kind of trite situation by . . .'

'You're thinking of . . .'

'Of none of his stories . . . and all of them,' says the Poet Criminologist. 'Except that here, instead of finding ourselves with that simplicity of the humdrum, life has to go and commit the unforgivable sin of piling up an excessive quantity of storybook inessentials.'

'That's precisely what I said to Gustav Zhorn. "Very well," he replied, "let's keep things in their true proportion. But how can we neglect Karl Knigh's wealth, and the almost incomprehensible bonds that hold the unbreachable Knigh family circle together? So, forget Reunion, forget the yacht," Zhorn continued, "let's take the situation in its bare essentials: an old man marries a young woman and on the very night of her wedding the bride runs off with her husband's youngest son. Take this paradigm, and transpose it in time and space; the fact of it's there, in its eternity. Humiliation of the old man. Justifiable panic of the bride, whose flight's natural, isn't it? Cats, dogs, seals . . . that's the way Nature behaves. And Lolotte is nothing other than Nature bursting into the lives, which go against nature, of old Knigh and his family," Zhorn concluded,' says the Literary Expert.

XXIV

' "Don't believe a word of Gustav's stories!" Rosa said to me a little later when we were alone together. "Gustav is capable of inventing anything, especially about those close to me. He can't stand anybody, neither me, nor Kurt, nor you, no one! He adores himself and is only happy in his own company. What he told you about Franz and Lotte is untrue. The marriage in Reunion, untrue! The *Uranus* has never been in the waters round Reunion. Don't you see, he was having you on? Reunion! He must have thought that an amusing irony. Reunion!"

'While she was speaking to me,' the Literary Expert goes on, 'she kept casting worried glances at the doors and windows of the lounge where we were sitting by a big log fire. All of a sudden, she whispered, "He's putting our heads under water, he's slowly suffocating us, he's preventing us from breathing, I can't take it any more. Everything he tells you about me, about Kurt, is untrue, totally untrue, I want you to know that and not to take any notice of him," Rosa insisted.

' "But why . . ." I tried to interrupt her.

' "You mean, why don't we leave him? We're too seriously bound to him, that's all. Don't try to find out more. If you've read my books, especially the last one, you ought to guess what ties bind us, and will firmly bind all three of us until death. Our secret is in my writings, as well as in Kurt's. You only have to read them as they should be read. My writings say what I myself cannot say." '

'So what do they say, these writings?' the Investigator says impatiently.

'That's exactly what I've been trying to work out. She spoke of her writing by comparing it to pleating, of which all you see is the pleated edge. "I write in pleats," she said, "and each pleat is pressed in with an iron set on maximum. You think you're seeing the same creases all the time but it's up to you to work out which crease determined the rest and which of all my pleats is the true one. Kurt and I have been creased once and for all. It's up to you to work it out." Rosa spoke in a spasmodic way, as if what she had to say came to her in waves, or "pleats",' the Literary Expert goes on, 'yes, it was as though a welter of ideas, words, sometimes complaints built up inside her while she tried to tell you something that wouldn't come . . . and all at once it came. Her whole body would writhe, and words that were often difficult to understand in the way that she'd put them together took you by surprise. Have you read the poems of Emily Dickinson?'

'Yes, indeed,' says the Poet Criminologist. 'A wonderful lunatic who lived in a state of terror, and sang, "as the Boy does by the Burying Ground", she wrote, " − because I am afraid."'

'Well, believe it or not, there was a little of that madness in Rosa. Without Kurt, without that childhood love which had quite naturally taken possession of their bodies in adolescence, Rosa was destined never to accept physical love other than in the form of a terrible enslavement of the imagination.'

'I see now in what way she might have resembled Emily Dickinson,' says the Poet Criminologist.

'Except that Emily Dickinson revelled in her erotic fantasies, whereas Rosa, with the help of Kurt's desire, and no doubt also impelled by slow persistency towards an impossible goal, had experienced, asked for, perhaps obtained what one such as Emily had only known in her little private torture chamber locked up tight again round the whiteness of lilies. And always there was Death, a completely different Death from the one that Lotte referred to. Lotte kept talking about a woman who was one of the living dead, whereas Rosa lived in Death, as if a part of her body was already familiar with the coldness of the earth.'

'But nearly all the great woman poets . . .'

'You're right, they're buried up to their chest as they write.'

'Their eyes catching the sunlight, and the lower part of their bodies petrified in the granite of a tomb. You know, Dickinson liked to come towards you with a lily in her hand?'

'Rosa by contrast didn't come towards you. She waited for

you to plunge the depths of her malaise. "I don't understand the purpose of your thesis," she said to me. "What connection can you possibly find between Father's almost solemn books and those of Kurt, Franz, myself and our chosen father Julius?"

' "But none at all," I replied.

' "And I know you met Lotte in Geneva, as well as in Paris. What did she say to you? And what about all Gustav's nonsense, how are you going to deal with that?"

' "We'll see," I replied, "I think I'll use it, because *everything* must go into a thesis."

' "What do you mean by everything?"

' "*Everything,* and perhaps even especially what apparently has nothing to do with the thesis in question."

' "But don't you see that Gustav will say anything. He hates the whole Knigh family. Myself and Kurt included, I assure you. He came down on us like the Angel of Sin. He caught Kurt and me in his talons, and held up our dark mirror to us. We're naked and enchained in his dark mirror. He keeps us deep in a damp cave and we rattle our chains without complaint."

'She was sitting on a low sofa, with her legs tucked under her, and every sentence was delivered as though brought about by the sudden variations in the fire, which caught her in irregular flashes of light. "Franz too . . ." she said, leaving her sentence hanging, unfinished.

' "Franz?"

' "Yes, Franz too . . . he tried to trap him."

' "Who?"

' "Gustav of course."

' "How do you mean, trap him?"

' "As with all the others: Father, Lotte, and even Julius – he trapped every one of them by his blackmail or by setting them against each other. God sent the Devil down on us. The irresistible Devil. And we're grateful for it . . . So? What thesis could accommodate confidences like this?" she asked, laughing.

' "Well, mine," I replied. "There's no place in the world

more open than the open terrain of a thesis such as can be written today."

'"You know what Scott Fitzgerald said about the asphyxiating work of writing? 'All good writing is *swimming under water and holding your breath.*' That's what Kurt and Franz and I, the so-called Knigh children, are trying to do . . ."'

'It's truly remarkable,' the Investigator once again breaks in, 'to see how at every stage we run into these kinds of metaphors. Is it possible that writing is like . . .'

'Drowning! Many people say so,' says the Poet Criminologist. 'But you know how it is with metaphors . . . They call Scotch 'water', and so on. Let's get back instead to your Rosa Dickinson and to how they all ended up underwater, exhausted to death? While you were describing your conversation with Zhorn, I had a rather funny notion about Lotte and Franz. I pictured a lovely sunny day, blue skies, blue sea, silver-spangled as they say, all around, stretching to the horizon, in a perfectly closed circle, with the *Uranus* at the centre, its engines cut. They're all swimming around the yacht – yes, the entire Knigh family. And then Franz climbs back aboard, immediately followed by Lotte. What I mean is, that instead of escaping the oppression of the Knigh family by leaving the boat – as Zhorn would have us believe, the son taking his father's place on the very night of his wedding – acting on this same impulse, but in reverse, they escape on to the boat, pulling up the ladder behind them – and they've made it! They haven't planned anything. I see them rushing to the forbidden cabin . . . throwing themselves on the paternal bed, the altar on which this time the sacrifice takes place in broad daylight, while the father's cries reach them through the hull of the motionless *Uranus*.'

'Very funny,' says the Investigator. 'And then what? Beware of allowing your fantasies to enter into an investigation that deserves the most scrupulous rigorousness. According to you, here we have two on board and five swimming around the yacht with its unscalable sides. How, from this simple equation, do we reach that terrible zero of a completely empty boat. I'm quite willing to imagine the adulterous couple engaged in some erotic madness, consummating what has been designated as incest and therefore taboo in human society since time immemorial. But what do you do with them next? Granted that the drowning took the same time as that lovemaking wrested from the myths so dear to old Knigh. Granted anything you like, but what Angel will drive them out of this supposed Eden of yours? They blink in the sun. They lean over the side: everybody's gone! What then?'

'Well, for a criminologist like me, the question is this: how long will a "diabolical couple" such as this survive their crime without destroying each other? In criminology, this problem has always been analysed with the most meticulous attention. The answer has never varied. It's the same today as it is in the Bible. Adam and Eve were not driven out of Eden: it's God that they eliminated – that's what criminological analysis tells us – but Eden was also destroyed at the same time that they destroyed themselves, of course.'

'So, according to you,' says the Literary Expert, 'no survival without the Eye of the *Outsider*.'

'That's certainly what criminology teaches us – that little-known science, but surely of all the sciences the one closest to poetry. What misdeed are Adam and Eve charged with? They threw God overboard and found themselves alone on the deck of the *Uranus*. With no *Outsider*. And believe it or not, God found it very amusing to be driven out of Eden. He turned his back on Eden, which he abandoned to mankind. And what did mankind do for centuries? Tried desperately to reintroduce into their Eden now become hellish this expelled *Outsider*. For centuries and centuries they laboured to reconstitute God from the void, and little by little the Eye opened, Someone was watching man again. Then slowly the Eye closed, and humanity eventually perished, humanity finally destroyed itself.'

'What are you trying to get at?' says the Investigator, losing patience.

'The inevitable demise of Lotte and Franz because there was no longer any outsider to give life to them, do you see?'

'My friend, what on earth are you talking about?'

'About myself of course! About my wife and child, about us. I think that we've been wrong to isolate ourselves, that by expelling any outside gaze, by shutting ourselves away in the heart of an emptied universe, with the sole purpose . . . without any purpose to tell the truth . . . so much so that I'd reached the point . . . Oh, I'm sorry . . . forgive this moment of weakness. Yes, I was thinking, while the Literary Expert was talking about Lotte and Franz, I was thinking that only an outside gaze can deter, can restrain you, that an Angel at least is needed as a prevention. Something we don't have these days. As there was no outsider and no Angel, all they could do was, in their turn, to jump overboard. But do go on, please. I interrupted you with my nonsense.'

'Not at all,' says the Literary Expert, 'on the contrary. Rosa, as it happened, believed in Angels. Yes, in Angels such as Rossetti painted and described in his poems. "If no Angel restrains us, humanity is going to plunge to its death. Every line of my writings," she told me, "yearns for the Angel but succeeds only in giving life to the Devil. My writings are possessed by Devils, as Kurt and I are possessed by the Devil of the flesh. At once its creatures and its masters, we have at our disposal the magic ring but we don't want to use it to get rid of him who keeps us so securely on a chain."'

'We shouldn't take this woman too seriously,' says the Investigator. 'Don't you see what pleasure she took in knowing that she was being listened to by the young researcher that you were at the time? This morning we seem to be losing our way. We should keep theology of any kind out of this mystery. And no Angels! No biblical, esoteric or fantasmagorical explanations! On inspection, the white modern yacht found drifting at sea turns out to be empty. Why?"

'It seems to me that our friend the Literary Expert isn't listening to you any more. What's he reading with such extraordinary attention?' says the Poet Criminologist.

'Indeed, while you were talking, I was absentmindedly reading this poem of Kurt's left lying on top of one of his manuscripts. I daren't believe that there may be hidden within it . . .'

'Another acrostic?'

'Yes, but this one seems to give us a lead. Just look at this W here.'

H
Y

> Total emptiness all around   Look, friend, where we lie   At twenty paces
> Overheard dark ominous skies   unmourned   Soon you'll find
>   Our watery tomb unmarked   The first-born son
> Rival siblings lost at sea   Our names unrecorded   Explains all
> Expect no funeral pyres   Kindred bones worn smooth   Read the note
> Abyss of stinking lime   by waves   Now we're gone.
>   extinguished sun
> Deathward-spiralling distant
>   comets
>
> W
> H
> Y

'It sends shivers down my spine,' exclaims the Poet Criminologist. Twenty paces from the stern lies the reason why. If it hadn't been written already, there'd be nothing to prevent us believing that some ghost has just written this poem in reply to your question. It's as if they're all here, around us, invisible but very much present, and listening. Are you sure this poem really was on top of that pile of manuscripts?'

'I assume so,' says the Literary Expert. 'That WHY caught my attention. And while you were talking, I absentmindedly glanced through these verses. I confess to feeling quite disturbed.'

'I suggest we go over to the *Uranus* immediately,' says the Maritime Affairs Investigator.'

'You're right, it's the best thing we can do. Take the poem. It may be that once we're on board, we'll find other valuable clues in it. Already I see how though not why becoming clear,' says the Poet Criminologist. 'Let's assume it was Kurt Knigh. Forget why for a moment, since there's a why for every one that died; let's limit ourselves to how. Suppose it was Kurt acting on his own. They're all swimming around the yacht that lies motionless in the sun. Kurt climbs back aboard, alone. He pulls up the ladder, goes and shuts himself below deck, and without taking any further notice of the cries, pleas, desperate scratchings on the hull, he writes a few poems revealing his secret. This is why and how I, Kurt Knigh, have decided to put an end to the Knigh literary family. As I write these lines, I can hear them moaning and thrashing the water more and more feebly. From time to time I go back up on deck and count them. Father, Julius and Rosa were the first to go under. On the second day I saw Franz desperately holding up Lotte, and Gustav circling round them trying to push them under the water. He was shouting. I think he had been driven mad by all that swimming and scratching the hull of the yacht in vain. Every time I leaned over, Franz and Lotte looked up at me imploringly. If Gustav had drowned before them, I would certainly have let down the ladder. I think that despite my terrible resolution I would have saved them. But Gustav's demented cries prevented me. Finally, Lotte and Franz disappeared; it was the evening of the third day. Only Gustav Zhorn remained now. He was lying on his back, floating, and laughing silently. "Come on!" he said every time he saw me appear above him. "Jump in!" On the fourth day . . . or rather the third night . . . I don't remember now . . . no, the fourth night, he was still floating on his back but no longer reacted. Only his eyes and teeth were visible in the dark. I shone an electric torch on him. He was pale, and apart from his wide-open eyes and the rictus on his face, you'd have thought that he was surely dead. But does a dead man float on his back? Is he going to remain like that for ever, lying on the surface of the sea? I'm going to try and restart the *Uranus*'s engines and shake him off. Then I'll see it through to the end . . ."'

'Stop it! Wake up!' cries the Investigator, shaking the Poet Criminologist by the sleeve. 'Come back to your senses!'

'Why did you interrupt me, I was doing brilliantly. You can't imagine the experience I've just had! He was inside me, speaking through me.'

'Who? What?'

'I saw everything, I tell you, I was Kurt, his spirit was within me! Why did you break the contact between us? I was alone on the yacht and had restarted its powerful engines. But then, following, there in its wake, was Gustav Zhorn, his body rigid, as though laid upon the water, being sucked along by the whirl of the propellers. Gustav was following, following the *Uranus*. I increased speed and it was only after half a day's sailing that I managed to shake him from my wake. Then I went down into my cabin and till my energy was exhausted wrote a considerable number of coded poems in which I confessed what couldn't be said otherwise. Then I dragged myself on to the deserted deck and stood there, remembering the others with a mixture of regret, deep melancholy and secret joy. Gathering my last remaining strength, as they say, I slipped overboard and drowned immediately.

'Well? Convinced?' the Poet Criminologist concludes, laughing bizarrely. 'Come on, let's go over to the yacht. I'd be very curious to board her and find what Kurt's poem promises us.'

XXV

Here they are on the deck of the *Uranus*. They have climbed the iron ladder and all three of them are now making for the stern.

'Calm down,' says the Investigator to the Poet Criminologist, 'stop running round in all directions. Twenty paces? But twenty paces from what point? Here we are at the stern. I'll draw a cross with a piece of chalk, and count twenty paces.'

'No, not like that,' says the Poet Criminologist, extremely agitated. 'Let me do it! There! Twenty paces from the stern to the control room. Ah, leave me alone, I feel I'm being guided. It's there, I'm sure of it. What did I tell you? There's something here! Look, a piece of paper stuck behind the axle of the helm. Come on, my friends! Let's open it on deck.'

1X9L	1X2R	5X4R	6X8L
3X1M	3X2R	1X1R	3X5R
6X1L	4X6M	4X17L	5X1L
3X4L			2X1M
2X9M			
5X5L			

3X1234567891011121314 15R

5X1L 3X6M 2X2M 5X1R 4X4M 4X1L 2X4L 1X5R 6X6R

'Terrific!' says the Literary Expert. 'We're still left in the dark.'

'It seems that these numbers ought to provide us with the key,' says the Poet Criminologist.

'The key? I doubt it, but they may tell us on *whom* we should focus our attention.'

'Here's some paper and a pencil,' says the Investigator.

'Now, let's proceed methodically. So? What do you think? We have here four columns with a series of numbers combined with letters. M. R. L. X.'

'Let's leave aside the columns, shall we, and start by working out what the letters mean. It seems to me that all these numbers and letters refer to Kurt's poem.'

'That's obvious,' says the Poet Criminologist. 'We have four different letters. Let's forget the X for the time being. That leaves us with M. L. R.'

'How can we relate these three letters to the three columns of poetry?' says the Literary Expert.

'But nothing simpler!' says the Poet Criminologist.

'Stop getting so excited,' says the Investigator, 'and don't say everything's simple when everything seems to me to be getting more complicated.'

'Don't you believe it! In criminology nothing's simpler than the apparently complicated, just as nothing's more complicated than the apparently simple. I could cite you numerous extraordinary cases whose incredible complications concealed . . .'

'I think I've got it!' says the Literary Expert. 'All you have to do is look at the poem. R, L and M stand quite simply for Right, Left and Middle. From there on, nothing could be simpler and more perverse. The X isn't the letter X, but the mathematical symbol.'

'Meaning?'

'Well, you take 1 by 9 in the left-hand column. That gives you the letter T.'

'And why the letter T?'

Well, see for yourself: the ninth letter in the first line of the left-hand column . . . and so on. For the two bottom series we just have to follow the same procedure.'

'You're right!' exclaims the Poet Criminologist. 'We go to 3 Right and there are the fifteen numbers for the line: 'The first-born son'. Kurt of course. His signature, as it were. Wait, wait! Now read this! The final series gives: A MURDERER! 'The first-born son A MURDERER.' As for the rest, decoding it is just child's play. Let's see: TODAY'S THE DAY

CIAO. That *ciao* seems to me a tease, which in my view would suggest a completely different guilty party.'

'What do you mean?' says the Investigator tetchily.

'I get you,' says the Literary Expert. 'You think that someone other than Kurt fooled around . . .'

'Blurring the trail at the very last moment. Yes, that's my hunch.'

'And who are you thinking of?'

'I see Zhorn, yes, Gustav Zhorn. What's happening? They're all swimming around the immaculate-white *Uranus*, water and skies of blue all around. How hot it is in the midday sun! They've all climbed down the ladder to get into the water. How cool and refreshing it is! They're enjoying their swim. But then Gustav says to himself: it's now or never! Quick, climb the ladder and pull it up after you. Good, at last, all of our dear literary family are in the drink!

'"This is your last swim!" You shout down at the others below, who begin to laugh and call you all kinds of silly names. "I'm not joking!" you shout at them, increasingly irritated by their absurd confidence. And so, leaning over the rail, lighting one cigarette after another, you watch them splashing about.

'"Hey, Gustav, that's enough! The joke's over!" old Knigh calls to you, out of breath. "Come on, now, lower the ladder!"

'"No way!" you reply. "Time's up for you and your dear family of writers!"

'And you throw your cigarette so that it lands and fizzles out in the water just in front of the great writer's nose. You can see that he's really exhausted. And now Rosa and Kurt in their turn are shouting at you in angry voices. Rosa says that she's cold and you can see she's clinging round Kurt's neck. Julius is calm. He swims calmly and all of a sudden he says: "Zhorn, that's enough! I order you to lower the ladder, I've got terrible cramp in my leg!"

'So you get the ladder, unhook it and throw it overboard. They all yell, suddenly realizing that you're not joking.

'"This is the last act of my play!" you shout at them. "Your so-called 'failed actor' is going to wait until you've all drowned before he jumps in as well. But before that he wants to have some fun. He's going to play around with your various manuscripts. The 'failed actor' is going to tamper with the writings of the dead, to falsify, doctor and swap your texts around. The 'failed actor' is going to assume power over your texts!"

'That's what you shout down over the rail at them while they swim with raised heads, getting increasingly out of breath. Hours pass. Karl and Julius support each other, groaning, treading water; from above, they look as if they're dancing. Kurt and Franz have swum round the yacht. You rush over to the port side! They're clinging to each other. Ah, look, Franz is helping Kurt to climb on his shoulders, but they sink.

' "Leg-ups won't work, my dears!" That's what you shout at them. And since they start to insult you, you return to starboard.

'Ah, no sign of Julius any more. Ah, yes! He's gone under, but with a last thrust he resurfaces, swallows water. And this time sinks for good. Good-bye, Julius. A few hours later you lean over and notice Karl Knigh. He's swimming with ever greater difficulty, panting and scratching the hull. What's he doing? He looks as if he's trying to write something on the side of his yacht.

' "No more letters! No more symbols!" That's what you shout at him, leaning half overboard. "Your so-called 'failed actor' is going to play havoc with your letters and symbols! Hah-hah!"

'He's sunk at last. They've all sunk at last! And now you say to yourself: "Let's do some tinkering!" Where will you start in finishing them off?'

'For heaven's sake, stop getting so worked up!' cries the Investigator to his friend the Poet Criminologist.

'Let him be,' says the Literary Expert. 'It's quite possible that . . .'

'No, it's not possible!' the Poet Criminologist cuts him short. 'That's the way it was. I saw it all! Gustav Zhorn took over me, I was Gustav Zhorn, and if you hadn't woken me from my trance we'd know more about the manuscripts and those coded poems that are perhaps just another obstacle on the mystery trail.'

'Do you sincerely believe the manuscripts have been tampered with?'

'If things happened the way that everything suggests they did, if the Knigh literary family was condemned to remain in the water until overcome with exhaustion, and only one of its members was insane enough to doom them to drowning . . .'

'You think that he wouldn't have contented himself with just this crime, but would have also . . .'

'As you say, taken pleasure in introducing changes, in tampering with the texts so that the Mystery would remain for ever sealed. As I said to you the other day: Why was Oedipus spared by the Sphinx? Because he was the only one who refused to give an answer. All the travellers who tried to give an answer were devoured by the monster. Nothing more natural! A mystery solved is no longer a mystery. And if there's no Mystery: there's Nothing.'

'And so you think that . . .'

'Absolutely! The last person left aboard the *Uranus* could only have blurred the trail even more. Leaving behind nothing but a conclusive Why? It's in the natural disorder of things. That doesn't prevent you from studying the Knigh family manuscripts more than ever before. And the more they were tampered with, switched around, doctored, the more intense the study of them will be. The least fragment will become a relic, nothing will be left to chance, and I assume that with the passage of time this mass of writings will become both a philosophical and hermeneutic curiosity. The Knigh family will have been long forgotten. Legends will say: *They were six plus one. They went off on a boat filled with their writings, which they abandoned. One morning they got up and said: "Let's go, the time has come!" They set out upon the water and walked to the far side of the ocean. Three investigators searched for traces of them in vain. The sea's memory had not retained the imprint of their footsteps.*'

'You really think the last word has to be fabulous?'

'If life's nothing but a story, certainly. If life isn't a story, then there's no last word.'

XXVI

'Well!' says the Investigator to the Literary Expert. 'Today we've relaunched the *Uranus*. Let's take advantage of this sunny day to go out to sea. That way perhaps we might get a better idea of what might have happened.

' "Why don't we try a classic reconstruction?" my friend the Poet Criminologist said to me yesterday evening. "Why don't we all put to sea on the *Uranus*? Let's set sail with the Literary Expert and head out for the open."

' "Excellent idea!" I replied and immediately issued the necessary orders. So, isn't it wonderful to see the *Uranus*'s sides and superstructure rising between the clear-blue sky and the still sea, where they are reflected upside down? Come on, let's take the tender and row across this water that even our oars cannot disturb. As we approach this white cliff-face we can imagine how desperate the efforts of those swimming around it must have been. No grip at all, nothing! Ah, there's the rope ladder! You climb up, I'll follow. In a short while my friend the Poet Criminologist will join us and we'll set sail. I bet he won't be alone. His wife will be with him, I hope, and why not the child? I'm also expecting my inseparable companion in separated inseparation.

' "Let's give the Literary Expert a surprise," my friend the Poet Criminologist said to me yesterday evening, "let's set sail for the unknown. When the circle has closed around us, when the horizon has placed us at the centre of the world, then perhaps we'll understand the power of mystery."

'In a moment they're going to cast off from the quayside in the second tender, and join us aboard. We'll raise anchor and my companion in separated inseparation will come and stand beside me while I pilot the yacht. Her hair will blow in the wind and I shall screw up my eyes. I like having my companion beside me when we sail together, happy to remain silent. As for my friend the Poet Criminologist, I imagine he will have installed the child and his wife in the prow of the yacht. There he'll remain, standing behind them, with one hand resting on his wife's shoulder, and with the other holding the child as upright as possible so that he can see the sea as well as the big birds circling round the boats.'

And to conclude, he adds:

'As for you, my dear Literary Expert, I want you to know that I've had the Knigh family manuscripts replaced in the different cabins where we found them, respecting as much as possible their original disorder. So, while we sail, you can continue to decipher them, without end.'